Paladin

Terri Daneshyar

Book One of The Light Stone
Series

To Jenny

Thank you for the
inspiration. Enjoy.

Temi Daneshyaz

Prologue

Darkness swamped him, suffocating him. Sinking ever deeper into the black he clawed frantically, trying to gain a hold and slow his descent.

'I see you boy. Come to me. It is time.'

'No! Leave me alone. What do you want with me?'

'I want your soul.'

Screams echoed in the night as his consciousness was caught by his tormenter. He felt his shoulders shaking violently.

'Jadeja, Jadeja, come back, come back.'

This voice was familiar. He reached out with his mind and saw a flicker of light, the faintest of glimmers.

'To me, to me,' came the dark voice again.

Garnering all his strength, Jadeja turned his face to the light and felt its welcoming call.

'I'm coming Master, I'm coming.'

His sweat soaked tunic made him shiver which helped to rouse him from the dream that had threatened to engulf him. He opened his eyes and was relieved to see the Shaman-Master standing over him.

'I will have you boy.'

'OUT' he screamed. 'OUT.'

The Shaman-Master laid his hands on Jadeja's forehead and pushed the voice back into darkness. Jadeja sat up, noting the dreamcatcher and the familiar shelf of books. *My room,* he sighed, but the tightness of his grip on the Master's hand gave away his fear.

1

Sensing the danger, Caderyn ran. Ancient cries and howls filled the air. He got away just before a large wolf landed in the clearing, its tongue tasting the air for his scent. Before it had time to alert its master an arrow pierced its heart. Stopping only momentarily to check that the creature was dead, the young bowman continued on his way, following paths long abandoned, letting instinct keep him safe and guide his way. His wiry frame making it easy for him to move amongst the trees.

When he reached the three rendezvous stones he sat on the first. Satisfied that no enemy was near, he stilled his mind and body and reached into the spirit realm for his orders. His master's voice filtered into his mind.

'Caderyn, the moment all three of my Paladin are gathered, meet me at Simniel. The quickest way, spies are everywhere. I have an important mission for you.'

'Yes, Master Shaman. I have just killed one of them. We will be with you by nightfall.'

The link broken, Caderyn became aware of a heaviness on his shoulder and noticed the black hairy leg of a giant spider whose weight pushed him backwards. He was momentarily unnerved, then he smiled as a young woman now stood before him, shrouded in a black cloak which hung down in several overlapping layers like multiple legs, making even her human form appear spider-like. Turquoise hair and purple multi-faceted eyes another indication of her identity as a daughter of the Arachne, the spider people.

'Eilidon.'

'Still outwitting you, Mr Intuitive. What news from the Master?'

'We must travel speedily to Simniel as soon as Suremaana arrives. He awaits us there.'

Eilidon was about to reply when her senses tingled.

'She's here.'

A barely discernible movement in the undergrowth made Caderyn turn to see a girl dressed from head to toe in snakeskin, her long dark hair and light brown skin blending perfectly with the clothes. She carried a large dead rat in her hand.

'An enemy spy. I caught him before he had time to report our meeting.'

'Thank you Suremaana. Now that you are here we must head straight to Simniel. The master has urgent need of us,' said Caderyn.

'Then allow me,' she replied.

Eilidon stood and wrapped her cloak around her. Caderyn found a large spider sat on his shoulder again. He slung his bow across his body and stood still, allowing Suremaana, now a snake, to wrap herself around him, then squeeze so tightly that he could hardly breathe. They began spinning and spinning, until he felt himself being sucked underground, travelling fast in complete darkness. Seconds later, just as he felt that his lungs would burst, they emerged above ground in the stable of a traveller's inn. Suremaana and Eilidon were girls once more.

'Excuse me,' muttered Caderyn and turned and threw up.

'Every time,' laughed Suremaana, but her laughter was short-lived.

2

Eilidon was the first to react. She felt the creature's presence before she saw it. The silver blade flew from her hand and hit its mark. She pulled the body of a large dragonfly from the wall, put it in a pouch, wiped her blade and sucked up the blood that remained.

'Snack.'

'Gross!' groaned Caderyn.

'One less dargon to trouble us,' she said.

'Let's just hope you got it before it called to its masters,' said Suremaana. 'Come on, let's move.'

With Caderyn leading, the three Paladin approached Simniel, a large market town teeming with people.

'We need to avoid the town gates,' he warned. 'We don't want to alert anyone to our presence.'

'There's a small culvert under one of the side walls. I'll slip through, then drop you a rope over the side. It will be easier for me.' said Eilidon.

The other two agreed. As they neared the gate they mingled with the horses and carts of fellow travellers, then slipped off, unseen, to the side. It didn't take them long to find the culvert, a drain carrying the filth from the town out into the meadow. Eilidon changed into her spider form. 'Wait here for me until the light fades,' she said and scuttled through the gap.

'Great, we'll just hang around by the bad smell then, shall we?' muttered Caderyn.

'Better than being one,' said Suremaana.

'Hey!'

Suremaana leaned back against the wall, listening keenly for the sound of anyone approaching. She only picked up the steady stream of footsteps on the road, nothing moved in their direction.

Eilidon went easily through the culvert, the revolting smell having no effect on her spider form. She emerged inside the walls and was immediately on high alert. It was market day and the town was full.

Checking carefully, she threw out a silken thread and hoisted herself onto the armour of a passing guard, secreting herself just under the scabbard that he carried on his back. From there she could see and hear all around her.

At first there didn't seem to be anything out of the ordinary, just traders and townsfolk going about their business. The guard turned a corner and she picked up a scent of ill favour coming from a small insignificant house at the end of the street. Swinging a thread, she caught the thatch just as the guard passed it, then crept under the eaves and along the exposed roof beams. She felt the negative will pressing down on her, a heaviness in the air that drained her energy and made her less cautious than she should have been. Too late, Eilidon realised that she was falling. She tried to release a thread, but had no strength. With the smallest of sounds she dropped into the inverted dreamcatcher, its distorted patterns clearly the cause of the negative energy. She struggled briefly knowing that it was futile, then passed out.

When she came to, she was human again, tied up and sitting in a darkened corner.

'If she is here the other two can't be far away. Our dargons did well to warn us.'

'Yes, a pity we lost one. She will pay for that.'

Eilidon tried to focus on the voices. The first came from a small, hunched figure, with withered hands. He was dressed in the dark brown goatskin of a Jhankril, a follower of negative magic. The second of her captors was tall, with raven-black hair. His face was pinched and thin, mean looking and he had a scar from his left ear to the edge of his mouth.

'The Jhankhira will be pleased with us,' said the hunchback. 'We have a fine prize for him.'

Eilidon froze. The Jhankhira was very bad news. Once he was a Shaman with great healing powers, but he had been subjugated by an evil spirit he was trying to keep at bay. This was a most dangerous enemy. The Shaman Elders had long questioned themselves as to why they had not seen the signs of his vulnerability before it was too late.

'How long till night fall?' asked the hunchback.

'An hour, maybe two. I'll get some food before the Jhankhira arrives. You guard the prisoner. If she wakes, the dream snarer will soon put her under again.'

The tall man left. Eilidon feigned unconsciousness and prayed that her friends would come.

3

'Sitting here is pointless and tiresome. Come on, let's go into town. I'll give us an aura to distract the guards.'

'Is that wise Caderyn? If the enemy's dargon are abroad they may pick up on it.'

'I'll keep it light and brief. We only need to slip past the gate. Hopefully that won't be long enough for anything to pick up the vibrations.'

Suremaana remained wary, but agreed to the plan. Twisting and writhing she wrapped herself around his waist like an ornate snakeskin belt. Caderyn stilled his mind and body, and began an ancient chant, calling on the spirits to shield them from detection. It took only moments to complete the ritual. He sprinted for the gate and slipped inside.

Once they were safely past, Caderyn ducked down an alley and shed the aura. Suremaana resumed her human form.

'What do we do now?' she asked.

'Head for the culvert. Eilidon will go back there.'

They left the alley and made their way along the town walls until they arrived at the drain.

'I thought she would be back here by now. Can you pick up a trail?'

Caderyn knelt. He found silken threads alongside a heavy footprint.

'I think that she may have hitched a ride,' he said. 'Let's see where these tracks lead us.'

Fortunately for Caderyn the guard's boots were quite distinct from those of the townsfolk so he was relatively easy to follow. Suddenly Suremaana froze.

'Down here. Be ready.'

She had picked up the same sense of foreboding that Eilidon had felt. Without warning she pushed herself and Caderyn flat against the wall and covered them both in his cloak. To anyone passing all that was visible was the wall of the house. Her reaction was timely as the tall raven-haired man passed right by them. Suremaana watched and noted which building he entered. She was about to move when she noticed a distortion in the air. A shadow that most people would have missed.

'The Jhankira's men. It is not safe for us.' She sounded nervous.

'We have to find Eilidon. She must be in that house, but if the Jhankira is exerting his will over the building we won't be able to enter undetected. Unless...' Caderyn paused. '...How close can we get?'

Suremaana tested the air with her forked tongue.

'We can get a little nearer.'

She led the way, continuously detecting the air for the essence of the Jhankira. Caderyn followed cautiously behind her. She entered the house neighbouring the Jhankhira's. Luckily the occupants were not at home.

'We can't go any nearer or we will be caught in the shadow of the aura.'

'This will do,' answered Caderyn, sitting cross legged on the floor. He remained perfectly still, facing the building that held his friend, hands resting on his knees, palms upward. He began calling on the spirit of a Khadroma, a sacred being, to come to his aid.

Suremaana was always amazed at his stillness. As a snake, she could stay motionless, but not in human form. Even his breathing had slowed right down. She watched, as he communicated with the spirits. Then he jumped up and she toppled backward, surprised by the movement.

'She is in the back corner. There is an inverted dream catcher making her drowsy and keeping her in human form. You will need to be lightning quick. In, out, away.'

He pricked his finger with an arrow head and squeezed a drop of blood. Suremaana held the droplet on her tongue, then transformed, slithering away to rescue their friend.

Caderyn slumped to the floor, all energy gone.

Eilidon had drifted into unconsciousness again, her senses dulled by the negative energy filling the room. She was awoken by her tall captor kicking her.

'Wake up changeling. Our Master is on his way.'

He bent down so that she could feel his breath on her face.

'Quite pretty for a spider.' His hands began to move down her body. She spat in his face and was rewarded with a ferocious slap that left her cheek red and stinging.

His companion laughed.

'I don't think she likes you.'

The raven-haired man turned to his fellow captor.

'She doesn't have to like me for what I've got in mind,' and he licked his lips in anticipation as he reached over to take a red-hot branding iron out of the fire.

Eilidon now fully awake, knew immediately what he was going to do. She had no intention of letting him brand her with the sign of the dargon, forever binding her to the Jhankira's will. She pushed herself back against the wall as if the solidness of the building would save her and tried desperately to return to her spider form, but the dreamcatcher prevented it. With rising panic, she awaited her doom.

Her captor's black eyes reflected the red heat of the metal as he lifted the branding iron out of the fire. In that moment, the floor opened, Suremaana spat the drop of blood on Eilidon who instantly transformed into a spider and jumped into the mouth of the snake. Before either of the men had time to react the ground closed and they were gone.

4

Caderyn heard the cursing and smiled. He was up immediately. Drawing his cloak around him he exited the building through a rear window. Crouching low, he ran swiftly and silently looking for safe-haven. He was running so fast he almost fell over the cat curled up on the step. Surprised that it hadn't moved he realised that it was a carving. He knocked twice, paused then knocked three more times. The door opened silently and he stepped within. The two girls were sat waiting for him.

'What kept you?' smiled Eilidon, but he could see the relief in her eyes.

'You were lucky this time but your escape will anger the Jhankira. His dargon will be everywhere.' The voice came from a man in his thirties wearing a brown tunic and a wide leather belt studded with shells, sitting to the right of the girls.

'Master Shaman.' Caderyn bowed.

'Please sit, we have much to discuss.' The Master indicated a cushion facing him.

There was a movement behind and a dark-eyed young man similar in age to the Paladin, emerged from a back room with a bowl of steaming broth and passed it to Caderyn.

'My apprentice, Jadeja.'

The young man bowed and returned to the kitchen. Caderyn ate greedily, the invocation had drained him and his body craved nourishment.

The Shaman-Master looked at his guests.

'For many years, although the Paladin are highly trained fighters, their role has been largely as my ambassadors. You have all served me well, but my friends it now falls to you to complete a mission that may well put you in great peril.

Nine years ago, a powerful demoness was imprisoned in an ancient and sacred artefact, The Bottle of Isfahan. This small vessel is protected by three spirit guardians whose images are embossed onto it. However, the bottle can only hold her for a short time and so it was sealed in caves on the Island of Dura. The Jhankhira has broken through our layers of protection and retrieved the bottle, a sign that her prison is weakening. At Spring Equinox, I have to perform a ceremony of banishment to completely rid the world of this menace. To do this I must gather the four power stones and bring them to the Temple of Shang To. One stone is kept there, the other power stones are scattered in secret places and to retrieve them will require all of your skills. There is a power stone hidden here. We must find it before the Jhankhira. Not only does he want to stop the ceremony, he also wants to use the stones himself to release the demoness.'

'Then if we gather the stones at Shang To we are putting the temple in danger.'

'Yes Eilidon, we are, but without the banishment her prison will not hold, so we have no choice but to take the risk.'

'Why wasn't she banished nine years ago instead of being imprisoned?'

'An element we needed for the banishment was missing so we could only temporarily imprison her. We now have that element, which is why we must move quickly to stay ahead of the Jhankhira. You, with the help of my apprentice, have to stop him from finding the other three stones and bring them to me at Shang To. I must return there to prepare its defences and complete the ceremony.'

'Why us and not the Elders?' said Caderyn.

'Because the guardians on the bottle are a spider, a snake, and a bowman. Young as you are, I believe you were chosen by the spirits and you must answer the call.'

The Shaman-Master gave them a little time to digest this information before continuing,

'The writings say that the stones are hidden in plain sight but they only reveal themselves to Khadromas. We believe that the Jhankira has control over one of these celestial beings and he is manipulating it to do his will. Caderyn you recently communed with the spirits did they give you any instructions or show you anything?'

Caderyn shook his head.

'Look,' said Eilidon. 'Your wrist.'

Caderyn pulled back his sleeve and there tattooed in tiny black runes was a message. It read:

From the eye of the sun
I smile down on Simniel

'What does that mean?'

'It means, dear Eilidon, that you have a puzzle to solve. I will chant for you and mark you with the sign of the feather. That should protect you from a dreamcatcher.'

The Shaman-Master reached for the wide leather straps that held his hand bells and the heavy wooden beads engraved with ancient markings, each one representing a spirit. With these on, he began his chant, sitting cross-legged in the same way that Caderyn had done earlier. As he chanted, he rang the smallest of the bells six times, then the largest bell twice.

The air became still and a blue flame danced in the fireplace. Suremaana was about to speak when a look from Caderyn silenced her. The Shaman-Master was in a deep trance. A wisp of red smoke began to emanate from his shoulder. They watched mesmerised as the smoke moved steadily towards them, increasing in size until they could make out a large red bird. It was majestic, part eagle, part peacock. It stood before each of them in turn, fixing its gaze right to their hearts until it was satisfied. Eilidon shifted uncomfortably under the scrutiny of the bird. *Am I up to this task* she asked herself, once again allowing her self-doubt to surface? Each of them felt unsettled, they knew their deepest thoughts were being opened. The examination of Suremaana took longer, as if she harboured a secret she was not willing to give up.

When the bird spirit had finished, it began to diminish back to where it had come from. There was a movement behind the kitchen curtain and Jadeja stepped through just as it was disappearing, but not before it saw him, causing it to shriek and then vanish.

The noise brought them all out of their reveries and they turned to look at Jadeja who seemed as taken aback by the spirit's reaction as they were. Caderyn was on his feet holding an arrow to his neck. Eilidon had tied him up in silken thread.

'Who are you, that you would enrage the spirit so?' hissed Suremaana.

Jadeja looked from one to the other and shook his head.

'I…I…I am a simple apprentice. I hope one day to be a Shaman like my Master.'

'I don't believe you,' snarled Caderyn. 'A Khadroma would not react like that without reason.'

'I am…I am a simple boy working for my Master.'

While Jadeja was speaking, the Shaman-Master came out of his trance, unaware of what had happened with the spirit.

'Caderyn, what has my apprentice done that you must hold an arrow to his throat?'

'Master, as the Khadroma returned to the spirits, it saw your apprentice and screamed. We are trying to find out why.'

'The spirits are very good judges of people. Jadeja did you frighten it? What were you doing?'

'Nothing Master. I came to see if our guests needed more food.'

The Shaman-Master looked deep into Jadeja's eyes and laid his hands upon his head. The spirits were still near the surface and he called on them now as he probed his apprentice. Finally, he lifted his hands and smiled.

'They are satisfied. You may release him.'

'But Master.'

'Release him Caderyn. Eilidon there is no need for your bonds.'

Reluctantly Caderyn sheathed his arrow and Eilidon snapped the silken threads. Jadeja looked at them and then at the Shaman-Master.

'I am sorry Master if I have caused you and your friends distress.'

'You have not, but I see that the Khadroma has marked you too, which is good if you are to lead this hunt.'

Caderyn was about to protest but he saw the mark on Jadeja's wrist, a series of small red feathers with a black triangle at their centre. He looked at his mark. Pure red feathers, Suremaana's and Eilidon's the same.

'Why is he leading the hunt?' said Eilidon.

'It is not your place to question the spirits, Eilidon. He has been chosen and that is an end to it. You all now carry the blessing of the Khadroma, may it protect you on your quest.'

Eilidon thought that she detected the merest hint of a smile on Jadeja's face and vowed to herself to keep a very close eye on him. She could sense a vibration around him, but whether good or evil, at this stage she could not tell. She only knew that he was hiding something.

'I must eat and you must rest. Tomorrow you begin the search of Simniel. The Jhankira has not arrived yet, but his henchmen will be looking for you. They will not have enjoyed losing their prize.'

The Shaman-Master retired to a room at the back of the house. Jadeja was busy bringing food and drink to his Master. He indicated the stairs and the three visitors headed up. They found a large room under the eaves with blankets and cushions for them to sleep on. Once they were out of earshot they began discussing the day's events.

'I don't like that apprentice leading us. He has a strange vibration,' said Eilidon 'Watch him at all times.'

'The spirits must have chosen him for a reason,' said Suremaana.

'Maybe he has a link to the bottle too. All the same I don't trust him,' said Caderyn. 'Eilidon can you remember anything from the house you were held in?'

'Very little. Negative energy from the building. I climbed onto the roof and went inside. There was an inverted dreamcatcher ready. They were expecting me. When I came to, I was tied up in the corner. There were two of them. The raven-haired one was poised to give me a dargon brand.' She shuddered at the memory. 'He would have done so if Suremaana hadn't appeared when she did. Thanks by the way, even if you did spit blood in my face.'

Suremaana smiled. 'Anytime, but it was his blood that broke the will.'

Eilidon nodded at Caderyn, her gratitude tempered with the knowledge that the bond between them had now deepened and their fate was intertwined.

In a small backroom downstairs Jadeja studied the runes on his wrist. The black triangles that singled him out from the others bothered him. The Shaman-Master knew from his apprentice's furrowed brow that he was worried. For Jadeja the thought of travelling again filled him with trepidation. He felt sick. The road meant chaos and he didn't think he could cope with that again.

'Master, how can I lead them? They won't listen to me. They don't trust me. You saw how they reacted. Is there no one else? Why not send them without me?'

'Because it will take all of your combined strengths to complete this mission. I need you to do this for me, Jadeja, I have to be at Shang To. You have been marked. The spirits have granted you protection. The bird reacted as it did because you have a phoenix guard to keep you safe. You must take up the responsibility. And trust... trust, is something you must earn my young friend. They are fair-minded people and they have sworn oaths of loyalty.'

But not to me, thought Jadeja, *not to me.*

5

They were up at first light. Despite her ordeal, Eildon had slept deeply, Caderyn too, still exhausted from the incantation. Only Suremaana had been restless. Her encounter with the bird spirit had left her uneasy. *What had it seen within her? A weakness?* She was a proud daughter of The Serpentae, the snake people of Aribold and she could not countenance that she might not be as strong as the other two.

Whisperings in her dreams, *be watchful, take care,* had disturbed her rest and made her toss and turn all night.

When they got downstairs they found Jadeja up and waiting for them. Eildon eyed him suspiciously, still sensing the strange vibration that emanated from him.

'I have packed each bag with provisions that I think are suitable to your needs as well as a water bottle. My Master thinks that we should move around the town in pairs, a group of four will draw too much attention. I am happy to travel with the lady Suremaana.'

'No. Suremaana and Caderyn will go together,' replied Eildon.

'As you wish mistress.'

Eilidon watched him carefully, noting the disappointment in his voice. He unsettled her. She also had her own reasons for keeping a distance from herself and Caderyn, who now spoke.

'Be watchful for dargon. They will be looking for us and the power stone. Suremaana and I will take the old town to the north. You and Jadeja move south. Remember the words:

From the eye of the sun
I smile down on Simniel

So, we are probably looking for a sun rune.'

'That is most likely Caderyn,' said the Master, appearing from the back room.

'One thing, Master.'

'Yes Jadeja.'

'If the stones are only visible to Khadroma how will we find it?'

'Because, my son, you carry the mark of the Khadroma and the stone will know to show itself. Now hurry.'

Eilidon smiled to Jadeja and said, 'I hope you're not afraid of spiders.'

She transformed and positioned herself on his right shoulder, like a large spider shaped clasp. Jadeja winced momentarily, then he set off for the southern end of town.

Caderyn smiled to himself at Jadeja's discomfort, but Suremaana felt a pang of guilt for their treatment of this strange boy who was to be their travelling companion.

'Go carefully my friends. When you find the stone bring it to me and I will see that it remains safe.'

'Yes Master.' Caderyn bowed and they set off.

The old town was bustling with people as street sellers vied with each other for customers. In the central market, they were met with an explosion of colours, smells and sounds. Vendors called out to each passerby. The aromas of a hundred different spices assaulted their noses. At the bottom end were the silk merchants, stalls piled high with reel upon reel of brightly coloured fabric. Beyond them the tanners with their animal skins. The candle makers beyond them, where the smell of the tallow overpowered all else.

Caderyn and Suremaana were not looking at the stalls they were looking above at the tops of buildings. None were displaying any kind of emblem or sign that might be the one they sought.

'If the stone is looking down maybe we need a taller building. Does Simniel have a tower?' asked Suremaana.

'Of course. You genius. It's not going to be one of these. There's a look-out tower in the town wall. That must be what we need.'

Caderyn grabbed her hand and set off at a run towards the walls. Turning down a back alley they found their path blocked by the tall raven-haired man who had captured Eilidon. His eyes flashed as he tried to seize Caderyn, but he was too slow and he found himself constricted in the grip of a large snake, squeezing and squeezing the air from his lungs. Caderyn had an arrow at his throat.

'Where is your Master?'

The man laughed.

'My Master is not afraid of you, Paladin. You are nothing. Mere dots on the landscape. You cannot stop us. We know what you seek but it is well beyond your reach.'

Caderyn applied pressure and drew the arrow across the man's throat, breaking the skin.

'Tell me.'

Suremaana squeezed tighter. The man smiled.

'We see you. We are everywhere. You will not stop us.'

Caderyn ripped the man's throat open with his arrow. As he did so the blood poured out and transformed into a large black raven that flew away laughing.

Suremaana shivered. 'That was unpleasant. We must be more careful. If he was able to find us so easily there must be spies everywhere.'

Breaking his arrow in half and throwing the pieces behind him, Caderyn continued to the watchtower in silence. Suremaana's skin bristled and her snake's tongue continually tasted the air for any scent of enemy spies. Caderyn too was vigilant.

Eilidon and Jadeja made their way through the southern end of town. Here the streets were wider and less populated as this end of town was inhabited by the wealthier merchants and guildsmen, the sword makers, the shield makers, the gold and silversmiths. Eilidon noted how much taller and more ornate the houses were. Each one trying to outshine its neighbour. The passersby she observed were well dressed and better fed than their northern counterparts.

Jadeja, eyes darting nervously left to right, began to move amongst the people. He avoided all eye contact with anyone they passed, his dark fringe falling across his face to hide him from their glance. Eilidon felt his body flinch if anyone brushed against his slender frame as if each touch inflicted a wound. In his head Jadeja repeated the words, *I have nothing to fear, I have nothing to fear,* clenching his fists tightly, trying to hold on to what little courage he had.

'We're not being followed. There's no reason to be nervous,' she said.

Jadeja made no reply.

'We should look at the tops of these buildings, an emblem or sign maybe.'

Arriving at the end of a particularly fine street of tall timber framed buildings they turned a corner into a large courtyard surrounded on three sides by a magnificent four-storey building of dark oak timbers and windows filled with the finest coloured glass. The doors drew his attention being almost the full width of the central building and ornately carved with the figures and tools of every guild in the town. The grandeur of the building was breathtaking. Today it was also adorned with the flags of each guild, making it look like a giant sea clipper in full sail.

'The Master Guildhall,' whispered Jadeja. 'I thought if anything was looking down on Simniel it would be this building.'

Eilidon was grudgingly impressed with his thinking. 'I'll climb up and check the carvings near the roof.'

She swung out a thread and scuttled unseen up the timbers of the Guildhall.

Jadeja picked his way through the courtyard. The guilds of Master craftsmen met here to discuss the running of the town. Each guild took it in turn to oversee town business. Currently it was the shield makers and their crest could be seen on the flag that flew directly above the colossal doors to the building. Today the hall was busy with families as the guilds were selecting their new apprentices. Young men and women from the northern side were hoping to be chosen so that they could lift their family into the coveted ranks of guildsmen. The majority of apprentices came from within the guilds, but just occasionally an outsider would be picked if they could demonstrate an exceptional flair for a craft. Once a year the master craftsmen would open their doors for non-members to try their luck and today was Guilds Day. Because of the extra people present Jadeja could mix easily. He was used to navigating through crowds without drawing any attention to himself, even so he could feel his heart beating faster than usual. He felt a touch on his arm and recoiled, then a tremor in his mind, made him react. He took a sling shot from his pocket and fired a red stone high up the wall of the building. There was a squawk and a large black bird fell from the sky. Eilidon heard the noise and saw the bird fall, realising that it had been coming for her.

Jadeja ran forward to retrieve his prey before anyone in the throng could get it. His aim was true and the bird lay lifeless on the floor. Picking it up hurriedly, he dashed away from the crowded courtyard to a quieter street. There he took a tail feather while reciting an incantation and put it in an inner pocket of his tunic. Taking a knife from his boot, he cut open the bird to remove its heart and lungs. These he placed into a small jar which he sealed and chanted over, then pushed the jar in next to the feather. The body he discarded. Returning to the courtyard he found Eilidon waiting for him. He recoiled again, feeling the spider land on his shoulder.

'Nothing here. I hadn't sensed Raven. Thanks.'

'Because he was your captor and so was shielded from your senses by the Jhankhira. Luckily not from mine.'

And what senses do you have? thought Eilidon, studying this boy who could detect an enemy at that distance. *He is hiding something, I must watch him closely.*

6

The watchtower stood high above the town walls, manned at all times by members of the town guard. Not that this was a time of war, but it was prudent to be vigilant. Standing at the base of the tallest structure in the town, Caderyn and Suremaana were confident that they would solve the riddle.

'How are we supposed to see what's up there?' groaned Suremaana.

'I'll go,' smiled Caderyn. 'It's easy. Watch.'

Before she had time to protest, his cloak was off and he was ten feet off the ground. Laughing as she remembered how quick and nimble he was, she watched him climb, picturing the time they had first met three years ago. She was twelve and had not long been called to Paladin training. Sat under the guardian tree waiting for her orders from the elders, this brown-haired boy had swung down through the branches. He was the only human she had ever met who could negotiate this tree, the sharp spiky leaves making it virtually impossible to move through its branches.

'Hi, I'm Caderyn. You're one of the new trainees.'

'Suremaana,' she replied. How long have you been here at the temple?'

'All my life,' he laughed. 'My father is a guardsman.'

'Are you training to be a Paladin too?'

'Yes. I've completed the first year. One more before the final tests. Good luck.' And he sprinted away to join the combat class in front of the guardhouse where a turquoise-haired girl partnered him.

Now as she observed him, he ascended the watchtower with grace and agility, finding footholds where no one else would. His athletic build making light work of the distance. What surprised her was that none of the guards checking the many travellers entering the town, had seen him. Then she remembered that he was an incantation Master and he would have a spirit shroud to prevent him from being seen.

Caderyn quickly reached the top. From this vantage point he could see across the whole town. This would certainly be a place to smile down on Simniel, but as he carefully made his way around the outside of the structure he found no eye or sun that could possibly house a power stone. He sat back on his haunches on the very top of the tower, shoulders slumped, and looked out. None of the buildings were as tall as the one he was perched on. It was then that he saw it and let out a whoop so loud the people milling around Suremaana looked up. Luckily, because of his aura, she was the only one who could see him. He clambered down to her as fast as he safely could.

'Come on I know where we need to be.'

Without further explanation, he grabbed her hand and ran through the gates and out of the town.

'Why are you taking us away from Simniel?'

'Trust me, we will soon be there.'

Knowing there was no point arguing she followed on behind, enjoying the freedom to just run in open fields. The ground began an upward incline and their speed slowed as they went up a steep hill half a mile from the old town. Suremaana felt the incline in her calf muscles. As they neared the summit she saw where they were headed and finally understood when she saw an ancient oak tree, tall and grand with spreading branches that looked like welcoming arms. It was twice the height of a standard oak. There at the topmost part of the trunk was a large mask carved from gold. A round, smiling face surrounded by billowing waves of yellow, like golden curls, smiled down on them.

'There,' said Caderyn.

From the eye of the sun
I look down on Simniel.

Your turn.'

Suremaana became a beautiful serpent slithering her way up to the golden mask. Hidden behind the left eye was a large oval amethyst. Suremaana's head went into the deep-set eye socket and emerged with a stone between her jaws. Then she retreated down the tree to Caderyn. Placing the stone carefully in a red cloth with silver runes he dropped it into a leather pouch which he then hung around his neck, so that it was concealed within his tunic. 'We must remove all traces we have been here or the Jhankhira will follow us.'

Suremaana nodded and disappeared, 'Leave that to me.'

A few minutes later she stepped from behind the oak followed by hundreds of tiny vipers. They formed a chain up the tree, their tongues picking up all scent of Suremaana and eliminating it, then they followed the two of them down the hill and over the fields eradicating all trace that they had ever been there.

At dusk the vipers formed a ladder up and over the wall so that Suremaana and Caderyn could re-enter the town undetected. Suremaana then released them from their service and they vanished as quickly as they had appeared. 'Tracer vipers,' smiled Suremaana. 'Very handy for erasing scent.'

'You're full of surprises. Come on let's head back to the Shaman-Master.'

They made their way to the house, Suremaana tasting the air for enemy scent. A sharp tug on Caderyn's sleeve and a nod to the right allowed Caderyn to take out a dargon with his bow. These dragonfly-like creatures were a useful tool for the enemy, spying out the Paladin's movements and reporting back to the Jhankhira's men. It was too far ahead to have seen them, but even so they made several circuits of the alleys before arriving at the house. The cat that had been curled up the day before now sat upright, ears pricked.

'A spirit guardian' whispered Caderyn, when he saw the puzzled look on Suremaana's face. 'It adopts a pose to suit the time. If it is on alert, then we were wise to be careful.' Before they could knock, the door was opened by Jadeja who ushered them inside. The Shaman-Master stood before them.

'Do you have it? Do you have it?'

Caderyn showed him the stone. Relieved, he took it from them.

'Excellent. The Jhankhira is here. We must hurry. I felt his net spreading out through the town as he searches for it. Jadeja killed one of his followers today, Blackraven, the one who captured Eilidon.'

'We met him too. I gave him a taste of my arrows, but he transformed and got away.'

'Then we must hurry. I will take the stone to the Elders for safe keeping. You must head for the Artisans' Table.'

'Master, it is dangerous for you to go. Let me take the stone,' said Jadeja, placing his hands on the amethyst. It flared with purple light as the Master pulled it out of his grasp.

'No Jadeja you cannot. I must go alone. Your mission is to find the other two stones.'

'What if I can't?'

'You must! You are to lead the Paladin.'

Caderyn looked hard at the Shaman-Master.

'Jadeja will guide you. Trust him.'

'Yes Master,' said Caderyn, but he was not sure if he could.

Jadeja bowed and turned away. Eilidon stared at him. She had witnessed the flare and the stern way in which the Shaman-Master had spoken. *Why was the Master so determined to keep him away from the stone?*

'Pack away all trace of us. I must leave at once. Follow the river to the fork. Jadeja knows the way from there. Hurry and may the spirits guide you.'

For the first time they noticed that the Master was wearing his bells and jerkin and they saw his feathered headdress sticking out of his bag. He picked up his thumb stick and slipped out the back. He was hardly through the door when there was a loud hissing and spitting from the cat outside. Caderyn's bow was loaded, an arrow unleashed the second the door was open. It found its mark in the throat of a heavy-set man. As he fell his place was taken by another. This one was met by a dagger straight to his heart. A third was crushed by a giant python. Working as one fighting unit they took out the Jhankhira's men. Each dead man was replaced by another. All were met by a dagger or an arrow or a snake. In total fifteen men lay dead. 'Run!' shouted Caderyn. 'Run!'

Jadeja, feeling more inadequate than ever, witnessed the fighting, noting how they worked as one unit. He lingered momentarily, reciting ancient words then blowing on his hands. The bodies dissolved, leaving no evidence of the assault that had just taken place. He left the house. The cat curled up asleep on the front step; all was quiet again. As they ran, a discordant cry filled the air, the Jhankhira realising his prey had left. The sky blackened and they could feel his negative will spreading over them like a shroud, slowing them down.

7

Caderyn was the first to stop. His bow weighed him down as if it were made of lead.

'I'm sorry. Too heavy.' And he sat down.

Eilidon threw out silken threads and made a web above them. Jadeja pulled Caderyn under as his legs had stopped moving. Eilidon drew the web tightly around them and they felt the weight easing.

'It won't hold long. A brief rest. Then we carry on.'

Everyone nodded, grateful for the respite.

'How far to the river?' asked Suremaana.

'We must pass through the jewellery quarter, after that we can exit the town and pick up the river half a league from there.' Jadeja pointed north as he spoke. 'At this pace about a quarter hour.'

The moment he finished speaking they heard the twang of a thread snapping above them.

'My web weakens. Move.'

Wearily they carried on, while all around them silken threads pulled apart and they felt the downward force like the weight of a building on them. Slowly and heavily they moved forward, linked by a chain of spider thread to prevent anyone falling behind. Jadeja led the way, seemingly more immune to the negative pressure than the others. Eilidon's misgivings rose.

After what felt like an hour, they found themselves in an opulent quarter of town and they knew from their surroundings that they had reached the jewellery quarter. Each house they passed was more ornate than the last. Jadeja was unaffected by the elaborate carvings around doors and the gold and silver set with jewels atop the doorways or the heavy velvets and satins hanging at the windows. Wealth was everywhere but he barely noticed.

He led them on, stopping before the most magnificent house any of them had ever seen. Even Suremaana, who had grown up in a palace, was impressed, seeing the rich mahogany doors encrusted with emeralds and window frames made from gold, filled with glass panes that glistened with diamonds. She couldn't resist checking her reflection, enjoying the sight of her face surrounded by jewels. Jadeja rang the doorbell, a solid gold cat with emerald eyes. A small slight man opened the door. Looking Jadeja up and down, he ushered them quickly inside.

If the outside was magnificent the inside was more so. Jewelled furniture, gold tables, shimmering marble floors. Their host did not stop to let them admire the view, he rushed them through the hall and down a side passageway. This was far less ornate, hung only with tapestries of the finest silks. They did not have time to appreciate them. The man drew aside a tapestry of a bird in flight, claws outstretched. They followed him through this hidden door that led to a darkened stairway. Deeper and deeper they descended making their way through a labyrinth of dim oppressive tunnels. Eilidon stumbled in the darkness, bumping into Caderyn as they tried to keep up with their guide. Only Suremaana felt comfortable in this underground maze. The cool of the walls brushed her skin, the thin air having no effect on her. Jadeja felt his breathing becoming laboured. Something pulled at his mind. *Leave me alone* he thought. He pressed on behind the small man repeating the word *courage* to himself. Their guide stopped at a plain wooden door.

The man bowed. 'All speed to you and your companions, Jadeja. They will not find what they seek here.' He turned and left.

'Thank you, Mole. May the spirits guard you.'

'Who was that?' demanded Eilidon.

'A friend,' said Jadeja.

'A very wealthy one,' said Caderyn.

8

Exiting through the small wooden door the four travellers set off at great speed away from Simniel. The negativity had lessened the moment they stepped outside, allowing them to breathe and move freely. They ran fast without looking back until they reached the river.

'We must follow it southwards until we come to the fork,' said Caderyn. 'From there Jadeja, you will have to lead us again.'

They slowed to a fast walk, taking care to watch for dargon.

'I hope the Shaman-Master got away safely. There is too much at stake.'

'He will have taken secret ways out of Simniel and the spirits will have protected him lady Suremaana,' said Jadeja. 'He has many friends to help him.'

Eilidon led them to a small copse that she had seen up ahead.

'We'll camp here tonight. It's sheltered and the only cover for miles.'

The others agreed and moved under the small canopy of evergreen trees. Gathering leaves and sticks they soon had enough fuel for a small fire. Caderyn and Suremaana refilled the water bottles at the river. Suremaana transformed and slipped into the water, re-emerging with a large trout in her jaws. Three more dips later and there was a fish each.

'Supper,' she said.

Jadeja busied himself lighting a fire, placing large stones in its flames, trying to focus his thoughts on the task. His nerves were like taut strings. A twig snapping made him jump and his hand automatically reached for the small blade in his boot. He relaxed when he realised that it was Caderyn and Suremaana. She tried to catch his eye but he looked away, embarrassed. He wanted to sit with her and talk but he was awkward with people and had no idea how to start a conversation with this girl. Eilidon was nowhere to be seen. He followed Caderyn's gaze to the tops of the trees and saw a large silver web strung between the branches. Once all of them were settled the web expanded until they were completely enclosed.

'That should shield us for the night,' said Eilidon as she appeared from the edge of the copse. Caderyn smiled.

'Ever resourceful, which is why you're such a good Paladin. Sit down and eat, you must be exhausted.'

Eilidon winced at the compliment, however friendly his intention, she hated any signs of affection. Spinning a web that size had drained her and she slumped down by the fire. Suremaana sat brushing her hair and watched Jadeja, something drew her to him, a vulnerability behind the eyes perhaps, sadness, a sense of loss. She studied him as he expertly gutted the fish and placed them on hot stones he had removed from the base of the fire. As the stones cooled, he put them back in the fire and pulled out more hot ones. Soon the fish were cooked to perfection.

'Where did you learn to do that?' she asked him.

'When you travel, you pick up tricks to help you survive.'

'Have you travelled a lot then?'

'When I was a child.'

Jadeja took his fish and began eating, a sign that the conversation was over and then wished he could think of something more to say, but memories of his childhood were not something he wanted to dwell on.

The other three ate voraciously, adding bread from their packs to fill themselves up.

By the time they had finished eating, the only light was from the fire.

'I will take the first watch,' said Jadeja.

Eilidon's web building, had left her more tired than she cared to admit so she didn't argue. The other two settled quickly and were soon asleep. Again, Suremaana's night was punctuated with strange dreams and warnings of betrayal.

Once Jadeja was sure that they were all asleep he withdrew the raven feather from its hiding place. Taking six red stones from a small pouch in his pocket, he made a circle and placed the feather in the middle. Quietly, he began an incantation which drew a spirit from within the stones. Each one projected an upward beam of light. These lines met at a point forming a pyramid above the feather. Jadeja stared into the light then reached through and touched it. Instantly he felt the opposition of the Jhankhira's will pushing into his mind. He wanted to withdraw his hand but he kept it there, pushing back against the negativity until he saw the face of the Jhankhira.

'I see you Jadeja. You cannot run from me for ever. I am coming.'

A cold blade at his neck broke the connection.

'What are you doing?' It was Eilidon.

'Are you calling the Jhankhira to us?'

The noise awoke the other two. Seeing Eilidon with a knife at Jadeja's throat Caderyn sprang up.

'What's going on?'

'I caught him contacting the Jhankhira. Giving out our position no doubt.'

'I gave out nothing. I was trying to see if we were being followed.'

'By carrying out secret rituals. No wonder you offered to take the first watch.' Eilidon was incensed.

'It is better to do these things alone to avoid others being probed,' replied Jadeja quietly, unmoved by the knife at his throat.

'Put the knife down Eilidon,' said Caderyn. 'Are we being followed?'

'Not at the moment, but they know we found the stone. Dargon will be sent to track us as we hunt the next one. We should move at first light.'

Reluctantly Eilidon put down the knife.

'I don't trust you. I'll be watching,' she warned.

Jadeja gathered up his stones and placed the feather back within his jacket.

'I will not betray you,' he said.

'The Shaman-Master sent us with him. He would not have done so if he were an enemy,' said Suremaana.

'Wouldn't he? Shaman have been deceived before,' answered Eilidon. 'I'll finish the night watch. Get some rest.'

They lay down, Jadeja close to the fire, his back to Eilidon, eyes closed. He was used to being mistrusted. Subdued memories of being a small boy alone and abandoned came back to him, people wary, accusing him of thieving or spying as he moved from village to village trying to find where he belonged. He yearned for the peace that being with the Shaman-Master had given him. Now that had been taken and he was left with these three travelling companions who once again eyed him with that same mistrust. He curled up tightly, the amulet that he always wore around his neck, held firmly in his hand to keep him calm while he tried to sleep.

For the rest of the night, a large brooding spider sat on top of the web and watched and listened for the enemy. Although her main focus was outside the camp, a small thread gently touched Jadeja's back. Any movement from it and she would know that he was awake. *Caderyn and Suremaana may allow for your faults but I will not,* she thought.

At first light Eilidon woke them and they set off, taking care to cover the embers of their fire and bury the fish bones. She removed her protective web, deftly rolling up the threads and dropping them in the water to dissolve.

They followed the river for a couple of hours until the sun was fully up. Luckily the river bank was open and easy and they could travel quickly, reaching the fork in the river without further incident. The main artery carried on southward in a wide, channel. To the left was a smaller vein that snaked away through dense undergrowth.

'We must take the left fork,' said Jadeja.

'Pity,' groaned Caderyn. 'I should have known we wouldn't be able to travel the whole way unhindered.'

'If you tell me which way we are going I can take us underground,' offered Suremaana.

'That would not be wise. The Artisan does not like to be surprised. We must go on foot so that he is aware of our approach.' Jadeja spoke quietly but firmly.

'The hard way it is then. How far is it?' asked Caderyn.

'If we make good time we should be there by mid-afternoon.'

Jadeja began pushing his way through the foliage. Being seldom used the way was blocked by intertwined bushes and brambles. Blood spilled from Suremaana's fingers as they snagged on vicious thorns.

'My bow,' said Caderyn struggling to free it from the brambles.

'Ow, watch what you're doing,' said Eilidon when Jadeja let a thorny branch swing back in her face.

'My clothes are ripped to pieces,' said Suremaana.

'And you think nobody else's are? snapped Eilidon.

With every snag from a thorn the more frayed their tempers became, and their impatience to be free of their surroundings spilled over towards their guide. Eilidon was especially vitriolic in her criticism.

'Some guide you are Jadeja. By the time we get out of here we will all have bled to death.'

'My lady, I can do nothing about the state of the path we must follow. I can only lead you as fast as I can. We have evaded pursuit thus far, but our advantage will not last long.'

'Especially when you perform your secret rituals,' spat back Eilidon.

Caderyn shot her a look that said, *not now.* She was about to respond when their path opened. The river or stream as it had become, bent back on itself, heading off to rejoin the main artery. What lay before them was a man-made waterway, leading straight through flat land to a small pool. Everywhere bore the hallmarks of care.

Up ahead they could see a large wooden table with a bench on either side. It was not until they came level that they could see how unusual it was. Each bench was two feet high and carved with deep semi-circles. The back of each one was made up of six upright planks of varying heights. Each plank was topped with a large rectangular chunk of wood giving them the appearance of a line of people.

The table itself was inlaid with four rectangular metal plates set at right angles to each other and embedded in the corners. A large central plate also made from metal and raised from the table was fixed in place with four large bolts. Deep grooves were cut into each corner. Either side of the central plate, five triangles had been chiselled far down into the wood. Bolted to the table was a tall cylinder that held oversized metal tools: a poker, a long iron nail, a chisel and a tool for boring holes in wood. While they were admiring the work, an extremely large man with hands like anvils, bearing the scars of one who works with hot metal, came and joined them. His hair and beard were the colour of rust which seemed fitting. Even so, it was hard to imagine this leviathan being so skilled in intricate metalworking.

'I see that you are admiring my table.' His voice had a low and mellow timbre and his eyes glinted with pleasure as he looked at his craftsmanship.

'We have come for guidance, Master Artisan, if you would care to aid us.' As he spoke Jadeja bowed low and indicated to the others to do the same.

The Artisan looked at his group of visitors for some time without speaking.

'Who wishes to ask me?'

Jadeja motioned to answer but Eilidon spoke first.

'I would ask Master Artisan.'

He studied her carefully.

'I often have spiders at my table, but none that speak to me. Choose your seat. If you pick correctly, I will answer your question, but if you choose wrongly, you must answer mine.'

Eilidon nodded, then approached the table. She circled it twice. Although there were only two benches to choose from she had no idea which to pick. She stood at the end of the table and put a hand on each corner. On touching the wood, the deep grooves in the surface seemed to fill with silver liquid. The left side filled quicker than the right so that was the side she chose, sitting down on the bench of her choice. Instantly the rivulets of silver disappeared. Once seated she looked to the Artisan. He climbed onto the bench opposite in large lumbering movements like a giant bear sitting down with her.

'You have chosen well my lady. You may ask your question.'

'We seek a power stone. We have come from Simniel. Where do we go next?'

The Artisan pondered deeply. Reaching for the poker he began to follow the triangles on the table, all the while chanting to himself, eyes glazed. After tracing the outlines of the triangles three times his poker stopped at the third one.

'One and two have been removed. The third is at Porphyra's chair, for the one whose love will bear her there.'

Suremaana reacted to the name Porphyra, it was familiar to her, but before she could call out Eilidon spoke again.

'What is Porphyra's chair. I've never heard of it!'

'I have answered your question.'

'But I need more information.'

The giant man stared at her, 'Please leave my table.'

Banging her hands on the surface in frustration Eilidon stood up, as did the Artisan. He bowed to them then shuffled back inside his dwelling.

'We have to ask him another question,' said Caderyn. 'We have to know more.'

'I will take the test.'

It was Suremaana who spoke. 'Jadeja call him back out.'

Jadeja did as she told him and the bear-like man reappeared. Once again, he gave the option to choose sides, but in her eagerness for answers Suremaana did not study the table. Instead she sat on the same side as Eilidon.

The Artisan sat opposite.

'Lady of the Snakes you have not been wise. There will be no question to me. You must answer the question I put to you. Place your hands on my table.'

With mounting anger at her own haste and trepidation at what she may be asked, Suremaana placed her hands on the wood. When she touched the table, the deep channels turned into writhing snakes all making their way towards her, like a living blanket ready to smother her. She could not move or make a sound as the snakes began to cover her.

'Lady Suremaana, will you be true to the one who loves you or send him to his doom?'

She felt herself unable to answer. *Of course I will be true*, she thought to herself. *I am a loyal person. I would never betray my father.*

The Artisan now placed his hands on hers. The snakes disappeared, all bar one that bit into her arm sending venom shooting through her body. She tried to pull away but the Artisan's hands had her rooted to the table. Venom coursed through her veins until it reached her heart. She gasped as it hit. The Artisan looked within her. It was only a fleeting moment, but it was horrifying.

'You will be tested. It is not clear which path you will choose, but know this, choose wrongly and all will be lost.'

He released her, then turning to the others waiting quietly on the grass, he said:

'I will allow one more to sit at my table. You.' he pointed at Caderyn. 'Will you be worthy of my answer?'

He stood up allowing Suremaana to join the others, giving Caderyn the choice of seats.

'Did you see what he did to me?' asked Suremaana, still shaking from her ordeal.

'We only saw him with his hands on yours. You did look a bit blank, but that was all.' replied Eilidon.

'It is time to choose your seat Bowman.'

Caderyn moved cautiously towards the table. He circled it twice as Eilidon had done, then stood at the end and placed his hands on the wood and knew immediately where to sit. Once seated The Artisan took his place opposite him.

'Well chosen, Master Bowman. I see you know your wood.'

'The suppleness of this side reminded me of my bow,' replied Caderyn.

The Artisan nodded. 'You may ask your question.'

'Which path will lead us to Porphyra's chair?'

'You must take her path and traverse the Lake of Fire, walk the breadth of the Frozen Forest and enter the Garden of Yangchen. There you will find what you seek. The lady of the snakes will remember.'

'The Lake of Fire?' said Caderyn.

'Head to the east. If you are a true Paladin the spirits will guide you.' The Artisan stood up and bowed once more.

'May I ask a question?' said Jadeja.

The Artisan stood and looked at him and then shook his head.

'It is not time for you to sit at my table.'

Again, he bowed and left. Jadeja felt the colour rise in his cheeks.

9

'Why wouldn't he let you sit at the table?' asked Eilidon.

'One may sit only at his invitation. I was not invited.'

'But why?' probed Eilidon.

'That is for the Artisan to answer, not me.'

Eilidon was not happy with Jadeja's reply, but it was clear that she would not glean any further information.

'If we move further downstream we can make camp for the night. The Artisan does not like visitors to linger for long in his garden,' said Jadeja.

He led them on another mile or so before making camp at the end of the clear land, just in front of another overgrown trail. Their meal was prepared in silence, each one mulling over the events at the table. Despite being within the Artisan's domain, Eilidon still insisted on creating a web canopy.

'I prefer to be cautious,' she said.

Jadeja sat quietly, watching Suremaana as she lay on the ground, admiring her long brown hair. A strange feeling stirred within him. He desired to be near her but at the same time it scared him. She looked in his direction and he realised that he was staring. In order to hide his embarrassment, he said,

'I know the Gardens of Yangchen, but not its creators. Can you tell us about Porphyra, The Artisan said that you would remember?'

Suremaana sat up.

'Yes, yes, of course, It's coming back to me.'

The others turned to her, keen to hear more. She began her tale.

'There is an ancient legend among my people, of a Serpentae queen who loved a fierce warlord from the north. She had been basking in the sun as her snake self, the heat making her sleepy and distracted. The Warlord, Ancrobus, crept up on her and captured her, thinking that her snake skin would make a fine belt for a warrior. He tied her with silver which prevented her from becoming human so he had no idea who he had captured. He thought she was just a snake, albeit one he had never seen before. At the point of killing her, he looked into her eyes. Mesmerised, he was unable to strike the death blow. Feeling remorseful, he untied the snake and set her free, but in that instant of connection, Porphyra had seen into the man's soul and had lost her heart to him. She slid away, only to return moments later as her human self. She was the most ravishingly beautiful woman this warrior had ever seen. Tall and slender as a young willow, with eyes of the deepest emerald green. He too was lost.

Their love and passion were all consuming, but it angered both their peoples. He gave up his lands and she renounced her throne. Together they crossed the Lake of Fire and entered the frozen forest heading for the Garden of Yangchen, where they hoped to find peace. No families judging them, no wars to claim him. In the garden, he carved for her a throne, for she was his queen. He covered it in the finest green foliage to match her eyes. But the spirits were angry with her for forsaking her people and as she took her seat she pricked her skin on a stray thorn and a poison filled her veins. Distraught to see his lover writhing in agony as the poison sapped her life, he snatched her up and carried her to the centre of the garden where he lay down beside her and sucked the poison from her wound into himself and the two died together, entwined in each other's arms. It is said that a bed of green and black thorns grew over their bodies. To this day her chair sits empty and alone in the garden.'

'Nice story but it doesn't tell us where the Lake of Fire is or how we cross it,' muttered Caderyn.

'I believe we seek The Golden Lake of Ipsilon. It is three days from here across the Niniver Hills,' said Jadeja.

'I will consult the spirits and seek their guidance,' replied Caderyn.

'As you wish.' Jadeja turned away and lay down. He was used to being disregarded.

Caderyn sat cross-legged, hands resting on his knees, palms upwards. He stilled his body and slowed his breathing. He began chanting, drifting into familiar rhythms as he succumbed to a trance like state. Slowly the spirits called him into their realm. He saw the beautiful shapes and colours of half formed beings weaving in and out of his thoughts in time to the rhythm of his chanting.

When he finished, he smiled.

'Jadeja is right. The Golden Lake is where we go and yes Suremaana you can take us there. However, we must be cautious. You can take us to the edge of Ipsilon which is where we need to be. I will show you.'

He drew a map in the dirt showing Suremaana the directions. She nodded.

'I will have to make two journeys. The distance is great and we are four.'

Caderyn nodded. 'Eilidon and I will go first. You can come back for Jadeja.'

Suremaana agreed.

'Now I must sleep. It will take all my strength to travel that distance underground. Twice!'

'I will say a sleep incantation to make sure that you are well rested,' smiled Caderyn.

Closing her eyes Suremaana lay down, hoping that the words would quell the disturbing dreams that she had been having lately. Whether it was the incantation itself or simply the smooth rhythm of his chanting she couldn't tell, but a deep sleep soon enfolded her. Similarly, Eilidon and Jadeja were also slumbering. Caderyn smiled and was soon unconscious himself.

Although Suremaana slept, the words of the Artisan found themselves tumbling round and round in her head, mixed in with images of Porphyra and her dead lover. Even more disturbing were the scenes where her own head sat on Porphyra's body as she cradled her dead love. In the dream, Suremaana wept copious tears, but the face of her dead lover was always just out of focus. She awoke to find herself sobbing. Luckily for her, she was the first one up and so was able to hide her tears.

Once everyone was awake, they ate a meagre breakfast from the last of their provisions. As Caderyn ate, Suremaana looked at him.

'Are you sure that you want to eat that now?'

'I'm hungry,' he replied. Then looking at Suremaana he laughed. 'I see what you mean. Perhaps I will save the rest for later.'

Even Eilidon grinned. Seeing Jadeja's puzzled look she said: 'Private joke.'

Again, Jadeja felt the pang of being an outsider.

Breakfast being done, Suremaana looked at Eilidon and Caderyn.

'Ready?'

'Ready!' they nodded in unison.

Jadeja watched as a large serpent with a giant spider in its mouth, entwined itself around Caderyn then disappeared into the ground. Suremaana was right, it was a long distance and by the time they broke through just outside Ipsilon, Caderyn's lungs were screaming for air.

'Too far, too far,' he gasped and then promptly threw up. Eilidon laughed but Suremaana had already gone back for their travelling companion.

'She'll be all right, won't she? With him I mean?'

'The Master would not have sent him with us if it wasn't safe.' he replied.

'I'm not sure of him. Something isn't right. I mean what do we know about him? He's moved about a lot. Who are his people?'

'Eilidon I know that you are worried but the Shaman-Master has charged us to keep him safe.'

'But that bird spirit's reaction was so strong and unexpected. And why is his mark different to ours?'

Sighing Caderyn replied, 'I only know that the spirits wanted him to lead this quest and we must respect that and follow their wishes.'

'Okay, okay, but I don't have to like or trust him.' She folded her arms crossly and climbed into a tree to wait.

While they were gone Jadeja again took out the raven feather. As he studied it the black mark on his arm began to throb and he heard a dark and distant voice calling to him.

Jadeja, Jadeja. I call you to me. Come Jadeja. Come now.

He found himself slipping down, down into a deep unconsciousness.

'I can't. No,' he murmured.

Again, the voice called. *Jadeja. Jadeja.*

He was slipping into blackness unable to stop himself.

'Jadeja. Jadeja.'

This time the voice was softer, lighter, urgent.

'Jadeja. Jadeja are you okay?'

It was a girl's voice calling him back from the abyss.

'Jadeja.'

Slowly he opened his eyes to see Suremaana leaning over him.

'Are you okay? You seemed to be in some kind of trance.'

He smiled weakly at her.

'Yes, yes. Thank you. I was, I was…' Unsure of what to say next he stopped. 'Please let's go.'

Suremaana nodded and moments later he found himself encircled by a snake and disappearing into blackness once more. She brought them safely to where the others were waiting. When she released him, he stumbled forward, his face as pale as the moon.

'Are you alright? It can be quite unsettling the first time.'

There was genuine concern in Caderyn's voice.

Jadeja nodded. 'I may just need a few minutes to catch my breath.'

'I know what you mean,' laughed Caderyn. 'At least you haven't thrown up. That's my party piece.'

10

Ipsilon was a bustling trade centre. Positioned as it was on the edge of the Golden Lake where three rivers met, there were plenty of opportunities for commerce. The southern farmers brought their wheat and barley crops. The silk traders from the east brought the most marvellous array of fabrics and the western peoples brought their metal and wood working skills to trade and barter. Because the land around the lake was fertile, the townspeople of Ipsilon had many crops to trade as well as the fish from the lake. There were other towns along the shore, but Ipsilon was by far the biggest.

'We need supplies and somewhere to sleep. Do we have any money?' asked Eilidon.

'We'll soon get some,' grinned Caderyn.

'I don't see how unless you're planning on robbing someone.'

'Jadeja, a little faith. We will earn it.'

'And how do you propose to do that? There are no archery contests at this time of year.'

He looked at him quizzically. Caderyn winked at Suremaana. 'We shall do what we usually do in places like this. Snake charming.'

'What! No. You can't,' said Jadeja. 'The lady Suremaana is not some cheap circus act.'

'No indeed. Last time we earned 400 reema in one show,' replied Caderyn.

The look of horror on Jadeja's face made Caderyn and Suremaana laugh.

'Thank you for your chivalry,' smiled Suremaana, when she had composed herself. 'It really is okay. We have done this a few times and it is an easy way to earn our bed for the night.'

They set off to the town. There was plenty going on. The streets were full of hawkers trying to sell their wares. As they pushed through the crowds their ears were assailed by a cacophony of noise, multiple languages dancing together in the music of trade. Eyes were dazzled by a constantly changing array of stalls. Fine wrought iron goods, woven baskets, rolls of fabrics, intricate wooden carvings were just a few of the things on display. Caderyn stopped by one of the basket weavers and used the last of their coins to purchase a large basket, then dipping into a side alley he re-emerged with Suremaana, now a snake, curled up inside the basket.

Reaching the main market square, they found a suitable pitch. Jadeja watched as Caderyn spread his cloak on the ground then placed the basket carefully at the front edge. He wrapped a brightly coloured scarf around his head in the eastern style, pulled a wooden flute from his pack and sat ready to play. Eilidon took up the role of MC and began calling to the passing crowds.

'Ladies and gentlemen, here for one day only, we have Cadovan of the East to perform his amazing snake charming. Watch and wonder as he controls the snake and makes it dance to his tune.'

Eilidon was good at attracting people and soon there was a large crowd around them. Jadeja stood off to the side, disgusted that Caderyn was using Suremaana in this way. Once the music started however, and the beautiful snake emerged from the basket, he found himself mesmerised by the beauty and fluidity of her movements. She was like silk rippling in the wind. Up and down and round, twisting, turning, in time to the notes. It truly was magical. The crowd too, were stunned by the way this young man controlled the snake and made it dance. When the music finished Suremaana wrapped herself around Caderyn's shoulders and the crowd erupted into cheers. People began filling the basket with money.

'Thank you, thank you. We'll be back next year.'

Quickly gathering up the money they moved away from the square. Once they were well away from observers Suremaana changed back.

'How much did we make?' she asked.

'Wow, four hundred and fifty reema. The best yet,' answered Caderyn.

'It was definitely the lady Suremaana's dancing. She was spellbinding.'

They all turned to look at Jadeja, who found himself blushing under their gaze.

'At least we can eat, sleep and hire a boat for the morning,' said Eilidon.

'Are you sure that this is the right lake? I wouldn't call it a lake of fire.' Caderyn looked questioningly at Jadeja.

'Wait for this evening. You will understand where it gets its name. For now, we must find lodgings and I think that we should be on the lake shore. Follow me.'

They headed off to find suitable accommodation.

From the shadows behind them, a small boy slipped away unnoticed. Running quietly through the streets he met his paymaster at the rendezvous point and passed on his information.

'Four of them, two girls, two boys. They are lodging by the lake shore. Going to hire a boat,' he panted.

'You have done well. Here is the five reema. Now be gone.'

The boy took the money gratefully and disappeared quickly. He neither knew nor cared why this young man was interested in the four strangers. His only concern was that he would be able to eat for a few days now. Having paid off his informer, Rabten hurried off to the lake shore.

The lakeside taverns were noisy, brash affairs, full with fishermen fresh from unloading their catches, or merchants, here to buy or sell their goods. Jadeja chose an inn at the far end of the quayside. It was quieter than the others and looked a little less shabby. They paid for two rooms and ordered a meal of steaming hot fish stew and fresh bread. The fish had been landed that morning and tasted delicious.

'Once we cross the lake we make for the frozen forest. We will not be able to travel underground so we must take plenty of supplies with us, including furs. The forest is not somewhere to linger. We have to cross it in one day.' Jadeja spoke quietly.

'Why can't I take us underground and avoid the forest if it is so dangerous?'

'Because the tree roots would block your passage and the spread of the forest is too wide for you to go around. Also, we must cross the lake at first light to avoid being seen. We will need to find a boatman we can trust.'

'Why can't we cross at night if you're worried about being seen?' asked Suremaana.

'Because we would need a light and that could be noticed. Don't forget there are many spies abroad and not many travellers sail to the northern tip. I will go and talk to the boatmen.' Jadeja stood up to go.

'I'm coming with you. I'm good at seeing to the heart of a man,' said Eilidon, pointedly.

'As you wish, my lady.'

The two of them set off, leaving Caderyn and Suremaana to go and purchase the supplies.

Jadeja led Eilidon along the quayside where a huge variety of craft vied with each other for mooring space. There were so many different boats Eilidon wondered how they would know which one was suitable for their journey. The larger vessels heavily laden with goods were clearly not appropriate and fishing boats looked too flimsy to make it all the way to the northern tip of the lake, built as they were for inshore fishing.

Jadeja surveyed the scene. A small craft came into view. It was not much bigger than a rowing boat with only one sail, but it was tacking speedily into harbour and its master was adept at outmanoeuvring the larger vessels. Jadeja hopped down to the water's edge to greet the skipper. He was so quick that Eilidon was caught unawares and by the time she reached them, Jadeja was shaking hands on the deal.

'We have our sail,' said Jadeja.

The young skipper smiled and held out a hand. Eilidon was briefly taken aback to see that it was a young woman.

'I am Erin, skipper of The Maybird.'

Eilidon took the proffered hand and looked her straight in the eye. She saw a steeliness in the gaze and sensed courage, but nothing to alert her spider senses.

'Would you care to board her?'

Eilidon nodded and lightly jumped aboard. Despite its size the boat felt sturdy and well balanced. As the sail caught the evening breeze, she saw a small red bird painted in the corner and was reminded of the bird spirit that had scrutinised them before they left the Shaman-Master's house.

After a few more exchanges over the departure time and the fee, Eilidon and Jadeja headed back to the inn.

'You've made a good choice. Next time don't go ahead without me.'

'I am sorry my lady but I wanted to secure our passage. Erin does not stay ashore for any longer than it takes to resupply her boat and I did not want to miss our chance.'

Eilidon was about to respond but hesitated. Turning sharply, she detected a movement in the shadows behind them. She ran back and peered up the narrow street they had just crossed. Nothing was visible. Running her hand up the corner of the building she recoiled as if she had been punched.

'We've been followed. We must take more care. The Jhankhira probably knows that we're here. We have to warn the others. One will travel less visibly than two.'

She transformed and Jadeja once again had to carry a large spider on his shoulder.

The arrangement was to meet the others at the end of the quay at sunset. Keeping to the shadows and with

Eilidon's senses on high alert, Jadeja took a circuitous route through narrow alleyways, many piled high with rubbish. Frequently checking for any sense of being followed he felt on edge, not helped by the presence of the spider on his shoulder. *What is it about spiders that makes me so afraid? After all, they are so much smaller than me and very rarely are they malicious.* Irrational he knew, but their ability to disappear as fast as light and reappear just as you had forgotten about them played havoc with his nerves.

He liked order, probably because for most of his life there had been none. As a wandering child, his life had been nothing but chaos and uncertainty, until the Shaman-Master had found him and taken him in. From then on, he had taken comfort in keeping the Shaman-Master's home and life in order. Now here he was again on a chaotic and dangerous journey that he hadn't wanted to take, and with a mission he was unsure that he could complete. His Master had insisted that he go. He knew the Shaman-Master must have had good reasons for sending him, but he could not quell the feelings of rejection that kept surfacing. *Why did he not keep me with him? What have I done to disappoint him?* He looked at the runes on his wrist and wondered again about the Khadroma's reaction to him and sighed heavily.

He turned a corner and bumped right into Suremaana knocking her off balance. He reached out to help her to her feet. Eilidon launched off his shoulder and landed on a dargon perched on a roof above them. In seconds, she had it bound and rolled in a silken web like an Egyptian mummy heading for a sarcophagus. Only this particular insect was headed for her stomach.

'My apologies dear lady. I was not paying attention.'

To his dismay, he thought that she was crying. He soon realised that she was laughing.

'Your face,' she chuckled.

Blushing heavily, Jadeja took her hand and she jumped to her feet.

'You should be more careful, you could hurt someone,' snapped Caderyn.

'I'm all right,' said Suremaana. 'You should be more worried about that dargon that Eilidon is busy pocketing for later,'

Eilidon, human once more, looked up.

'We've been followed to Ipsilon,' she said grimly.' I felt the presence down at the quay. This dargon is further proof of the need for caution.'

Caderyn nodded, 'We have the supplies and furs, so we can leave at first light.'

'Oh my, look. Look.'

They turned to where Suremaana was pointing.

'Now I understand why the lake is named as it is. It truly is on fire.'

As they turned, the setting sun cast a shimmering golden glow on the water so intense, that the lake really did seem to be alight. Red and gold, mixed with the rippling surface of the water, enveloped all the boats and the harbour. It seemed as if the entirety of the lake was immersed in flame. They remained enthralled by the beauty of the scene. Only Jadeja was unmoved.

'Come, we must return to the inn and get some sleep. It is not safe to linger here.'

'Just one more minute. It is the most beautiful sight I have ever seen,' said Suremaana.

'We cannot my lady. There are spies about.'

Jadeja pulled his cloak around him and waited. It was Caderyn who broke the spell.

'Jadeja is right. We must head back now.'

With a last look back at the fiery water, they made their way to the inn.

11

Once they were safely at the inn, Eilidon encased each room in its own web.

'It will allow us some protection from spies. I just hope it's enough.'

'Thanks,' said Caderyn. 'I am going to consult the spirits to see if they can guard us as we cross the lake.'

'That will not be necessary,' replied Jadeja. 'The vessel we are taking is a protected one.'

'And how would you know that?' said Eilidon.

'Because I have sailed in her before and I know her captain is….' he hesitated. 'Is blessed.'

He would say no more.

'That may be so, but I will feel more reassured after I commune with the spirits,' insisted Caderyn.

'As you wish, but I assure you it is not required.'

Jadeja turned to go back to the room he and Caderyn were sharing. Suremaana smiled at him as he left.

'Thank you for showing us the lake. I have never seen anything so beautiful.'

Jadeja nodded at her and left.

'You shouldn't be so hard on him,' she said to the other two.

'Maybe,' answered Eilidon, 'But there's something not right about him. Well, not clear anyway.'

'I think that he is just lonely,' replied Suremaana.

'Like that orphan child at Aramathea that you took a liking to. The one who inveigled his way into your affection and then robbed us while we slept,' said Eilidon. 'You are so naive Suremaana. I know you grew up cossetted from the world, but you've been a Paladin long enough now to know that people are not always what you see on the surface.'

'I may have had a privileged background but at least I don't always expect the worst of others.'

'And I do?'

'Yes Eilidon, you do.'

'It's safer than trusting someone before they've proved themselves worthy.'

'But you are not even giving him a chance,' said Suremaana. 'What do you think Caderyn?'

'I think that Eilidon is right and we should be cautious. However, the Shaman-Master trusts him and that ought to be enough.' He did not sound fully convinced though.

Caderyn sat down in the centre of the room, crossed his legs and stilled his mind and body, calling the spirits to him. They did not respond. He chanted for over an hour but no spirits answered his call. He stopped and opened his eyes.

'They are not answering me.'

'Has that happened before?' asked Eilidon.

'No.'

'Maybe Jadeja is right and they are not needed and that is why they are not answering you,' said Suremaana.

Caderyn wasn't sure.

'Either I am being blocked or they are needed elsewhere.'

After that, the night was a restless one for all of them. Caderyn was disturbed by his lack of communication with the spirits. Jadeja simply could not sleep. Suremaana was again troubled by dreams of betrayal and Eilidon dreamt of Jadeja calling out to the Jhankhira and bowing down in front of him. She awoke to see him leaning over her, shaking her and recoiled from his touch.

'Please hurry my lady, the boat is waiting. I'm sorry if I startled you.'

'Where are the others?' asked Eildon groggily.

'They are downstairs. The lady Suremaana said that she could not rouse you, so I offered to try.'

Eilidon sat up crossly and put on her boots. Grabbing her things, she followed Jadeja down to the others.

'Morning sleepyhead,' grinned Caderyn. 'Sorry we had to disturb your beauty sleep.'

Eilidon punched him in the arm by way of reply.

'Quickly,' urged Jadeja. 'We must be on our way.'

Keeping to back streets and alleyways, they made their way cautiously to the quayside, where Erin and The Maybird were waiting to cast off. Eilidon was surprised to see that the sail was still furled. Catching her puzzled look Erin said,

'We must row out of the harbour. My sail is well known and we don't want to be followed. We have half an hour before it will be light enough to notice a boat leaving.'

She sat each one of them at an oar.

'I take it that you can row?' she asked.

They nodded.

'Good. Then once you have stowed your belongings under the seats we can go.'

Erin set them to a rhythm and then took the tiller to steer them carefully through the boats that were rather precariously moored up in any available space, and out around the last long wooden jetty. They found the boat so light that it glided quickly and easily through the water. Rounding the last jetty and free from the protection of the harbour, they felt the wind blowing across the water. Erin sprang to the mast and with the speed and grace of a dancer unfurled the sail in moments. Immediately the wind filled it and Maybird shot forward.

The sudden movement caught Suremaana unawares and she toppled backwards. Jadeja caught her as she fell. For a brief moment, their eyes locked.

'Thank you.' she smiled.

'You're welcome,' blushed Jadeja, holding her gaze for a fraction too long. An awkward pause followed, then they each sat back down in their places. He felt a strange fluttering inside his belly as he watched her back.

The Maybird turned out to be a fast and steady craft and Erin was an extremely adept skipper. The wind played with them, frequently changing direction, so Erin was constantly adjusting the canvas. It seemed to Eilidon that the bird in the corner of the sail was actually flying. Indeed, that was so, because it was a spirit guardian that travelled with Erin and her boat, keeping them on a safe course.

Caderyn enjoyed the sensation of the wind on his face. It reminded him of bowman training, when he had had to sit in a high tower with the wind swirling around him and still shoot his arrows accurately at a moving target. After many cold and painful hours, he had learnt what others could not, how to move with the wind and counteract its effects on his arrows. When he eventually came down, the Elders knew that this son of a temple guard, was a Paladin of the Bow. Watching Erin skilfully handle her boat, he knew that she too was in tune with the flow of the wind.

Eilidon, on the other hand, felt every movement of the boat and couldn't settle, so she transformed and spun herself a web underneath the seat, where the threads could absorb the motion and she could remain still and calm.

The lake was vast, stretching far into the horizon. Jadeja sat back with his face to the wind and watched the huge black and white gulls above them swooping and soaring, happily catching the currents of air underneath their wings. The sun rose, its warm rays beaming onto the boat. He allowed himself the luxury of relaxing. The water glistened like a highly-polished mirror. Looking back, he could see the lake polka dotted with brightly coloured sails as the vessels moved from town to town along the shore. No other boats were as far out as them.

He went and sat with Erin when the wind allowed and they talked like old friends. Despite herself, Suremaana looked on and felt a pang of jealousy. Although she would never admit it to anyone, she had enjoyed the compliments and the extra attention that this strange young man had bestowed on her. Caderyn spoke and broke her reverie.

'Those two seem to know each other quite well. I wonder what the connection is?'

'Perhaps we should ask him,' she replied.

As if reading their thoughts Jadeja moved back towards them.

'Forgive me ignoring you, but Erin and I were talking of the time she carried the Shaman-Master and I across the lake. She wanted to know how he is.'

'Why didn't you say that the Master had travelled with her? I would not have tried to invoke the spirits if I'd known,' muttered Caderyn crossly.

'I did tell you that it wasn't necessary, but you chose not to believe me,' answered Jadeja calmly.

'But you didn't tell me why.'

'Perhaps you should have a little more faith in my choices.' He looked Caderyn straight in the eye as he spoke, goading him to respond. He was about to, when Suremaana interjected.

'You are right Jadeja. We should show a little more belief. It's just that we have always worked as a trio and it is not easy to let another person in. Especially when he is a stranger to us.'

Jadeja looked at her.

'Thank you, my lady. I appreciate your support.'

He turned and moved back to sit by Erin. Caderyn stared at her and shook his head.

'You're too trusting Suremaana. We still need to be cautious.'

'Maybe so, but he seems genuine to me.'

Caderyn shrugged and turned to check that no one had followed them across the lake. Having satisfied himself that they were alone, he sat back and watched the bird spirit as it skilfully guided their sail. Lulled by the rocking of the boat he fell asleep.

It was Eilidon that woke him. Her senses had picked up a warning as she sat in her web, instantly she was human and alerting the others. Erin too had seen it.

'Caderyn wake up! The gulls.'

He roused himself and looked quizzically at her. She was pointing behind. Turning to look he saw that the gulls that had previously flown freely high above them, were now flying in formation and heading straight for them. As he watched he saw a large black bird in the centre that appeared to be commanding them. His bow was in his hand immediately. Erin too pulled a bow and a large sheath of arrows from the prow of the boat. Jadeja took the tiller.

'There's something in their claws,'

Caderyn loosed an arrow as the first rock fell.

Erin and Caderyn fired arrow after arrow into the flock as the Maybird was deluged by rocks. Suremaana and Eilidon tried to swat them away with the oars. Jadeja tacked from left to right to try and dodge the missiles. Many hit their target and the little boat rocked dangerously.

Caderyn noted that Erin was as good a bowman as she was a sailor. Her arrows were fired with precision and she took out several of the attacking flock. Many birds fell, but not enough to hold off the assault.

'We're running out of arrows,' he yelled.

'The hull's damaged. I'll try a web but it won't hold long. Another blow will sink us.'

'Look out,' yelled Suremaana. Jadeja turned the tiller just in time to avoid more rocks hitting the boat.

'My webs can't keep the water out,' shouted Eilidon.

Caderyn took his final arrow and aimed it at the black gull, knowing that if he took that one out the attack would end.

'Wait!' shouted Erin. She spoke to the Maybird's spirit guide.

'Now!' she screamed.

Releasing his last arrow, Caderyn saw the Maybird's spirit flying beneath it, guiding it home.

He looked to Erin, touched his heart and bowed. She acknowledged his tribute.

A violent shriek filled the skies. The arrow plunged into the chest and the large black bird plummeted to the water. As it fell, they could see Maybird's spirit wrestling with a larger black spirit. The two were intertwined as they hit the water and disappeared. Erin let out a desolate cry and collapsed to the floor.

With their leader fallen the remaining gulls dropped their stones harmlessly and flew back to land. Suremaana took the tiller from Jadeja while he handled the sail. Eilidon patched up any further breaches in the hull the best she could and bailed water.

Caderyn lifted the unconscious Erin and laid her gently in the stern of the boat in the only dry place that he could find. Once there he said the ritual words to ease the parting from her spirit and guide her to the land beyond. He alone recognised the enormous sacrifice she had made in releasing the spirit from Maybird to ensure that his arrow succeeded. In saving them, Erin had sacrificed herself. At the moment of release, he had seen that she was a Shabtoe, a spirit, sent to live within a human until called upon to return. When the call came, it was swift and painful and the human left behind would have their very being torn asunder. Most died within minutes of the separation. Those that survived were just empty shells, doomed to have a living body but no living soul, destined to die a long and lingering death as the physical body wasted away. He hoped that Erin would pass peacefully. He sat and prayed for her. When he had finished, he turned to see silent tears falling from Jadejas' eyes.

He knows, thought Caderyn. *Why would she have shown herself to him?*

Puzzled by this new knowledge, he stared long and hard at Jadeja.

What am I not seeing? he asked himself. *What don't I know?*

Between the bailing and the handling of the sail they managed to guide the little craft to the northern shore of

68

the lake. It was only when they landed that the girls realised that Erin had not recovered.

'She is gone. She was a Shabtoe. We owe her our lives,' said Jadeja.

The girls bowed low to honour her and uttered their thanks.

They disembarked. Caderyn lay Erin gently in the heart of the boat, then he and Jadeja pushed Maybird back out onto the water.

'May the spirits guide your sail one last time,' prayed Jadeja. 'Your sacrifice will be honoured.'

The wind then filled the sail and took the craft out from the shore on its final journey. Caderyn fired a flame that landed in the prow of the boat. The Paladin and Jadeja bowed low as the little vessel caught fire and sank beneath the water.

In sombre mood, the four travellers set off towards the mountains.

12

After the bustle and noise of the southern town, the northern shore of the lake was eerily quiet. No people, no animals and no vegetation. The shingle beach led to a rocky path through a dry and barren wasteland.

'What happened here?' asked Eilidon. 'Why's it so empty?'

'The spirits have abandoned this place,' replied Jadeja. 'Many years ago, a rare golden spirit, Nahm Kha, one destined to be a great unifier, was ensnared by Songaara, The Destroyer, a dark being. He put her in a cage and set her on the lake shore and began to drain the light from her and pull her power into him. Many warriors, many Paladin and many spirits tried to free her, but the cage was impenetrable. Destruction and death were everywhere. They had to find a way to stop the Destroyer. If he consumed the light of a golden one his power would become immeasurable. Realising that she would not escape, she tempted the Destroyer. She flattered him and appealed to his vanity, telling him that if he took her power he would be strong but if they made an alliance, together they would be unstoppable. She almost convinced him, however at the moment of their union, Nam Kha shed a golden tear. Seeing this the Destroyer knew that he had been deceived. He tried to annihilate her, but she was too clever for him.

A mighty battle ensued that burnt and scarred the land. Nam Kha realised that the only way to win was to destroy them both. Selflessly she surrendered to him and offered herself up, knowing that his greed and lust would ruin him. He accepted her surrender. Filled with a potent mixture of hate, desire and revenge he ravished her. In that moment of fusion, Nam Kha's spirit overwhelmed him. The meeting of their two energies caused an explosion, and fire that consumed them both. So great was the conflagration that the earth was scorched beyond healing. The land is left bare as a warning to those that would follow the dark ways. Nothing lives here and none cross the lake.'

Suremaana shivered. Thinking she heard a whisper she looked behind. Nothing was there.

'Let's hurry then. I don't think this is a place to linger in.'

The others nodded. Jadeja led them forward, their footsteps echoing on the rocky path. Even as they walked Suremaana could not shake off the feeling that they were being observed.

'Are you sure no one ventures here?' she asked Jadeja anxiously.

'Yes, my lady, quite sure.' He felt guilty deceiving her, but it would do no good to let them worry about the watcher. If they moved quickly and quietly they might evade attack. *Perhaps I should warn them,* he thought. *At least that way they will be ready for a fight.* He couldn't decide and pressed on.

Feeling a little reassured, Suremaana walked beside him. She tried to make conversation but something about the emptiness made her stop. Somehow her voice sounded harsh and unwelcome. She felt as if the rocks were chastising her for breaking their silence.

'Stop!' ordered Caderyn.

Jadeja halted immediately and turned to Caderyn who remained quite still with his eyes wide, staring in to the distance but seeing nothing.

'The aura is on him,' explained Suremaana to Jadeja.

Caderyn's vision had become distorted by a series of white lights interspersed with flashes of colour. Each colour was a spirit bringing a message, usually in the form of a vision. The others could not see the lights they could only see the rapid movement of Caderyn's eyes as he read the meaning.

Eilidon shuddered. 'Attack!' she screamed.

She threw a web over Caderyn to camouflage him. Almost immediately a Griffin, half dragon, half eagle rose from the rocks in front of Jadeja, stretching out its enormous talons to tear his body to shreds. Eilidon threw a blade which sliced deeply into one of its legs. It hesitated, allowing Jadeja to draw his sword, slashing at the creature in a frantic attempt to protect himself.

'Go for the wings,' he shouted.

Eilidon threw her blades into the wings trying to bring it down. One or two tore the skin but the giant enemy resisted the onslaught.

'No difference. Need Caderyn's bow.'

Suremaana, now a snake, launched herself onto one of its mighty legs, coiled herself around and sank her fangs deep into its flesh, filling its veins with venom. The griffin faltered momentarily, allowing Jadeja to slash it across the body. Suremaana uncoiled herself but before she could get away the bird caught her in its beak and threw her violently onto the rocks.

'It's coming again. I'll try and land a blow on its underbelly,' said Jadeja. He planted his feet firmly and raised his sword above his head, bracing himself for the impact. Free of the snake the griffin rose up and circled above them on enormous wings, out of reach of their blades. Suddenly it dived down on them. The vicious beak raked down Jadeja's arm as he valiantly held his ground trying to drive his sword through its flesh. Eilidon tried to disable it with a web around the wings. It was too powerful, tearing the threads as if they were as light as gossamer.

Sensing the advantage, the creature flew up once more, circled and then began its final, bloody assault on them. Eilidon and Jadeja stood together, blades in hand, ready for the attack. They saw the creature recoil, then heard its death shriek, as it plummeted to earth. Turning they saw Caderyn, bow in hand.

'Sorry I took so long,' he grinned. 'The spirits sent new arrows. And thank you for the safety net.'

Eilidon saw her web in a heap on the ground.

 She nodded.

Jadeja also acknowledged his gratitude.

'I'm sorry. I should have warned you it might appear.'

'You knew,' screamed Eilidon. 'You knew and you let us cross here unprepared.?'

'I hoped we could make it across without detection. I didn't want to worry you.'

'If we're under threat then we need to know. You keep too much from us, apprentice. The Shaman-Master was wrong to put you in charge.'

Jadeja winced at her verbal attack, feeling the truth of her words, then slumped to the ground.

'He's bleeding out, quick bind his arm.'

Eilidon wound threads around Jadeja's wounds. Caderyn said a few words of healing over him and hoped that it would be enough.

'Where's Suremaana?' he asked.

It was only then that Eilidon realised that she was missing.

'She bit the griffin. I don't know what happened.'

'I'll find her. You stay with Jadeja. And try not to get aggressive with him.'

Eilidon glared back, but she knew she had to keep her anger in check.

He did not have to search for long. The greens and golds of her snake skin stood out among the rocks where she fell. Gently picking her up, he carried her back to the other two.

'Is she… is she dead?' said Jadeja.

'Not yet, but this is not good.'

'Can we save her?' asked Eilidon.

'Perhaps, but not here. We must move quickly. Jadeja can you walk?'

He nodded, 'But I cannot carry my pack and we can't leave anything here for the enemy to find.'

'Obviously,' said Eilidon. She spun a net and wrapped it around hers, Jadeja's and Suremaana's packs, then attached a cord and tied it round Caderyn's waist.

'I'll carry Suremaana. You pull the packs.'

As gently as she could she coiled the snake around her body, securing her with threads. Once she was satisfied that Suremaana would not move, she nodded to the boys and they set off. Jadeja struggled to his feet and moved slowly forward, feeling weaker than he had anticipated. Caderyn hoisted his own pack and then braced himself to take the weight of the other two dragging along behind him. Their progress was slow and laboured. Jadeja tried hard to fight the dizziness brought on by his blood loss.

'I'm sorry,' he said. 'I need to rest a moment.' Caderyn passed him a water bottle and he drank greedily. He looked across at the unconscious Suremaana and felt guilty for his weakness.

Caderyn, also tired from hauling three packs, was glad of a break. They reached the base of the mountain where they found shelter between two large rocks. Eilidon span a web over the top and around them so that they were inside a rocky cocoon. Jadeja collapsed, exhausted. His wound had opened again but he had said nothing in his anxiety to leave the scorched plains and save Suremaana.

After spreading the furs on the ground Eilidon laid Suremaana carefully on them, before once again, grudgingly, binding Jadeja's arm.

'How is she?' he asked.

'Not good.'

Caderyn knelt over Suremaana and gently ran his hands over her body. He could see that the colours of her skin were fading. Touching between her eyes, he began a healing chant, calling on the spirits within him and sending his life energy up and out through his fingers into the snake. Although he was a natural healer, he sensed that he was failing. At last, exhausted he stopped.

'I can't reach her. I don't know if it's because she is in snake form or if I am just too late.'

'There must be something else we can try,' said Eilidon.

Caderyn shook his head.

Jadeja saw the beautiful snake slipping from life. *This is my fault, he* thought. *I led them here. I knew the danger. I can't let her die, I just can't.*

'Let me try,' he said. 'I know some healing from my time with the Shaman-Master.'

'Please,' said Caderyn.

Eilidon raised a hand to protest but Caderyn silenced her.

Jadeja shuffled over to Suremaana. He looked at this beautiful fading snake and felt his emotions in turmoil.

'I'm sorry. I will save you,' he whispered.

He reached into his jacket and took out the small red stones he carried with him. Placing them in a circle around Suremaana, he closed his eyes and began to summon a phoenix spirit. The bird looked questioningly at Jadeja.

'You called me?'

'Yes.' He pointed to Suremaana. 'You must save her.'

The bird looked at her, then spoke to him.

'I am your Khadroma. I was sent to protect you. The risks to you are great. You know that you are hunted.'

'You must save her. I command you to save her.'

'If I do this, then your life will be in her hands.'

'I understand,' replied Jadeja. 'Please bring her back.'

The bird bowed to him. 'I am obliged to obey you.'

Then turning to Suremaana, it enveloped her in a red flame. The fire appeared to consume her body. Eilidon yelled and tried to grab Jadeja, but Caderyn pulled her back.

'Wait! Watch.'

The flames ate away at Suremaana's snake skin until it was quite dry and blackened. Once this was done the phoenix reformed and disappeared. Jadeja gathered up his stones and sat, deep in thought, gazing at Suremaana, willing her to regain consciousness.

The blackened snakeskin began to split, underneath they could see a new, golden one. Suremaana began to stir, she sloughed off the burnt skin and a beautiful red and golden snake emerged, then transformed. She opened her eyes and smiled at her friends.

'What happened?' she asked. 'Why are you looking so worried Eilidon?'

Caderyn rushed forward to hug her.

'I thought we'd lost you,' said Eilidon. 'The griffin. Caderyn couldn't save you.'

'Yes, I remember now. I gave him a taste of my venom. The rest is blackness. If not Caderyn then who?'

'Jadeja saved you,' replied Caderyn.

Suremaana leant over to Jadeja, who had stayed behind the others.

'How can I repay you for this?' she asked.

'You wouldn't need to repay him if he'd prepared us,' said Eilidon.

Feeling the truth of her remark, Jadeja lowered his head.

'My lady, I am pleased to see you recovered.'

She looked deep into his eyes.

'Thank you. Thank you. I will not forget this.'

He smiled and just for a moment he let himself hope that she meant it.

13

Later that evening, after they had eaten and Suremaana was well recovered, Caderyn took Jadeja to one side.

'What are you?' he asked, 'That you can summon a sacred bird to aid you?'

'I am just an apprentice. My Master has taught me many incantations, including the one I just performed.' Jadeja replied.

'No, no no.' answered Caderyn. 'Only a fully trained Shaman can learn that one.'

'It is possible to learn as an apprentice, if you study hard and have a deep focus. My Master took me through the ritual many times until I could perform it. He felt that it was important for me to know it and so it has proved. Although, that is the first time I have done it alone.'

Caderyn was not satisfied.

'The bird questioned you. I saw it. That bird was meant for you, wasn't it? That's why it stopped.'

Jadeja said nothing, but something in his expression gave him away.

'Jadeja, if the Master taught you that incantation to save your own life you have opened yourself up to peril.'

'The lady Suremaana needed help. We would have lost her without the phoenix.'

Caderyn, who was always fair-minded, looked at him with a new respect.

'You are a strange one Jadeja. You lead us into danger unprepared and then perform an act of selflessness. I don't know what to think of you, but I am your Paladin and you can be sure that I will perform my duties.'

Jadeja bowed his head in thanks.

'Now you must rest,' ordered Caderyn. 'You are wounded too and that I can help with.'

'I cannot lie, I am exhausted,' muttered Jadeja.

He went and lay on his furs and was immediately asleep. Caderyn said restorative prayers over him while he slept.

The three Paladin talked briefly about the battle and Jadeja's healing work. Eilidon threw a binding spell on her web and hung delicate glistening droplets on it at various points around them.

'If there is any movement they will fall and wake us,' she said. 'So I think we can risk sleeping.'

Soon all of them were slumbering.

Dawn broke without incident and feeling much refreshed, they packed up. Jadeja was relieved to see that his arm had begun to heal thanks to the efforts of Eilidon and Caderyn. The most remarkable change was to Suremaana. He had to stop himself from staring. Her hair, which had been the colour of dark chocolate was now a glorious flame red, which shimmered in the sunlight. Eilidon also stared when she saw her. Noticing her reaction, Suremaana questioned her.

'What's wrong? Am I scarred?'

'No. Your hair. It's...it's'

'Beautiful,' said Jadeja. 'Stunning.'

Suremaana glanced down at her long plait.

'Oh. Oh!' she repeated. 'That's unexpected. Where's my mirror?'

She pulled a small mirror from within her cloak and held it up, examining her new hair carefully. Caderyn, who up to then had remained silent, now spoke.

'Suremaana you have been marked by the bird spirit. This is a blessing and will give you renewed strength. It is also a reminder of a debt that you owe.'

He grinned and then added: 'It also makes you look amazing.'

Suremaana blushed and Jadeja shot a jealous glance at Caderyn who was now busy with his pack and failed to notice.

Once they were ready, Caderyn led the way.

'The spirits in the aura showed me a path that will take us around the mountain rather than over it.'

'I know of no such path,' said Jadeja.

'It is a spirit way.'

Jadeja looked at the strong and confident Caderyn. *The Master should have chosen you to head this mission,* he thought. *You are a natural leader. No one questions your authority, whereas I am doubted at every turn.* His mind turned inward and clouds of self-doubt gnawed away at him. *I'm going to fail them. I've already endangered them. Master, why did you send me?* He retreated further and further into himself, only brought back by the gentle touch of Suremaana on his arm.

'Are you okay? You looked troubled.'

'Yes, yes. I'm fine. Thank you.'

She smiled at him and he tried to imagine what it would be like to hold her hand. *Don't be so foolish, she would never look at you that way. If she is going to like anyone it would be Caderyn, he is all the things I am not. It was Caderyn that killed the griffin. It was Caderyn who took out the black crow and now it is Caderyn who has been shown the way by the spirits. He is the leader not me. I don't even know why I am part of this mission. They clearly don't need me or want me.* Caderyn's voice brought him back to the present.

'We must bind ourselves together. Eilidon if you could do that please.'

Eilidon duly obliged by spinning a thread around everyone's left wrist and then joined them onto a long light rope. She saw Jadeja lifting the flimsy thread as if questioning what use it could be.

'Don't be fooled by its weightlessness. If tested you will find that it's as strong as steel,' she informed him.

The binding complete, Caderyn led them on. Jadeja continued muttering to himself. At the base of the mountain they saw the first signs of the land healing. Small tufts of coarse grass had taken root amongst the rocks and as they climbed they began to see more and more vegetation appear. After half an hour of climbing they reached a small plateau teeming with wild flowers in a myriad of colours. It was in stark contrast with the land below. Even the air felt lighter.

'This is the healing gate,' said Caderyn.

'I have heard of it,' answered Jadeja. 'The spirits came here to renew after Nam Kha's battle.'

'They have certainly done that,' said Suremaana gazing at the wondrous array of colour. There were flowers in every hue imaginable. Hot pinks and reds mixed with deep blues. Bright oranges mingled with yellows. Purples and whites, indigos, teals, golds all in differing shades.

'It's so beautiful,' she said.

'It's just flowers,' said Eilidon, who was unmoved by the beauty of the place.

'Well, we must walk amongst them,' said Caderyn. 'Quietly now. And stay on my path. Do not stray.'

They walked in single file through the meadow. Suremaana was behind him, then Jadeja, with Eilidon at the rear. Walking amongst the flowers they all noticed how uplifted and renewed they felt. Jadeja's arm healed up completely and Suremaana felt herself filled with vigour and strength. Eilidon and Caderyn also felt stronger and calmer.

The deeper they walked into the meadow the taller the plants became, until they could not see where they were headed. It was only Caderyn's spirit vision that prevented them from getting lost. Soon the flowers towered above them and moving forward became increasingly difficult. What had at first been open and welcoming now became overwhelming and oppressive. The air was heavy with the scent of the flowers and the more they breathed it in the more soporific the effect.

It was Eilidon who dropped first. Jadeja felt the sharp pull on his binding as she fell. He called to the others who stopped immediately. He knelt over Eilidon and shook her but she was in a deep slumber and he could not rouse her.

'Take her pack. I will carry her.' ordered Caderyn. 'We must hurry before we are all overcome.'

Of course you will carry her, thought Jadeja. *I'm just the bag man.* He took the pack and Caderyn hoisted Eilidon over his shoulder and their journey continued. Suremaana and Caderyn chatted easily and once again Jadeja felt out in the cold. To fight the tiredness, they sang or asked each other questions, anything to keep their minds alert. Feeling his knees give way Jadeja called to the others to rest a moment.

'I'm sorry. Rest,' he said.

'Here, drink some water,' offered Suremaana, 'And splash your face.'

He took the bottle gratefully and drank deeply.

'Thank you, my lady, that has helped.'

Using all of his energy to fight the fatigue, Jadeja forced himself to his feet and they carried on.

Caderyn found himself weakening under the weight of his burden, but he pressed on, knowing that without him they would all be lost. He stumbled, getting slower and slower until he felt his knees buckling. He staggered forwards, semi-conscious, putting his hands out to break his fall, slipping into darkness. Instead of landing amongst the meadow flowers he fell face down onto snow. The sudden cold snapped him awake as the other two blundered out behind him.

14

The contrast from the warm vibrant colours and smells of the meadow to this ice white expanse was enough to bring all four of them to their senses. Even Eilidon, who had been unconscious, revived very quickly. There before them was a forest of ice. The trees stood like bare white skeletons rooted to the ground. Everything was covered in snow, which lay white and undisturbed, as if that too was a warning to visitors. *No one comes here. No one enters. I am untouched.* There was no movement, no breath of air, just stillness. Silence. Extreme cold.

Suremaana had already started to shiver.

'Put on your furs,' said Jadeja. 'We have to cross through without stopping. The cold is unforgiving, as is the forest. It does not appreciate being disturbed.'

'I don't think I feel like stopping here. It gives me the shivers. Literally,' said Caderyn.

'It is not a place to joke about. Many have perished in there trying to reach Porphyra's garden. When we set off, we must stay close and whatever you do, do not touch the trees.' Jadeja was firm.

'Why not?' asked Eilidon.

'They may look benign, but each tree holds a frozen spirit desperate to get back to the realm of the living. The warmth from your hand may just be enough to waken one. If that happens, be prepared to run as if your life depends on it. Because it will.'

Having given his warning, Jadeja strapped on his pack and prepared to lead them. *I'm the only one who fully appreciates the dangers of this place,* he thought. *I must lead them safely.* The amulet at his neck flared, he felt its warmth. *Courage, Jadeja, courage,* he told himself, but his knees still shook and bile rose in his stomach. With a final check that their furs were tightly around them, he advanced into the forest.

The silence hung in the air like a menace. It was hard to understand that something so benign could feel quite so threatening. Jadeja set a steady pace and they made rapid progress. There was no conversation. Even the sound of their breathing seemed to echo amongst the trees.

Eilidon noticed that although all the trees appeared the same, if you looked closely there were different markings on each. She could see fine black lines etched into the trunks. She wondered what they meant. The age of the tree perhaps, or the age of the spirit held within. Being a spider, she felt an affinity with trees. They were places of shelter and safety. Good for hiding in or resting. Her people lived in a dense forest where their close alliance to the trees had made them caretakers. In return the forest kept unwanted visitors at bay.

She found herself drawn towards one of the trees and paused in front of it. The white trunk was split into three. The fusing of three bodies, forever joined in a nightmarish fight against the cold. Mist floated around the tree and briefly touched her face as she studied the markings on the bark. Her scrutiny was broken by a hand on her shoulder making her turn sharply.

'Eilidon! Move! Now!' There was an urgency in Jadeja's voice.

Reluctantly she pulled herself away.

'The three,' she muttered.

'Sisters, evil to the core. Locked together throughout time.'

'How do you know about them?'

'I…I know. Please come away.'

He shuddered and she wasn't sure if it was the cold or a distant memory that had caused it. Eilidon moved forward but not without one last backward glance. She was sure that she heard a barely imperceptible sigh as she left.

The deeper into the forest they went the more biting the cold became. Their furs were pulled ever more tightly around them, even so the cold penetrated their bodies like sharp daggers. Jadeja chanced to look behind and noticed that they left no trail. There were no markings at all in the snow to indicate their passing. The trees appeared to be closer together somehow, as if they were forming an impenetrable barrier preventing their return. With a deepening sense of dread, he continued on.

He wasn't the only one to feel unsettled. Eilidon's encounter with the tree of three had left her extremely edgy and with a strong sense of being watched. All notion of time was lost in the continuing whiteness. They had no idea how long they had been travelling. The cold continued to knive them and chill them through. Jadeja kept his pace as unrelenting as the cold.

'How much further?' panted Caderyn.

'An hour or so,' replied Jadeja. 'If we keep moving.'

Caderyn flexed his fingers. His bow hand twitched.

'I have a strange sense of foreboding that I cannot shake,' he whispered.

'That is the forest. The nearer we get to the other side the greater that threat will become, as the tree spirits sense their opportunity for freedom waning. Whilst we are here there is always the possibility that one of us may accidently touch a tree and release a spirit. Once we are through that opportunity is gone. Keep moving, we will soon be out.'

Seemingly in response to Jadeja's words, the trees closed in around them and their path became narrower and more twisted. Progress was slow and tortuous.

'Will this forest never end?' said Suremaana. 'I'm frozen to the bone, tired and hungry.'

'We will soon be through my lady and then you can rest.'

Jadeja tried to sound reassuring but she could sense the weariness in his voice. She carried on, taking care to avoid the encroaching trees.

Eilidon, had started to lag behind. Ever since her encounter with the tree of three she had found it increasingly difficult to keep moving forward. She felt like there was a force trying to hold her back, making every step double the effort. She hadn't said anything to the others so as not to alarm them, but she now felt that she had to.

'Caderyn. Jadeja. Stop!'

Sensing the urgency in her voice they turned.

'I feel like I am being pulled from behind. It is taking all my strength to keep going.'

Looking at her they could see the tiredness in her face.

'It was your encounter with that tree,' replied Jadeja. 'They have sensed a weakness in you. I think it would be better if you stayed behind me and Caderyn brought up the rear.'

Caderyn went to move to the end of the line. Eilidon started to walk past Suremaana, but as she did so, she felt herself stumble over an unseen tree root. Instinctively she put out a hand to break her fall. It hit the ground and touched an exposed root for the briefest of moments. Immediately they heard a deep sigh like that of someone waking up from a long slumber.

'Run!' urged Jadeja. 'Run and don't look back.'

There was a resounding crack from the tree that Eilidon had grazed. A slit appeared in the bark which then peeled back to reveal an inner skin, smooth and white like alabaster. The skin began to melt into a white liquid that oozed from the tree, reforming itself into a woman. There was no solidity to the shape. It moved like fog twisting through the air. The arms reached out long tendrils, feeling for the human who had awakened it.

They ran, dodging and weaving their way through the trees. Twice Suremaana almost fell, only Caderyn's quick reactions in grabbing her prevented her crashing to the ground and waking more spirits. More than ever they were all grateful for the hours and hours of combat training they regularly undertook. Jadeja knew the likelihood of escape was small but he kept his thoughts to himself, willing them on. They couldn't see or hear their pursuer but they knew beyond doubt that it was there. An icy mist like cold breath on a winter's morning reached out to stroke them. Frozen droplets clung to their garments as they ran, slowing them. Their packs also weighed them down but Jadeja had shouted at them to leave nothing.

'I can't. I can't keep going,' said Eilidon.

'You must. Not far,' panted Jadeja.

With their muscles burning and their lungs screaming at them to stop, they raced on until they had passed the final row of trees. All except Eilidon. She remained at the edge, tantalisingly close to safety but unable to move, her cloak frozen to the ground as the tendrils of the awakened tree reached it and began to bind it. She screamed to Caderyn, who turned to see the tree woman coming up behind her, the shape visible through the icy shroud that encased it, bonding itself to Eilidon's cloak. Bow in hand, Caderyn looked Eilidon straight in the eye and then released his arrow.

15

With the precision that only a bow master could muster, the arrow found its target at Eilidon's neck. The point of the arrow penetrated and broke the strap of her cloak allowing her to run free, just as the icy tendrils of the tree woman encircled the hood.

Terrified and relieved in equal measure Eilidon staggered into Caderyn's arms. The woman let out an agonising shriek as she realised her chance of freedom was gone and she felt her tree host pulling her back into the forest, once more to enter her icy prison.

Jadeja saw his hands shake and wondered at the calmness that Caderyn exuded. *I would not have kept my focus. My nerves would have taken over. If it was up to me, Eilidon would be lost.* Darkness filled his heart and he sank to his knees.

'It's ok, she's fine. We are all shocked but we're all here.'

He looked up to see Suremaana standing over him, her face full of concern. She took his hand and pulled him to his feet. He usually recoiled from human contact but he liked the feel of her hand in his. He wondered, *did she like it too?* His thoughts were interrupted.

'Come on Jadeja. I was the one captured. Be a man.'

Eildon strode out, furious with herself for endangering them all and annoyed at Jadeja for showing his weakness.

Ahead of them lay open fields. Once they were well clear of the terrors of the forest, they set up camp. Despite her ordeal Eildon managed to build a protective web around them so they could light a much-needed fire. The warmth filled the web and began to seep into their bones. They ate hungrily. Although it had been less than a day since they had entered the forest, they all felt ravenous.

'Thanks, Caderyn, for saving me, again,' said Eildon.

'I would have done the same for any of us. Thank you for trusting me. If you had moved when I released my arrow... Well let's not think about that.'

'I knew your aim would be true. You are a Paladin of the Bow. I did not doubt you.' Even as she said these words Eildon knew that just for a split second, she had thought that she would die.

In an effort to lighten the mood Suremaana asked where they were to go next.

'It is about a half-day walk across this open country,' replied Jadeja. 'Lady Eildon may I check you for any traces of the ice spirit?'

Eildon shrugged. 'If you must. I'm fine.'

Jadeja took a red crystal on a leather thread from within his tunic. She watched him carefully.

'Please lie down.'

Jadeja held the crystal over her head.

'Try to keep as still as you can.'

He closed his eyes and began a Shamanic chant. The crystal remained motionless. Satisfied that she was clear he put it back in his jerkin.

'It would seem that you are undamaged,' he reassured her.

'I could've told you that,' said Eilidon, sitting up again. Nevertheless, when she moved a vision of the tree of three flashed into her mind. The shock of it unsteadied her and she toppled backwards.

'Are you ok?' asked Caderyn.

'Yes. Yes. It's nothing. Just a little dizzy.'

'I suggest we all get some sleep,' said Suremaana.

'No arguments here,' replied Caderyn.

They settled down for the night, confident that the web would be secure enough for them not to set a watch. Eilidon was the last to fall asleep, unable to shake off the terror of what had transpired. Although her outward demeanour gave nothing away, inwardly she was petrified and deeply shaken. *Weak, weak, weak,* she thought. *Never again.*

The next day dawned clear and bright, offering a cloudless sky to walk under. The fire embers were smothered and they were set.

'What about the furs? Will we need them?' asked Suremaana. 'Please tell me that we won't have to go back through that hideous forest again.'

'No my lady, we will take another route. I think we can leave the furs, but we must hide them,' replied Jadeja.

They dug a hole beneath a thorn bush and left the furs in it, covering the top with branches and leaves. Caderyn set a concealment charm over the site. Jadeja led them across the lush green fields. The going was easy and the warmth from the sun was in stark contrast to the ice and snow of the forest. They were crossing open land that was bright, verdant and calm. A fresh water stream offered them the chance to wash themselves and refill their water bottles.

A laughing Suremaana kicked water into Eilidon's face.

92

'Hey!' she shouted. Then grinning widely, she returned the favour. Jadeja got showered as he sat reorganising his pack. He stood up to protest, then he felt Caderyn's firm hand in his back and the next thing he knew he was face down in the stream. He came up spluttering to see the girls laughing at the indignant look on his face. He was about to protest again when Suremaana flicked water at him. He responded by pulling her over, then hurriedly tried to apologise.

'Jadeja!' she said, looking deep into his eyes and trying desperately to keep a straight face. 'I thought you were a gentleman.'

'Yes, my lady, forgive me. I don't know what came over me.'

Before he had time to say any more, she dunked him again. This time he came up laughing. They were all grateful for the break in the tension of the last few days and messed about in the stream until, drenched and exhausted they lay on the bank to dry off and fell asleep.

Eilidon woke first. The sun was high in the sky and her clothes were dry. She woke the others.

'Come on, time to move.'

Jadeja was immediately on alert.

'How long have we slept?'

'An hour maybe,' replied Eilidon.

'We must move quickly. We have been careless to leave ourselves so exposed.'

The anxiety in Jadeja's voice put them all on edge.

'He's right,' agreed Caderyn. 'We shouldn't have let our guard down.'

Hurriedly grabbing their stuff, they set off once more, following Jadeja as he led them onwards. He looked back at the Paladin and the easy way they were with each other.

Suremaana was laughing at something Caderyn had said and he felt the rush of jealousy again. *I'm always an outsider* he thought, feeling that familiar pang of loneliness. They walked until late afternoon, the light-hearted mood of earlier replaced by a much more cautious one. They had crossed the fields and found themselves facing a high wall overgrown with creepers. Jadeja began feeling his way along the greenery. His fingers moving rapidly as he searched for the way in.

'Can we help?' asked Suremaana. 'What are you looking for?'

'I am seeking the door handles,' replied Jadeja.

'Door handles,' scoffed Eilidon. 'You mean to get in we simply open the doors.'

'Yes, my lady. If we can locate the handles, we can open the doors to the garden.'

'How hard can that be?' asked Caderyn.

'It depends if the garden is willing for you to find them,' answered Jadeja.

'What do these handles look like then?' muttered Eilidon.

'They look like these leaves,' replied Jadeja, pointing to a cluster of bright green leaves curved and shaped like crescent moons.

'You will not find them by sight, only by touch.'

'Right let's spread out and work together. Eilidon and I will start down there and I'll mark our starting point with my bow. You two start over there and we'll work in towards each other,' said Caderyn.

They split up and began touching all the crescent shaped leaves. None felt like door handles, merely soft and flexible as leaves should. Jadeja and Suremaana worked together in silence. Occasionally they would catch each other's eye and

Jadeja would smile shyly at Suremaana, who beamed happily back. At one point their hands touched as they both reached for the same leaf. Instead of withdrawing her hand, Suremaana let it linger under Jadeja's fingers, feeling an inner glow at his touch. *Does she like me?* he thought and blushed awkwardly as he moved his hand away. His discomfort was short-lived because the next leaf she touched was firm beneath her hand, the one beside it also.

'I've found them,' she called out excitedly.

Suremaana pulled hard on the handles but nothing happened.

'May I?' my lady.

She nodded to Jadeja who placed his hands on hers and together they pulled on the handles until they heard a sharp click and a large pair of ivy-covered doors swung outwards. The other two came running up beside them.

'Welcome to The Garden of Yangchen,' said Jadeja.

What lay before them was quite magnificent. Suremaana entered first, noting the carefully sculpted lawns and flower borders ablaze with bright red roses. One lawn was in the shape of a serpent, bordered on every side with yellow and orange pansies. Another lawn was in the shape of a shield. This was edged with tall flowering purple thistles, their sharp spikes resembling men at arms. A large rectangular lawn had a tall palm tree at its centre, standing upright like a sentry on duty. Walking through, her eyes were met at every turn by more and more elaborate floral displays.

'This is really something,' said Caderyn.

'I had heard of its beauty, but I was not prepared for this,' said Suremaana. 'My father would love to see it.' Her voice trailed off as she thought of the home she hadn't seen for so long.

In its centre the garden had a beautiful pool, surrounded by willows hanging like curtains at the water's edge. Looking closely, they could see large golden fish swimming happily in the water. Jadeja heard a toad chorus coming from the undergrowth and smiled. Suremaana spoke again.

'This is more beautiful than I ever imagined. The stories tell that Porphyra and Ancrobus created a paradise, but I never dreamed it would be as wonderful as this.'

'Who tends it?' asked Caderyn

'It tends itself,' replied Jadeja. 'The garden keeps itself in order out of respect for its creators, who had lavished it with so much love before the spirits took their revenge.'

'I'm surprised no one has tried to claim it for themselves,' said Eilidon.

'Many have tried to find it, but the garden only reveals itself to those with a genuine need to visit. To all others, it remains hidden from view,' explained Jadeja.

'In other words, it knew we were coming,' said Caderyn.

'Perhaps,' replied Jadeja. He thought back to his previous visit here. He was only a child then, running scared, pursued by cruel masters desperate to recapture him. The garden had opened its doors to him and given him sanctuary. Those that pursued him unable to find or gain entry to this secret place.

'Where is Suremaana?' asked Eilidon, suddenly aware that she was not with them.

'She is safe. The garden will not harm her,' answered Jadeja.

Eilidon was not convinced. Her spider senses tingled.

'Something is watching us,' she muttered.

Suremaana had wandered off in the direction of a small knot garden. Its intricate pattern reminded her of a snakeskin. As she stood there looking at the diamond shaped layout of the little box trees, she felt something tugging at her. Her eyes followed the patterns to the centre where a mandala of intertwined snakes crossing over and under each other in a never-ending series of loops, formed the centre piece. The snakes were red and green and you could not tell where one ended and the next one began. Suremaana approached the centre and was surprised to find herself in snake form, having no recollection of the transformation.

Rising from the centre of the mandala was a golden snake, the most magnificent creature she had ever seen. She knew that this was Porphyra and bowed in recognition of this ancient queen of her people. Porphyra acknowledged the tribute then beckoned to Suremaana to approach. Suremaana obeyed, held as she was in the gaze of the snake queen. She began to entwine herself around the snake spirit.

The other three arrived at the knot garden in time to see Suremaana in a strange dance, for they could not see Porphyra. Eilidon was about to cross the garden to her friend when Jadeja held her back. She glared at him in protest but he pointed to the bushes and she saw that they were not covered in leaves but in hundreds of viperous snake heads.

'Only a snake may enter here,' he told her.

Realising the danger she had been about to put herself in, she nodded her thanks.

'There is nothing we can do except wait,' he said.

Suremaana and Porphyra remained locked in the centre of the garden. Porphyra sank her fangs into Suremaana and she felt a jolt like a thousand lightning bolts rush through her body and then a voice filled her mind.

You seek my stone. Are you worthy to retrieve it? You will have to sit in my chair and pass its test for the stone to reveal itself. You have strength Paladin, and a true heart. I believe the chair will spare you, but only if you do not falter. You have loyal friends. The chair will test them too. This is what you must do.

Porphyra whispered instructions then removed her fangs and let Suremaana go.

Thank you for remembering me, were the last words Suremaana heard before the snake queen melted back into the mandala and the never-ending loop. She remained motionless for a while, absorbing the event that had just passed, then slowly and gracefully Suremaana exited the knot garden and became human again. Her friends approached her full of concern.

'What just happened?' asked Eilidon.

'Porphyra spoke to me. She told me how to find the stone.'

'My lady, are you okay, you seem pale?'

'I am fine Jadeja. Please do not worry.' She squeezed his hand reassuringly.

'Come, we must find the chair. It is at the far end of the pool.'

They walked back to the water and around its edge until they arrived at the top end. There, on a dais, was a large green chair. It looked like it was draped in a heavy velvet, but closer inspection revealed it to be a covering of thick moss. In front of the chair on a bed of shells were five silver orbs of varying size.

'One of these is the stone we seek,' said Suremaana. Caderyn went to pick one up.

'Wait!' ordered Suremaana. 'You cannot touch them. It is certain death. Only one to whom the stone has revealed itself can touch them and then, only the one containing the stone.'

'I will ask the spirits to help us,' answered Caderyn.

'They already have,' replied Suremaana. 'I must take the test. Only if the chair finds me worthy will the stone be revealed.'

'Let me take it,' offered Jadeja. He couldn't bear the thought of her being in any danger.

'No, Jadeja. I have been chosen. Your loyalty to me will also be tested. All of you, whatever you see, whatever happens to me, you must remain where you are. Draw no weapon and make no move. You must not interfere or come to my aid. Do you promise? My life and our success depends on it.'

Jadeja made to protest again, but Caderyn stopped him.

'If this is what we must do then you have my promise.' He laid his bow on the floor as he spoke.

'Mine too,' added Eilidon, laying her knives on the ground.

Reluctantly Jadeja promised and lay his slingshot and sword down.

'Thank you,' nodded Suremaana. Then she hugged each of them in turn, making Jadeja blush at the contact. With a deep breath, she walked up to Porphyra's chair, bowed once, then sat down.

She looked as regal as any queen of the Serpentae. Her new red hair glistened like burnished copper in the sunlight. Jadeja was enraptured by her beauty. He had never seen a girl so magnificent. *Please let her pass this test,* he thought.

For a few moments nothing happened. Suremaana sat calmly in the chair smiling at her friends. Suddenly a golden snake shot out from behind her and wrapped itself tightly around her throat, binding her to the chair. More snakes appeared, each one tying her by the wrists, ankles and waist until she was unable to move. Watching on, the others saw the chair turn into a writhing mass of snakes, filling them with dread.

The snakes held no fear for Suremaana, she was a Serpentae and knew they would not harm her. However, she was not prepared for what came next. The vegetation that covered the chair began to move and reform into the shape of a huge warrior. He stood before her, sword raised and she knew that she faced Ancrobus, Porphyra's lover.

'You have come for my wife's jewel. I will not release it unless you prove worthy. Will you challenge me?'

Jadeja, seeing what was happening tried to rush forward, but Caderyn grabbed his wrist.

'No!' he ordered. 'We promised. She is a Paladin. She can do this.'

Jadeja fought his instincts and remained still. All he could see was the enormous figure of Ancrobus bearing down on Suremaana, striking her over and over with his sword. Blood ran everywhere and her screams filled his head. He wanted to save her. He couldn't bear the thought of her being attacked in this way. With all his inner strength, he held on to his promise. Closing his eyes, he began to chant, focusing on the words, repeating them over and over so that he didn't have to watch.

Suremaana, meanwhile, looked Ancrobus in the eye and replied.

'Mighty Ancrobus, our need is great or we would not have entered your garden. I must take the jewel with me, so yes I will challenge you.'

Ancrobus bowed. 'I accept your challenge.'

Suremaana transformed and coiled herself around Ancrobus's neck.

He pulled her off with ease but as he did so she flicked him violently in the eye with her tail causing him to release his grip. Instantly she was human again, scissor kicking him. He was ready for her and took the blow, slashing at her with his sword. She dodged the blade just in time, then ran at him launching herself through the air and wrapping her legs around his neck. He stumbled, but quickly released himself. The two of them continued to kick and punch, landing blow after blow. His strength was far superior to hers, but her agility and speed were matchless.

'You fight well,' acknowledged Ancrobus. 'But I see that you are tiring. A girl like you would never be strong enough to defeat me.'

Caderyn too, saw that Suremaana was weakening. He watched her opponent land blow after blow. His enormous fists pounding her body with ever increasing force. Blood poured from her eyes and mouth as the beating continued. Ancrobus laughed as he overpowered her, knocking her into unconsciousness. She lay collapsed on the ground, unable to resist any longer. Ancrobus raised his fist to land the fatal blow. Instinctively, Caderyn reached for his bow. The arrow was nocked and ready. The bow string drawn back, primed for firing. Every fibre urged him to release his arrow and save Suremaana, whose battered form lay still on the ground. At the last moment, the runes on his wrist flared, reminding him of his promise. He slackened his hold and let his arrow fall.

Suremaana said nothing in reply to Ancrobus's taunt. She knew it was true. Her strength and energy were waning, while that of her opponent remained full. Deciding to try one more move she gave herself room and came at him in a series of fast somersaults, aiming for the backs of his knees. Finding her target, he went down, but before she could land her next blow he was up, sword raised above her for the final strike.

Eilidon shouted a warning. Too late. The sword came down. As she watched, the sword sliced through Suremaana. She called again and without realising, reached for her blades to attack. She was poised to throw them when she heard Suremaana's warning.

'Whatever happens you must remain where you are. Do nothing.'

Reluctantly, she put down her weapons.

Suremaana had seen his move and transformed just as the blade crashed down. In that moment, she saw how to defeat her enemy. Ancrobus raised his sword again, as he did so, she sprang forward and slid herself through the loops on his scabbard, turning herself into a snakeskin belt. Completing the knot around him she rendered her opponent motionless. His sword fell harmlessly to the ground.

'You have claimed your victory. You may take your seat again,' said Ancrobus.

Suremaana slowly unwound herself from his waist, releasing her opponent and returned to human form. She sat in the chair and Porphyra appeared and stood beside her lover. The two of them bowed low to Suremaana, then Porphyra touched Suremaana's hand and said: 'Choose your orb. I will guide you.'

Then she and Ancrobus embraced and disappeared.

Jadeja watched as Suremaana studied the silver orbs and passed her hand over each one in turn. She chose the second of them. When she picked it up, the orb melted so that it looked like she was wearing a glove of liquid silver. Turning her hand over, she revealed an emerald stone.

16

Holding the stone high, Suremaana moved away from the chair and sat down wearily. Her friends sat silently with her.

Jadeja spoke, 'I saw that warrior strike you again and again. I wanted to rescue you. I thought you were dead.'

'Me too,' added Eilidon. 'I saw his sword slice through your body when you were a snake. I reached for my knives.'

'I had my bow,' said Caderyn. 'He was beating you to a pulp with his fists. It was horrific.'

'They were all tests, illusions, pushing you to keep your word. Porphyra told me that the chair would test your resolve. That's why I had to make you promise. I had to defeat Ancrobus on my own. If you had attacked, I would have died.'

'I came so close,' replied Caderyn. 'I was ready to fire. The runes on my wrist reminded me of my promise just in time.'

'My lady, are you really unharmed?' said Jadeja.

'A little bruised, but essentially I am fine. Thank you.' She smiled warmly at him and he felt the colour rise in his cheeks.

'More importantly we have the stone.'

'Well done Suremaana.'

It was Eilidon who spoke. Suremaana bowed her head, acknowledging the compliment.

'I communed with Porphyra in the knot garden. She questioned me and looked deep within. If she had not thought me worthy, she would not have let me sit in her chair. I believe that only a serpentae could have taken that test, which is why I was chosen.'

Eilidon asked, 'Where do we go next? I think we should take the stone to the Elders for safety.'

'Should we not try to find the next stone first?' suggested Caderyn. 'I can try to ask the spirits for guidance.'

'Maybe we could split up. Two of us deliver the stone and two continue the search,' said Suremaana.

'Whatever, but we shouldn't linger here. It doesn't feel safe.'

'The Garden of Yangchen is a peaceful place, lady Eilidon.'

'It may be to you Jadeja, however my senses are telling me otherwise. I felt it at the gate and I feel it...'

Before she had time to finish speaking a large wolf-like creature sprang from the bushes landing on Caderyn, tearing at his flesh with razor sharp fangs. Eilidon reacted immediately, drawing her knife across the creature's throat.

'Thank you,' mouthed Caderyn, throwing the creature off him and trying to staunch the bleeding from his shoulder.

'There'll be more. Suremaana hide the stone. Go. Leave. We'll fight them.'

Suremaana transformed with the stone in her mouth and slid off through the undergrowth as the next pack struck.

This time they were ready. Six wolves attacked. Six wolves died, taken out with blade, bow and slingshot.

Jadeja barely had time to draw breath before the birds came. Huge black crows dived down on them in a massive cloud.

'Cover me,' shouted Eilidon and she transformed and began making a huge web. While she spun Caderyn and Jadeja shot down bird after bird, but they were heavily outnumbered.

'Hurry Eilidon, we are running out of arrows and stones,' said Jadeja swivelling round to avoid losing an eye to a diving bird. He kicked it as it passed him, before reloading his shot and taking out another. He saw Caderyn take another blow on his wound causing him to drop his bow. Jadeja ran and killed another crow just as Eilidon threw out her web and the birds found themselves trapped in the sticky threads.

'Run!' she shouted. 'Won't hold long. Find cover.'

They ran through the garden looking for any place that might afford shelter.

'There,' yelled Jadeja, pointing to a small arbour at the edge of a particularly beautiful rose garden. They reached the shelter just as a large swarm of dargon appeared. Eilidon had a web over the entrance in moments, holding them at bay while Jadeja began an incantation to repel them. Some of the dargon squeezed through the roses growing around the arbour. These were swiftly dispatched by a blade or an arrowhead.

'Who is sending them? They must have a spirit guide? And how did they get in? I thought the garden was protected?'

In answer to his question, Caderyn saw a figure appear on the lawn. The man was tall and dressed in black which matched his long hair that was billowing out behind him. The whole left side of his face also appeared to be black.

The nearer he got they could see that it was a skull tattooed on his face.

'Rabten,' whispered Jadeja.

'You know him?' shouted Eilidon.

'He is the Jhankhira's messenger and a formidable opponent.'

'I take it you've faced him before,' muttered Caderyn.

'Once in battle, before that he...' Jadeja's voice trailed off, paling at the memory. Even as he spoke Rabten called up another wave of dargon that formed a deadly swarm around him.

'You have something I want Paladin. Hand it over and I will grant you a mercifully quick death, rather than a slow and painful one.'

'You don't get to decide how we die,' shouted Eilidon, defiantly.

'My dargon will fill your feeble bodies with poison and I shall enjoy watching you writhe around in agony. Now hand over the stone.'

'Never,' she replied.

Rabten howled and released the swarm. Jadeja saw the first dargon pushing through the arbour. More followed, faster now and faster. Jadeja was the first to be stung, recoiling as dargon venom entered his blood stream. Reacting to the pain he fought like a madman to keep them at bay. The sheer pressure of numbers threatened to overwhelm them in their confined space.

'This is impossible,' he said, then he heard a second droning. He looked to see what else was coming for them and saw a swarm of giant bees flying purposely towards the dargon, who fell, as the bees stung them. Seizing his opportunity, Caderyn emerged from the arbour and began shooting arrows at Rabten. Each one was repelled. Eilidon tried with her blades.

'It's no use, you are simply wasting your weapons,' yelled Jadeja.

Rabten sneered at them. Seeing that his dargon were being overrun by the bees he summoned an army of man-sized gargoyles. Each deformed face more hideous than the last. They formed a V-shaped attack formation and advanced.

'Give me what I want.'

Caderyn, Eilidon and Jadeja stood together.

'We must give Suremaana time to get away,' ordered Jadeja. 'We can hold them off for a little while.'

They prepared to fight.

'The answer is still no,' replied a defiant Eilidon.

'Then die.'

He waved his fist and the gargoyle army advanced. Caderyn's arrows took out the first line. Eilidon's knives the next. Jadeja's slingshot took more, but they were heavily outnumbered. Caderyn drew his sword and began hacking at them.

'This is hopeless,' panted Jadeja.

'Not while we are breathing,' answered Caderyn.

They heard a mighty war cry coming from behind them and Ancrobus appeared with an army of soldiers whose armour was reinforced with spikes. They wore purple helmets on their heads.

'Look! Look! They are from the shield garden,' shouted Caderyn.

Indeed, at first glance they did look like an army of giant thistles.

'Who dares defile my garden?' roared Ancrobus.

He advanced towards Rabten, while his soldiers engaged the gargoyles in battle. The thistle soldiers were precision fighters, dancing past the clumsy fists of the gargoyles before striking down their opponents. Caderyn and Eilidon felt the battle rush return and retrieved their arrows and knives, rejoining the combat with renewed vigour. Jadeja faltered, deafened by the clash of swords on shield and splitting of stone as gargoyles were destroyed. Terror at the memory of Rabten, the intensity of the fight and Suremaana undefended left him paralysed.

Ancrobus and Rabten were embroiled in fierce one to one combat, blades flashing. Ancrobus repeatedly made contact but each time he hit, his blade was repelled by a shield of dark energy.

'You can't defeat me old man,' taunted Rabten. 'Your sword has no power over me.'

Jadeja stared. For all his strength, Ancrobus was having no impact on the Jhankhira's man.

The gargoyle army was being driven back by the soldiers and the Paladin, who now advanced towards Rabten. His army defeated, he retreated. Taking a small gong from inside his cloak he beat it in an irregular rhythm. The sound resonated all around and brought Ancrobus to a standstill.

'Be gone warrior; back to your resting place,' ordered Rabten.

With each beat of the gong Ancrobus weakened as it drained his power. He was helpless to stop it. Rabten raised the gong high and with one final strike Ancrobus and his soldiers disappeared.

Smiling triumphantly, he once more advanced towards Caderyn and Eilidon. Jadeja retreated within the arbour and retrieved the feather and innards of the raven. Taking the heart, he placed it on the feather and began an ancient invocation. As he spoke the words the spirit of Raven emerged and gazed steadily at Jadeja.

'I have summoned you to attack Rabten. I am your slayer. You must obey me.'

Raven's spirit bowed to him then turned towards Rabten. Spreading out its wings it flew directly to its target. He didn't see it coming. The bird struck him cleanly in the heart. He stumbled, confused momentarily. The raven circled, poised to swoop again. This time Rabten was ready for it. Using a net inlaid with black runes he threw it in the air and captured the bird and smiled.

'I have you now Jadeja. You have overstretched yourself this time.'

Jadeja began to release the link between himself and the bird. Even as he chanted, he could hear Rabten's voice in his head.

It's too late, little one. I have you now. I have the spirit you summoned in my thrall and its link to you is all I need to have you.

Jadeja's words became more urgent. Already he could feel Rabten invading his mind. He pushed him back, releasing Raven and fell down, exhausted.

Feeling the break in the link a furious Rabten let out a howl of anger. Caderyn and Eilidon seized the opportunity to advance on him while he was momentarily distracted. An arrow pierced his shoulder, mirroring the wound the wolf had inflicted on Caderyn. He staggered backward, stunned at his vulnerability, then before another arrow or blade could penetrate, transformed into a crow and flew off.

Caderyn dropped to his knees, drained. Eilidon looked at him.

'Your wound's open and you've lost blood. I'll stitch it. I don't think he'll come back. He's injured.'

Caderyn was too worn out to argue.

'Where is Jadeja?'

Eilidon realised he was not with them. Inside the arbour, they saw his unconscious body lying on the ground, a heart and feather next to it.

'Is he alive?' asked Caderyn.

Eilidon felt his neck for a pulse.

'Yes, but barely. I can't see any wound.'

Seeing the heart and feather Caderyn realised what Jadeja had done.

'He sent that raven to attack. When it was captured Rabten must have tried to take Jadeja as well.'

'Why would he want Jadeja?'

Caderyn shrugged.

'I don't know, but the Shaman-Master did say we were to protect him. We don't appear to have managed that.'

'He's still alive,' said Eilidon.

'Maybe, but he is clearly harmed.'

'So are you. I must sew up that wound. Then I'll tend to Jadeja.'

Caderyn took off his shirt. The gash was deeper than he realised and now that the adrenalin of the battle was over the pain hit him.

'Wait here. I'll find healing herbs.'

Eilidon ran off and Caderyn allowed himself the luxury of closing his eyes, exhaustion overwhelming him.

Eilidon quickly found the herbs she wanted. The garden sensed her need and guided her towards the plants she required. When she returned to the arbour, she found a guard of thistles at the entrance. She acknowledged them and they parted to let her through.

Caderyn stirred as she entered. Eilidon spread out the herbs she had brought. They included camphor to reduce

111

infection and brolax to induce deep sleep, this she gave to Caderyn straight away.

'Eat this.'

He was too tired to put up any resistance and ate the leaves that were offered. Moments later he was unconscious. Eilidon cleaned the wound and put on a compress of camphor, lovage and witch hazel. With deft fingers, she created a net covering and then stitched the wound. Next, she turned to Jadeja, checking him for any physical wounds she may have missed. Satisfied that there were none she began mixing a compound of mint, lime and salvia flowers with water from her flask.

Raising Jadeja's head she carefully managed to get some of the liquid inside him.

'That was brave,' she whispered. 'This will restore you.'

Knowing that both her patients were likely to remain unconscious for some time and having a guard at the door, Eilidon transformed and scuttled off through the roof of the arbour to find out what had happened to Suremaana.

17

Unaware of the ensuing battle, Suremaana headed straight for the knot garden. Fortunately, she had escaped unseen, however she knew that it would not take the enemy long to discover that the stone was missing. At the mandala Suremaana called out to Porphyra.

'My lady of the garden, my need is great. I call upon you one more time to aid me if it pleases you.'

Her request was answered immediately and Porphyra rose once again from the centre of the mandala.

'My garden has been violated. They will not have my stone. Follow me Suremaana and I will lead you to safety.'

'My friends?' asked Suremaana.

'Ancrobus will help them. Come.'

Porphyra led her out of the knot garden, through a wall of gladioli and into an apple orchard swarming with bees, moving rapidly from blossom to blossom, until they turned and flew off in one giant cloud.

'It appears they are needed elsewhere,' said Porphyra.

Suremaana prayed that her friends were okay. Something fell and landed near them.

'Dargon. We must hurry. Our snakeskin will keep us camouflaged and my bees will make sure that no more of those things come near us.'

The two snakes slithered rapidly through the garden. There was no time for Suremaana to admire the designs or the blooms. They arrived at a dark and shady corner. Moving through a bed of hostas, Suremaana heard the sound of running water.

'An underground stream,' explained Porphyra. 'It will take you far beyond the plains and into the province of the Serpentae. From there you can find your way...'

'...Home.'

Porphyra nodded. 'My people always hoped that one day I would return. They never understood how I could love someone from the warrior race who wore snakeskins as trophies, but Ancrobus' spirit is ancient and although when we met it inhabited the body of a man, I saw that his true self was a serpentae of Aramansus, the oldest known snake people. I knew that we were meant to be together. When we made this sanctuary, we found this stream and I followed it back. When I realised where it led, I told Ancrobus to fill it up and cut it off in case anyone found it. Wisely, he told me to leave it, believing that one day we would have need of it. That day has now come. Hurry Suremaana, take my stone to safety, away from the dark forces that pursue it.'

'Thank you. I will be sure to tell my people that you are and always will be a true queen of the Serpentae.'

Porphyra bowed and moved a large flat stone to reveal the source of the waterway. Suremaana entered the water and was gone. Porphyra put the stone back and ordered the plants to grow so thickly around it that the entrance could not be discovered.

The underground stream flowed swiftly and Suremaana found herself travelling far and fast. As a snake, she was very comfortable in the water and being used to travelling underground she was not fearful. The stream flowed down at first, deep into the earth, then levelled out and turned south. In some places the water course became squeezed between rocks and she had to move carefully to avoid getting trapped.

All the time she thought of her friends, hoping that they had survived the attack. To her surprise, it was Jadeja she worried about the most. She hated to admit it, but she was attracted to him. Her feelings both angered and pleased her. Angered, because her mind was invaded by thoughts of the strange young man who was always so polite and courteous and flattered her so kindly. It made her feel weak and undisciplined. She had been trained to put personal feelings aside. At the same time, she enjoyed the warm feeling she got when she remembered the touch of his hands on hers as they had opened the garden gate, or how she felt when he held her gaze.

A sudden twist in the direction of the stream shook her from her daydreams. A sharp right turn was followed by the water bubbling upwards and opening out into a circular pool. The sound of roaring water met her ears. Surfacing, she found herself just behind a waterfall cascading down a rock face into a freshwater pool which was surrounded by tall orange flowers. Suremaana knew immediately where she was.

'Home,' she sighed out loud.

She swam under the waterfall and out into the centre of the pool. The water was sparkling, clear and fresh and she transformed and paddled around happily before climbing out onto a small patch of shingle on the right-hand bank.

Bending over to wring out her hair she was surprised to find a spear in her back.

'Who dares to swim in the royal pool?' came a man's voice. 'Only those of royal blood are allowed to enter here.'

'Then you will find that I am permitted,' answered Suremaana, turning to face her inquisitor.

The young guardsman looked somewhat confused.

'I am Suremaana, daughter of the king. To whom am I speaking?'

'I am Simeon, guardsman of the lake.'

'Well, Simeon, please put down your spear and escort me to my father.'

'Yes, my Lady Suremaana, forgive me. I did not recognise you.'

'I have been away for some time,' she smiled. 'There is nothing to forgive. You were doing your duty.'

Simeon bowed low, then led Suremaana up a rocky path and onwards to the royal house.

King Surreman was overjoyed to see his daughter again, although somewhat taken aback at her new copper coloured hair. They hugged and hugged and talked and talked, so much to catch up on. When he heard the story of her hair he spoke gravely.

'We owe that young man a great debt. To sacrifice a guardian spirit for another is an act of extreme nobility. Tell me more about him.'

'There is little to tell Papa. He is apprentice to the Shaman-Master. Where he is from or who his people are, I do not know. At first, we were wary of him, but he has proved himself an ally to the Paladin.'

'He certainly has, my darling daughter, even if you now have the flame hair of a northern tribeswoman. Surprisingly it has made you even more beautiful. If that is

116

possible.' He smiled warmly at Suremaana, who bowed politely at the compliment.

'We must celebrate your homecoming and decide what to do with Porphyra's stone. Go to your chambers and freshen yourself while I have the kitchens prepare us a feast.'

Knowing it was pointless to protest, Suremaana bowed and took her leave, returning to her chamber, a room she hadn't seen for over three years. Not since the day she was chosen to serve the Elders and taken away to train as a Paladin, the elite order of ambassadors, whose task is to represent the Shaman-Master on Temple business. Always young, the Paladin are picked for a unique gift that each possesses. For Caderyn it was his intuition and affinity with the bow. For Eilidon, her enhanced spider senses and herblore. Suremaana's skills lay in her ability to travel underground, a gift only bestowed on a limited number of the Serpentae and her fighting skills. Trained in the art of hand to hand combat, she had proven time and again to be faster, fiercer and more intuitive than any of her opponents and teachers.

It had been a painful goodbye when the Elders took her. Just twelve, she was the only child of the king. Her mother had died two years after her birth so she had always been cossetted by him, protected and loved, given every privilege associated with her status. However, she was headstrong, wilful and refused to sit and be pampered. Instead, she ordered her servants to bring her the best physical trainers and the best teachers of Serpentae lore. Day after day she kicked and tumbled and ran and jumped, learning every technique that could be taught, plus some that couldn't. Her skills and courage astounded her

117

teachers. Never backing away from a new move, her physicality amazed everyone.

Suremaana would rush to show her father every new move that she mastered, drinking in his praise. She adored him and when he gasped in shock as she showed him yet another daring move, she would run laughing into his arms and tell him not to worry, she knew what she was doing.

For her father however, her skills were a source of sadness. He knew that the Elders would come for her and he dreaded that day. Watching her become stronger made his heart ache. This child was his world and her departure would leave a gaping chasm.

A month after her twelfth birthday the Elders arrived. The king begged them not to take her, offering them anything they wanted. Ancient artefacts, a whole army of Serpentae, his best warriors. It was useless and he knew it. Suremaana was gifted, marked and he had to let her go.

That evening they sat together and he told her that the Elders were here for her. She looked at him.

'Papa, I knew this day would come. I am strong. I have my mother's skills. I love you Papa. I will make you proud. It is an honour to be chosen. We are blessed. Truly.'

'I know my child. I always knew, from the moment of your birth. You are the child of a Paladin. It was always your destiny to follow in her footsteps.'

Suremaana bowed low.

'When do I go?'

'You leave in the morning my dearest one. It is an honour, but you already make me proud.'

When he reached the door of her chamber she called out.

'Papa.'

He stopped and she ran to him and hugged him as tightly as she could for as long as she could. Finally letting go, he bent and kissed her forehead.

'Goodnight my child. I love you.'

Suremaana watched the door close behind him, then ran to her bed and cried copious tears.

The next morning she left with the Elders. While many at the court wept to see her leave, she kept her emotions inside and walked from the palace with her head held high and her heart in pieces.

Now she entered her chambers as a Paladin, a chosen warrior and ambassador, and stood there looking around at the familiar yet distant room of her childhood. A golden gown was laid out on the bed and a hot bath scented with the finest rose oils awaited her. Hesitating for only moments, her clothes were thrown off and she stepped into the warm water.

Bathed and dressed, Suremaana rejoined her father in the banqueting hall. When everyone was seated King Surreman clapped his hands and servants appeared with silver salvas piled with the most delicious foods: sweetbreads, saffron rice, stuffed mice, golden corn, tender fillets of fish from the pool, ice flowers dusted in fine sugar, chocolate and cinnamon dates and a multitude of other delicacies. The wine was served in golden goblets and there was plenty of it.

'Father, this is too much.'

'Nonsense. I haven't seen you in over three years. I think that we are allowed a little celebration.'

He clapped again and a band of musicians appeared followed by a troupe of dancers.

Suremaana sighed, and allowed her father this indulgence. She sat back and let herself be Suremaana, daughter of Surreman, Princess of the Serpentae, for the rest of the evening.

That night she slept in her sumptuous bed, covered in the finest of silk sheets. She awoke to find a floor length shift dress of emerald green silk and a long copper waistcoat that uncannily matched the colour of her hair, laid out on the ottoman at the foot of the bed. For her feet, the softest leather sandals that fitted like a second skin.

Once dressed she looked at herself in the mirror admiring the beautiful young woman looking back at her. She wondered what Jadeja would think of her dressed like this. She hoped that he would like it, then blushed at the notion.

There was a knock at the door and she opened it to find the young guardsman from the pool.

'Forgive me Your Highness, but the King has ordered me to escort you to his council chamber,' he spluttered, staring at this beautiful young woman.

'Then we had better hurry,' she replied, stepping outside into the corridor. 'Come on. The king does not like to be kept waiting.'

'Yes, yes. Follow me.'

Walking briskly, he took her quickly to the council chamber where the king and two Elders were waiting.

'Greetings dearest daughter. May I present our visitors. Hamroon and Gardeer from the Shamanic Council.'

Suremaana bowed to each of her visitors in turn. Hamroon was a small round man with a full beard. His smile filled his face and he was genuinely pleased to see her. She remembered him from her training days. He had prepared all their meals and eaten plenty himself.

'Dear girl. So good to see you. Still stick thin.'

'Thank you Hamroon. And yes, despite your best efforts.'

Her second visitor she was less familiar with.

'I am Gardeer of the Lake and it is good to see you again.'

Suremaana bowed, noting Gardeer's appearance. She was tall and willowy and seemed to sway as she spoke, like the rushes at the edge of the lake. Indeed, her long hair was the same deep brown as a bulrush.

'We have come to escort you and the stone to the Temple of Shang To, the Shaman-Master is waiting. He believes that if we move quickly we can reach Shang To before the enemy traces your whereabouts.'

'Let me provide you with a troop of my best guardsmen,' said Surreman.

'That would draw attention to us. We must be as unobtrusive as possible. Three travellers will draw less attention,' replied Gardeer.

'The Shaman-Master will need all his Paladin present to counter the Jhankhira's forces. Where are the other two?' asked Hamroon.

'I left them in Porphyra's garden. We were attacked. I was sent away with the stone to keep it safe. We should send help.'

'That is not possible, Suremaana. Surely you understand that?'

'I'm sorry Gardeer, right now, I can only see my friends being attacked and I don't know if they survived.'

'They took the oath of the Paladin. They knew what that meant,' replied Hamroon.

'Yes, but Jadeja didn't,' she found herself shouting. 'Jadeja didn't.'

121

'The young man of whom you speak is the Master's apprentice. He is well prepared for battle,' Gardeer tried to reassure her. Suremaana shook her head.

'You don't understand. He bestowed his guardian spirit on me to save my life. He is vulnerable.'

Hamroon and Gardeer exchanged glances.

'This is unexpected information. We will have to pass it on to the Master,' said Hamroon. 'Now do you have the stone?'

Suremaana brought the stone out from the pocket of her waistcoat. The giant emerald sparkled in the sunlight streaming through the windows.

'The snake's eye,' said Surreman. 'The jewel of my people. Not seen since Porphyra left the kingdom. You did well, Suremaana, to retrieve it.'

'We had to pass a test. She communed with me, we became one so that I would know how to finish the task.'

'Then you have been blessed if Porphyra trusted you. Many of our people have tried to bring back the eye,' said Surreman, gazing covetously at the jewel.

'She knew our need was great and she knew that I would return it to her.'

'What!' exclaimed Surreman.

'I promised her that I would return it,' replied Suremaana. 'It is hers by right.'

'It is our people's by right,' shouted Surreman.

'No!' replied Suremaana. 'It is the Queen's, only to be bestowed on another if she chooses. She chose Ancrobus.'

Her father was furious but realised now was not the moment to argue. Regaining control of himself he said, 'Then you shall keep your promise my daughter.'

Suremaana bowed, but a slight feeling of unease settled on her.

Hamroon and Gardeer took the emerald and wrapped it in a green cloth heavily embroidered with secret runes.

'This will prevent it from being detected by the Jhankhira while it is travelling. The stone gives off a strong energy when it is not in its protective case that can easily be traced by those with the right skill,' explained Hamroon.

'Then they will know that it is here,' said Suremaana.

'Luckily you travelled by water. That will have hidden it from view. The palace walls will have kept it shielded up to now. We must be on our way. We leave in an hour,' said Gardeer.

'Then I had better get ready,' Suremaana replied. 'Father if you will excuse me.'

Surreman nodded and she headed back to her chambers. There she found more new clothes laid out for her. A soft white shirt, leather breeches and waistcoat. To finish, an outer jacket made from green snakeskin, the royal colour. She fingered the jacket. Serpentae shed their snakeskins three times in their lives, just like a normal snake. These sheddings were a ritual, a rite of passage that everyone went through. The skins were then kept and used within families for special garments. They were highly treasured by the people. For royalty, there was one extra shedding that took place on the day they ascended to the throne. It marked the end of their old life and the start of their new one as ruler of the Serpentae. These skins were the most precious of all. Suremaana recognised that this jacket had been made from her father's ascension shedding.

This is very special, she smiled to herself gratefully. Putting it on she mouthed 'Thank you Papa.'

The jacket moulded to her body and truly became a second skin. Luxuriating in its touch, she stood quietly thinking of her father. There was a knock at her door.

'Come in,' she called.

The door opened and Surreman walked in.

'I see you found your new clothes,' he smiled.

'Thank you, Papa. I am honoured that you had this made for me.'

'It is I who am honoured that you can wear my skin. I am so proud of you my daughter, your mother would be too, knowing that you had followed in her footsteps and become a Paladin.'

For a long time they looked at each other, then she ran to his arms and hugged him so tightly. Just for that moment she was a little girl again, holding on to her papa the same way that she had done the night before she left to start her training.

'Come now, this is no time for sentiment. You are a Paladin with a job to do.'

'I had hoped to stay with you a little longer Papa. I have been away for an age.'

'I know my darling. I too wanted to keep you, but the Shaman-Master's need is greater than mine. Until you have completed your time as a Paladin, we must accept that we will not see much of each other.'

'I love you Papa. I will not stay away so long this time.'

He smiled at her, trying not to show the tears in his eyes. Surreman stayed with her as she gathered up her things and got ready to depart. The time moved too rapidly for them. The hour was soon up and she had to leave. They walked together to the courtyard where Hamroon and Gardeer were waiting for her on sturdy mountain ponies.

Suremaana and her father said their final goodbyes, then she mounted her pony and left.

18

Eilidon left the arbour and headed for the knot garden. As a spider, it was easy for her to move about unseen, so she arrived without any problems. Now though, she had to get to the mandala in the centre without coming to the attention of the snake bushes. She decided that she would have to swing from bush to bush at speed so that she passed them before they noticed her.

Safely at the mandala she then had another problem. How was she going to get Porphyra to talk to her? After sitting there for ten minutes she decided that the best way was simply to ask.

'Queen Porphyra, I am Eilidon, Paladin to the Shaman-Master and companion to Suremaana. I come to thank you for sending Ancrobus to help us. Without him we would have been overwhelmed. I also ask if Suremaana got safely away.'

For a while nothing happened and Eilidon was beginning to feel foolish for talking to a plant. Then the mandala opened and Porphyra appeared.

'You may speak to me as a human. My snakes will not harm you.'

Eilidon transformed and stood before the queen, who eyed her carefully.

'You are a brave one. I can see that, and loyal. Yes. Suremaana escaped unharmed. I cannot tell you where in case the enemy is listening, but be sure she is a long way from here.'

'Thank you,' replied Eilidon. 'I'm sorry we brought the enemy here.'

'He would have come anyway. He wants my stone. His plan depends on it.'

'We have to find the other power stone. Only... only I don't know where to look. Caderyn's wounded and Jadeja...Jadeja's beyond my help. I don't know what Rabten did to him, but he's deeply unconscious.'

Eilidon fell silent, despair and exhaustion washing over her.

'Come,' said Porphyra kindly. 'We will attend to your friends.'

She led Eilidon through the knot garden and back to the arbour, where Caderyn was just beginning to stir. The thistle guard bowed low and allowed the two ladies through. Seeing Caderyn awake, Eilidon ran to him and checked his wound.

'It appears to be healing and I am much rested. Thank you.'

'Then I have repaid some of my debt to you,' replied Eilidon.

Caderyn looked puzzled. 'There is no debt.'

'Blackraven,' said Eilidon.

Caderyn shrugged. 'Like I said. No debt.'

Porphyra was bent over Jadeja, who remained unconscious. Becoming a snake, she wrapped herself around his body, sinking her fangs into his neck. Her body began thrashing about, throwing Jadeja with her. The giant snake appeared to be consuming their companion. Without warning a black liquid began oozing out of one of Jadeja's ears, where it reformed into a crow. Porphyra released Jadeja and spat venom at the crow which shook and squawked, before dissolving into the ground, instantly killing the grass that it touched.

Porphyra returned to her human form.

'A mind locker,' she explained. 'It will have entered while he was linked with Blackraven. It was holding him unconscious, trying to bond him with the enemy. He has great strength. Most would have succumbed by now. He will remain like this for a day or so, but he will recover.

We must move you. This location is known and even though the enemy has fled, he may try to come back here. If he can get through a second time,' she added.

Porphyra then ordered the thistle guard to carry Jadeja to a small copse, where two hammocks were slung between the trees. Jadeja was placed in one, his face the pallor of death.

'I'm afraid you two will have to share,' she smiled. 'Now eat, there is an abundance of food here.'

Plates of apples, pears, berries and nuts were under the hammocks.

'Eat and rest. In a day or two I will send you on your way.' Then she was gone.

Caderyn and Eilidon looked at each other and then piled into the food. The flavours were intense, bursting in their mouths, filling them up and revitalising them. When their appetites were sated Caderyn ordered Eilidon to sleep in the hammock.

'I am fine on the ground,' he said.

She would have none of it.

'You take the hammock, I'll spin a web, more comfortable for me.'

He could not persuade her, so in the end he lay in the hammock with an intricate web above him, gently swaying with his movements, a large spider relaxing in its centre. Whether it was exhaustion from the battle, the food or the comfort of their surroundings, they could not say, but they slept deeply and peacefully.

She didn't know how it happened, but at some point, during the night Eilidon had dropped from her web and returned to her human form. She awoke to find herself lying next to Caderyn, his arms wrapped tightly around her. Sitting up, she moved quickly before he roused and found her there. He woke shortly after and stuck his head over the side of the hammock.

'Morning sleepyhead. How is the shoulder?'

Caderyn felt his wound.

'Surprisingly, okay. It has knitted together well. Thank you. Is there more food? I'm famished.'

'Typical boy,' said Eilidon. 'Always thinking of your stomach.' She tossed him an apple.

He ate it quickly, then climbed down for more.

'Porphyra said she'd send us on our way. Do you think she knows where the next stone is?'

'Maybe,' said Caderyn, with his mouth full. 'This food has such incredible flavour. I've never tasted anything as good. Here have some more.' He passed Eilidon a handful of apricots.

'Thanks. Should we check on Jadeja?'

'She said that he would sleep for a day or so, probably best to leave him for now. We'll check him this evening. Let's just enjoy this place while we can.'

He stretched languidly.

'I don't know about you, but I feel like a swim. I wonder if there is a pool near here?'

In answer to his question a thistle guard turned up.

'My mistress said to take you to the healing pools. Please follow me.'

'What about Jadeja?' asked Caderyn.

'Your companion will be safe here,' replied the guard. 'This way.'

Caderyn and Eilidon followed the guard through the trees until they reached an open glade with a series of interconnecting pools. Steam was rising from the water.

'The healing springs,' said the guard, who then bowed and walked off.

Caderyn stripped off his clothes and dived into the water. It was warm and comforting and he felt it wash away the dirt and grime of the battle.

'Come on in,' he called. 'It is so warm.'

Reluctantly Eilidon began removing her outer garments.

'Turn around,' she ordered.

Caderyn duly obliged and she removed the last of her clothing and stepped into the waters. The warmth enveloped her like a soft blanket and she immediately relaxed, feeling a mountain of care leave her body.

While she was happy to just let the water hold her, Caderyn swam about, testing the wound in his shoulder. She admired the tone of his muscles and the grace with which he moved through the water. He had always had a natural ease and fluidity in his movement. He was handsome too, she thought, but without being aware of it. There was no arrogance about him. No swagger, that she had seen amongst the other young men she had encountered, particularly the suitors who came to her father, all of whom had been dismissed. When the invitation came from the Elders to train as a Paladin she had seized it with relish, happy to leave home, leave a life she felt stifled by. Her father had been furious at her, wanting her to marry and remain among the people, but her mother understood, recognising the wanderlust in her daughter's eyes.

'Go and be who you need to be,' she had said. 'Just don't let the road become your master.'

Eilidon thanked her and left her home with a sense of optimism she had never felt before.

She was pulled from her daydreams by Caderyn calling from the bank.

'I'm heading back now, so you can have some privacy.'

She waved, realising that she hadn't even noticed him get out of the water. *How long have we been in here?* she thought, noticing her hands had gone wrinkly.

Slowly swimming to the bank, she got out of the water. She felt cleansed, not just externally but internally too, as if a burden had been lifted from her. With a deep sigh, she lay on the ground and slept.

Caderyn returned to the hammocks to check on Jadeja. He was still asleep but his expression was less pained.

'Sleep my friend,' he said, and was surprised to find that he meant it. Jadeja was becoming a friend and a reliable one too.

He felt the aura surround him. The flashing lights and bright colours before his eyes conveying a message to him, showing him the next path. In amongst the lights he saw the Shaman-Master's face.

'When you have retrieved the fire stone bring it straight to me at the Temple of Shang To.'

'Yes Master.'

'You will be hunted. Hurry. Is Jadeja safe?'

'Yes Master. He is sleeping.'

'Good. He will need all his strength. Guard him well, Paladin. Keep the enemy away from him.'

'Yes Master.'

The Shaman-Master melted back into the aura. The spirit messengers dissipated, allowing Caderyn to see clearly again. He was surprised to find Jadeja standing in front of him. He jumped up and hugged him. Jadeja was taken aback by this, unused as he was to any physical contact.

'You had us really worried. Rabten sent a mind locker to you, fortunately Porphyra was able to release you.'

'That would explain the numbness in my brain and why I have no recollection of anything after I sent out Black Raven.'

'Yes, we found you unconscious after the battle. Eilidon gave you a sleeping draught, but it was Porphyra who knew the real problem.'

'I hope I didn't give anything away to the enemy. I thought I could match Rabten but it seems I was wrong.'

'No, that bird you sent really helped to weaken him.'

Jadeja realised that they were alone and his body tensed.

'Suremaana, Eilidon. Are they…?'

'They are fine. Suremaana has gone. She took the stone and is far away from here. Porphyra wouldn't tell us where, but she escaped.'

Jadeja unclenched his fists.

'And Eilidon?'

'Is here,' she said, walking into the copse. 'Good to see you awake.'

'Thank you lady Eilidon, thank you, I feel much better.'

'You should bathe in the healing pools. I'll show you.'

131

He protested at first but Caderyn said that she was right. They both took him.

'We'll go back. When you want to return, a guard will escort you. It's quite safe,' promised Caderyn.

Jadeja looked around him. The pools did look inviting. *What harm can it do?* he said to himself taking off his clothes and stepping gingerly into the water. The warmth was surprising and he loosened up and lay back and let the waters engulf him. Thoughts of Suremaana filtered into his mind. He remembered how beautiful and queenly she had looked sitting on Porphyra's chair. He imagined her hand in his, then berated himself for his foolishness. *She would never think that way about me.* Still, the dream was pleasing. Underneath him a black shape was shadowing his movements, spreading out like a large oil slick, surrounding him with darkness. Suddenly he felt himself being pulled down under the water into this black morass. Desperately splashing and kicking, he fought for the surface. It was no use. The blackness held firm, rolling him over and over, tumbling him through darkness. He heard his name being called. Images of faces from his past flashed in and out of his mind as he tried to get away. He saw Rabten. Saw his face. Saw his hands reaching out. Then he saw Porphyra standing between them and slowly, slowly, Rabten's face melting away along with the blackness. *Am I drowning?* Unable to understand what was happening he saw the black mass being eaten by millions of tiny white lights until it had disappeared and he found himself back on the surface, which now had a green luminescence to it. *I must be dying. Please not yet, I haven't completed my mission. The Shaman-Master.* The tiny lights held him up and danced around him. Then gently, very gently they washed over him and carried him to the shore where Porphyra was waiting for him.

'Welcome Jadeja. You have been greatly honoured. The children of the light do not usually come out in such numbers. It would seem that they are drawn to you. Why would that be?'

Still disorientated Jadeja struggled to get his words out.

'Am I...am I... alive?'

Porphyra studied him carefully.

'Yes, young man you are alive. What are you?'

'I am the Shaman-Master's apprentice.'

'That may be what you are at the moment, but I sense that there is more to you than that.'

'Forgive me my lady but there is not. The Shaman-Master found me and took me in. He has been training me in the Shamanic laws. He says that I have a natural affinity with the spirits and I am a quick learner.'

'That I do not doubt, but there is something else. I sensed it when I freed you from the mind locker but I was unable to access it. My way was blocked.'

'I do not know of what you speak. I am a servant of the Shaman-Master and I was tasked to lead the Paladin to find the power stones.'

Porphyra held him in her gaze.

'You are tasked with far more than that.'

Jadeja shook his head, 'No my lady. I have only one mission to complete, if I can. I must return the power stones to the Temple of Shang To.'

He shuffled nervously under her scrutiny.

'You speak the truth, but only because you do not know who or what you are. Come, we will join the others. Follow me.'

Jadeja hurriedly put on his clothes, suddenly embarrassed by his nakedness, then ran after Porphyra, leaving a line of luminescence trailing behind him. The tiny creatures were reluctant to let him go.

'What happened to me in the pool? I was engulfed in blackness.'

'The waters sucked out the darkness from your clash with Rabten. Only I am surprised there was so much. I think perhaps you have encountered him before.'

'Yes, when I was much younger. He… he.' A vision of Rabten standing over him and beating him, flashed into his mind. 'I prefer not to think about it.'

'Do you feel lighter?'

'Yes. Much lighter. Thank you'

Porphyra smiled. 'You will have renewed strength as well. My senses tell me that you are going to need it.'

They entered the copse. Caderyn bowed to her.

'Mighty queen, we are honoured.'

'Thank you, Caderyn of the Bow. I return Jadeja to you. He has been cleansed by the healing waters. You may rest here one more night, then leave my garden.'

'We will depart at first light, Majesty. I know where we have to go.'

'I will not ask you, that way the enemy will have no need to try and enter here again. You have proved your worth, all four of you. At dawn, a guard will guide you out of the garden. My blessings upon you.'

They bowed to her, and then she was gone.

'Eat,' said Eilidon to Jadeja. 'This food will nourish you.'

He ate hungrily, surprised at the voracity of his appetite, while Caderyn explained to them where they had to go next. They settled down for the night. The two boys in the hammocks and Eilidon in her web. This time she stayed in it until daybreak.

At dawn they climbed down, ate breakfast, filled their packs with as much of the food as they could carry and followed the thistle guard to the edge of the garden.

19

Leaving the garden held different emotions for the three travellers. Caderyn was glad to go. Beautiful as they were, the gardens had felt stifling and enclosed, leaving them, allowed him to breathe freely again.

For Eilidon, it was a relief to leave. She had appreciated the beauty of the place but parts of it reminded her of home and that was a difficult memory for her.

Jadeja felt a deep sense of loss, like the sadness you feel when saying goodbye to a loved one when you're not sure if you will see them again. He didn't understand why he felt that way. The last time he had left the garden he hadn't felt so bereft. In fact, he had been happy to get away.

He was missing Suremaana greatly. She had always made him feel included, whereas Eilidon was colder, indifferent, only tolerating his presence. Suremaana had liked him and that was something he was not used to. Friendship was an elusive concept, but she had been a friend. He had hoped that she could be more than that. Now she was miles away and he had no idea whether he even entered her thoughts. He sighed so heavily that Caderyn stopped and turned around.

'Are you okay, Jadeja? If my pace is too fast I can slow down. I forgot that you have only just recovered.'

The genuine concern in his voice surprised Jadeja, it was not something he was used to.

'No, I'm fine. I am sad to leave the gardens, that's all. I felt an affinity with them that I had not experienced before.'

Caderyn smiled. 'A place can have that effect on you. The Temple at Shang To always does it for me. It's where I grew up so I always find it hard to leave. You've been through a lot in the past few days. It's bound to have an impact.'

He fell into step with Jadeja and they carried on chatting like the friends they were becoming, leaving Eilidon walking behind them. She watched them curiously, not sure whether she should be jealous or relieved. There had always been an unspoken bond between her and Caderyn, ever since they were trainee Paladin, an instant friendship based on an intuitive understanding of each other. The Elders had seen it and predicted a union, something she instinctively backed away from.

Being a Paladin gave her the freedom she craved, even though she had been required to stay in one place for three years while undergoing rigorous training and discipline, a life far more restricted than she was used to. The routine and the restriction only served to fuel her desire for freedom and increase her isolation from others. She made no friends because she didn't need or want them. Friendships meant ties and she wanted none of those. Caderyn had broken this code by always looking out for her and knowing if she was in trouble, helping her to finish tasks or releasing her from Black Raven. The fact that it had been his blood that freed her from the dreamcatcher

137

unnerved her because it was evidence of a deeper bond that she did not trust. Liberating her from the tree spirit had been down to his bowmanship, that she understood, but the blood link was something else altogether. Lost in her thoughts, she hadn't noticed that they had come to the banks of a fast- flowing river.

'This will take us to our next destination,' said Caderyn.

'Are we swimming?' she asked.

'Ha, I thought we might. I know how much you like water.'

Eilidon threw him such a look that he burst out laughing.

'I will call us a boat, if her majesty would kindly wait and allow me to do so.' He bowed extravagantly at her. She retaliated by throwing out a thread and tying him in that position.

'Now who's laughing Bowman.'

'Lady Eilidon. I believe Caderyn was joking.'

'Really Jadeja, you think? Back off.'

She pushed Caderyn down and stood over him.

'Say sorry, bowman, or stay like this for the rest of the day.'

'Sorry for what exactly? My sarcasm or referring to your noble status?'

'Both.'

Trying hard not to laugh at her indignation, Caderyn apologised and was duly released, whereupon he laughed so loudly that eventually Eilidon broke into a smile at her own petulance. Jadeja watched the whole scene play out with an air of puzzlement.

'Don't worry my friend, you will get used to her moods eventually.'

Jadeja felt sure that he wouldn't as he watched the two of them, now sitting comfortably together on the river bank.

'Shall I catch some fish while you catch us a boat?' offered Eilidon.

'An excellent idea. Jadeja you make us a fire and I will begin contacting the spirits.'

Soon they were all occupied, Eilidon was spinning a net to fish with, Jadeja gathering wood and kindling and digging a fire pit and Caderyn calling in the elements of water. Once again, he stilled his body and began his incantation, calling on the water spirits to assist them. A blue spirit appeared before him. It did not have a solid form, it was constantly moving like the waves on the seashore.

'I have answered your call Paladin. How can I help you?'

We require a vessel to carry us to Maur, if it pleases you to aid us.'

'Why do you wish to go to Maur's Temple?'

'We seek the fire stone. My Master has need of it. The Jhankhira also seeks it. Travelling by water gives us speed that we can't achieve on land.'

The spirit disappeared and Caderyn feared that he had offended it somehow. He remained still, anxious not to break the link. Eventually it reappeared.

'We will grant your request. When you arrive at the Temple of Maur you must release the vessels. They will only carry you one way.'

'Thank you. We are greatly honoured.'

He hardly had time to finish speaking before the spirit had gone. Breathing out deeply, he released himself from the trance and saw a small round coracle drifting in to the bank, then another, then another. Three tiny vessels to carry them down stream.

Returning with a net full of fish, Eilidon looked at the little boats in disbelief.

'We are sailing in those? Are you mad? They are too light and flimsy. The current will tip them over.'

'They are safe enough. We can tie them together, that should make them steadier. Besides, they are sent from the water spirits and it is not their intention to drown us.'

Eilidon remained sceptical, but a good lunch of fresh fish put her in a better mood.

'Our destination is two days from here,' said Caderyn. 'So keep your fishing net. We will have need of it. Now let's tie up these boats and get going.'

They attached silken ropes to each boat to hold them together but the current meant that they constantly banged into each other, resulting in a very unsteady and unbalanced ride. Later that evening when they pulled into the bank to rest for the night, they were exhausted and soaking wet.

'I feel like we have been fighting with the boats the whole time. It's as if they are arguing with each other over which one wants to take the lead,' said Jadeja.

'I have an alternative,' said Eilidon.

'What do you have in mind?' said Caderyn.

'They're trying to act as three individual boats. If I made a large net and we sat them in it, they become one boat rather than three.'

Jadeja and Caderyn looked at each other and both said, 'Brilliant.'

'How long will it take you my lady?'

'Probably a couple of hours, if it's to be strong enough, so you two are on dinner.'

'I think we can manage that,' said Caderyn. 'You just take your time.'

While the boys caught fish, made a fire and cooked them, Eilidon sat and spun, using all her skill to make the net strong enough to withstand the current. She even picked some bulrushes to weave into it for added buoyancy. As predicted, it took two hours to complete. The finished article was a piece of artistry, an intricate pattern of silk and reeds.

'Now all we've got to do is sit the boats in it,' she said.

'I think that will require all of us. And involve getting wet. We cannot bring the coracles on land so we will have to pass the net underneath them in the water,' said Caderyn.

Eilidon groaned. She was not overly fond of water.

'It's the only way,' replied Caderyn.

They stripped down to their undergarments and stepped in to the freezing water.

Jadeja recoiled as the coldness hit him.

'We better do this quickly,' said Caderyn.

Spreading out, each of them holding a corner of the net, they approached the coracles. Caderyn and Jadeja lowered themselves under the water and pulled the net underneath the boats, while Eilidon held her side round the first coracle. The boys quickly got their corners round the other two boats then watched as Eilidon gently tugged on a fine drawstring around the top edge of the net, pulling the three coracles together in to one. The little boats slotted together like the pieces of a jigsaw.

'Brilliant my lady. Well done,' said Jadeja, hurrying to sit by the fire and dry off.

'Yeah, not bad,' grinned Caderyn, sitting down next to Jadeja.

Eilidon smiled. 'Thanks. Move over and share that heat.'

Once they were dry, they settled down for the night. Having constructed the net for the boat, Eilidon was unable to provide a protective web so Jadeja took the first watch. Settling himself at the base of a willow tree, he drew out his flute. Made from the horns of a mountain goat, it played a sweet music, calling on protective spirits to keep the party safe. While he played, he watched the dance of the bird spirits that he had invoked, losing himself in the music and the movement. The melody drew other creatures to him. Fireflies circling around him, made it appear as if he had a halo of golden light around his head. Lulled by the dancing spirits, the flute dropped from his hands and he fell asleep. At dawn, he was rudely awakened by Eilidon roughly shaking his shoulder.

'Come on. Wake up. So much for taking the first watch.'

'I called up some protective spirits. They must have put me to sleep. Sorry.'

'Hmmph. Just get in the boat. Caderyn's waiting.'

Jadeja got to his feet, gathered up his belongings and then after a final check that their fire was out, he climbed aboard the little craft.

'She needs a name,' said Caderyn.

'What does?'

'The boat, Eilidon. Now that it's one vessel, it needs a name.'

'How about the coracle?' she muttered.

'Boring.'

They all tried to think of a suitable name, then Jadeja blurted out,

'Wayfinder.'

'Wayfinder. Yes. I like that. What about you Eilidon?'

'Yes fine.'

'Wayfinder it is then. Well done Jadeja. I name this boat Wayfinder, bless her and may she carry us safely to our destination.'

He saluted the little boat, then pushed her off from the bank. Now that the three coracles were properly joined, they floated together perfectly, picking up the current and moving with ease down the river.

'This is much better than yesterday,' said Caderyn.

For much of the day the river flowed at a steady pace. Jadeja felt much more at ease than he had done the day before. The green fields and rolling hills that they sailed past complimented his state of mind. In some places the river opened out into wide pools where wild ponies came to drink. He watched his companions, Eilidon trailed the net in the water and was able to land half a dozen good-sized fish, so supper was sorted. Caderyn sat in the prow scanning the banks for signs of the enemy. *Perhaps we will not be pursued,* thought Jadeja *and I can complete my mission.* But inside he knew this was a futile thought.

Wayfinder was true to its name and seemed to naturally find the best part of the current. Progress was quick and although they were alert for danger, none came. The two boys enjoyed the journey. Jadeja was glad of the opportunity to rest and regain more strength. Caderyn remained watchful, remembering the Shaman-Master's warning that they would be hunted. Eilidon however, was on edge. Her senses were heightened. She tried to put it down to being on the water. She was not a natural sailor, preferring dry land every time. Deep inside she knew it was more than the river. Something was haunting her and it had been since the frozen forest. Trying to relax, she let her hand trail over the side of the boat. The instant she broke the surface of the water, she felt the tug of ice-cold fingers and snatched her arm back into the boat. Caderyn saw her reaction.

'What's wrong?'

'Nothing. It was too cold, that's all.'

He wasn't fully convinced but she wouldn't say any more.

For the rest of the day he sat with his bow primed and ready.

That night they camped on the edge of a large pool that the river flowed through. It was peaceful and calm and the ponies came to drink. Their leader was a fine palomino. Jadeja approached him, palms open. The pony did not move. Their foreheads touched and Jadeja felt the strength and power of this magnificent animal flow into him. Similarly, the pony felt the fear and pain of the apprentice flowing back, and something else, something darker. Their thoughts passed from one to the other. The pony was about to break the link when a firefly landed on Jadeja's shoulder and he changed his mind.

'My name is Jadeja. I am apprentice to the Shaman-Master. My companions are the Paladin, Eilidon and Caderyn.'

'I am Chito of the Plains. Welcome Jadeja, Shaman apprentice and stone seeker. You may stay tonight, do not linger. Something follows you. My ponies have sensed it.'

'We have not, but I am expecting trouble at some point. How much further to the Temple of Maur?'

'You will be there tomorrow, but you must negotiate Myong Gorge. The rapids there are fierce. Your craft does not look sturdy.'

'Wayfinder is stronger than she looks. She was sent to us by the water spirits. She will manage the rapids.'

'Then I wish you speed and surefootedness. Rest tonight. My ponies will guard you.'

'Thank you, Chito of the Plains. We are deeply honoured.'

He stepped back releasing the flow, then bowed. Chito raised his head and whinnied to the ponies, who formed a guard around the camp.

Eilidon and Caderyn were waiting impatiently to hear Jadeja's news.

'They will guard the camp tonight. We will reach Maur tomorrow but we have to negotiate rapids,' said Jadeja.

'Great. I might build myself a web and travel that way.'

'No!' I mean, no,' said Jadeja, more gently. 'We are being followed and everyone has to be ready for an attack.'

'Who is following us? I haven't seen or heard anything.'

'I don't know Caderyn,' replied Jadeja, 'But the ponies are aware of something.'

Eilidon remained quiet. She had a strong suspicion of what hunted them. Or rather, hunted her. That night she slept as a spider in a tight cocoon web, her fear growing.

At dawn, Chito returned to see them on their way. He watched them until they rounded a bend in the river, then he whinnied loud and clear and galloped off, leading his herd away from the water.

Wayfinder found the centre of the current and hurried them on. Jadeja noted that the landscape began to change. The banks became rockier and the water course narrower, causing the river to flow quicker. The little boat seemed to feel more and more agitated, unsettled by the changing pace of the river.

'We must be getting close to the rapids,' said Jadeja. 'This is going to be bumpy.'

Eilidon gave each of them a silken thread that she had attached to the sides of the boat.

'It might be wise to tie ourselves in. And our packs.'

The two boys attached the threads just as Wayfinder was thrown forward into the roaring rapids. They were very quickly soaked by the plumes of spray as the turbulent waters poured between giant rocks. The little boat was alternately lifted out of the water or plunged deep, as the swirling current tossed them around like a leaf on the wind. The water became more violent and menacing.

'I don't like this,' screamed Eilidon. Then she saw a face in the rapids.

'There is something in the water.'

'What?' yelled Caderyn, unable to hear her above the roar.

Before she had time to reply the net holding the three boats together caught on a jagged rock, bringing them to a sudden stop and nearly throwing Jadeja over the side. It was only Caderyn's quick reaction in grabbing him that kept him in the boat. The water surged past them. Wayfinder fought to free herself from the rock. The power of the current pulled and tore at the little craft. Suddenly the threads of Eilidon's web snapped from the pressure, splitting Wayfinder into three again.

Caderyn's coracle sprang forward, bouncing and spiralling through the water. Jadeja was thrown backwards onto the floor of his as it shot forward like a stone fired from a catapult. Only Eilidon's boat had not moved, trapped as it was in the remains of the net. She drew a blade and began cutting at the threads until it could release itself. The current gathered her up and threw her forwards into the teeming mass of white foam. Except it wasn't white foam. It was white ice. She felt the fingers on her shoulders

146

pulling her backwards into the water. There in the tumult of the rapids she saw them, she felt them, she heard them. The sisters from the frozen forest. Three torsos melded into one body. Three heads focused on her. Three pairs of arms reaching out to embrace her.

'We have come.'

'We have come.'

'You are ours now.'

The arms began to close around her. The iciness of the water was numbing, she was unable to resist. At the last moment, the river squeezed her between two rocks and pushed her forward away from their grasp. Shrieking, they lunged after her. Now it became a race. The women riding the rapids, reaching out with their frozen fingers to grab Eilidon, who was left entirely at the mercy of the water which buffeted her between and over the rocks, the freezing temperature rendering her immobile and unconscious.

The sisters encircled her, spinning her round and round so it looked like she was caught in a whirlpool. They argued over which of them was to inhabit Eilidon. Each felt that they should be the one to be free. While they were pulling each other's hair, spitting and screaming and scratching, the river lifted Eilidon unnoticed, and threw her up to the surface and washed her downstream towards the bank.

By the time the sisters had realised what had happened she had safely landed on the shore. They shot after her. When they touched dry land, the sisters melted into a silver fog surrounding Eilidon where she lay. The ground frosted over at their touch as they built up an ice wall around her. Their excitement was palpable. This time they were sure they had their prey. With only one layer left to complete, Eilidon's icy tomb would be sealed. Before they could

147

finish, their way was barred by Jadeja, holding an amulet with an eagle on it.

'You know me. I am the bird wearer. The guardian. I bid you return to your prison where I placed you.'

The sisters howled and hissed and tried to grab him, but the amulet protected him. They pushed forward until their faces were nose to nose with Jadeja's. Unwanted memories of childhood torment dredged themselves up from the depths of his mind. The sisters laughed.

'Remember Worm.'

'Worthless maggot.'

'Remember how weak you are'

He stumbled backwards.

'I am the bird wearer,' he shouted lifting the amulet and chanting ancient magic, forcing them back to the river, away from Eilidon.

'She is not yours. Begone you hideous hags. You are not fit to walk this land.'

The sisters tried to resist him, shouting insults to undermine his confidence.

'Worm.'

'Puss ball.'

'Gobbit hole.'

'You weakling.'

'You are no match for us.'

Summoning all his inner strength, Jadeja blocked out their words and called forth the amulet's eagle spirit.

'Silence! Depart! Return from whence you came.'

The sisters, unable to resist the power of the eagle, were driven back to the forest, their sinister screeches echoing in his ears as they disappeared into the ether. The bird sat briefly on his shoulder and then melted back into the amulet once more.

Stepping out of the water, he hurried over to Eilidon who lay motionless on the bank.

20

Jadeja picked up Eilidon and carried her to dry ground, stripped her of her wet clothes and covered her in a thick layer of reeds plucked from the water's edge. He then dug a fire pit and started a small blaze. He dropped a piece of hartshorn and some eucalyptus leaves into the flames, wafting the resultant smoke towards Eilidon. The strong ammonia and eucalyptus mixture acted as a stimulant to help bring her back to consciousness. The sharpness of the aroma forcing her to revive.

Satisfied that she was coming around, he built up the fire, added some large stones to it, and went to look for Caderyn. He found two of the coracles washed up on the bank and tied them up. There was no sign of the third. He checked the two boats and was relieved to see that their packs had survived, glad now that Eilidon had suggested tying them in. He lifted them ashore, put them by the fire and set off downstream in search of his friend. The shore was tricky to navigate in places. Tall reeds blocked his way and he became increasingly worried that the third coracle had travelled on a lot further. He was beginning to think that he would have to go back and get a boat when he found it caught up in some reeds. Caderyn lay unconscious inside it, a large bruise on his right temple.

Jadeja lifted him out of the little craft and carried him back to the fire, taking off as many of his wet clothes as he could manage and wrapping him in bulrushes also. He went back for the pack and the coracle, which he carried over to the other two boats, before removing his own wet garments and drying off. Carefully removing the stones that he had placed in the fire, he spread their clothes on top, allowing the heat to dry them. As they cooled, he replaced them with others. In this way, he could constantly exchange hot stones and dry their clothes quickly. The methodical work calmed his anxiety after the encounter with the sisters. He had not expected to meet his childhood tormenters again. His hands shook as he fought to bring his emotions under control. *They are gone. You beat them again. They cannot harm you anymore.* Sensing his distress, the amulet flared again and he allowed its soothing warmth to calm him, while he waited for the other two to regain consciousness.

Eilidon was the first to fully wake.

'My clothes?'

'They are drying my lady. Don't worry the rushes will keep you warm.'

She looked at him.

'The water. The tree spirits?'

'I don't know what you mean my lady. I found you washed up on the shore. I was lucky, my coracle rode through the rapids safely.'

'In the water. I was thrown from my boat. The three sisters from the forest. They caught me.'

'I can assure you my lady that nothing had you but the water. Sometimes extreme cold can cause us to hallucinate. I'm sure that is what happened.'

Eilidon looked at him. He held her gaze.

'Perhaps you're right, but it was real to me. I've been haunted by them since we left the forest.'

'I think you will be safe now. These lands feel warm. A frozen spirit will not travel here.'

'Maybe. How is Caderyn?'

'He has had a blow to the head, perhaps you could suggest something to ease it.'

'Pass me something dry and I'll look.'

He handed her a shirt and she checked Caderyn.

'Can you get me some bulrush roots?'

Jadeja pulled up some rushes which she mashed with two of the stones before applying them to the bruise.

'This should reduce the swelling, but he may be out for a while yet.'

'I have fish cooking in the fire. Why don't we eat? I added some spice so they will warm our bodies from the inside.'

'Thanks'

The two of them sat close to the fire and ate the fish in silence. Eilidon studied Jadeja. Despite her misgivings about him he had once again proved his worth, and yet her senses still told her to be wary. Something blocked her from seeing into his aura. He was right about the hot food though, it warmed them up more rapidly than the heat of the fire alone. Just as they were finishing, Caderyn moaned: 'Aaaaagh. My head.'

Eilidon was up in a moment.

'Lie still. Let the roots do their work.'

He lay back down and looked about him. Noticing the clothes spread out he realised that they had been ashore for some time.

'The coracles?'

'They are secured on the bank. They're quite safe,' replied Jadeja.

'They have to be released. The water spirit only let us have them if they were returned when we arrived.'

'I will go and untie them.'

Caderyn looked at the sky and closed his eyes. The water spirit spoke with him.

'My boats have carried you as far as they can. You must free them.'

Opening his eyes again he spoke to Jadeja.

'Send them on their way.'

He left the camp and headed back to the water. He checked the boats for any of Eilidon's threads or any stray items of theirs, untied them and pushed each one out into the river, acknowledging their service and releasing them back to the water. The little boats danced on the current, then with the sound of tinkling laughter they sped on their way and were quickly out of sight.

As soon as Jadeja was out of earshot Eilidon sat beside Caderyn and recounted her experience in the water.

'Jadeja said it was an hallucination, but I'm sure it was real.'

'If the tree spirit had somehow entered your mind, Porphyra's healing waters would have cleansed it.'

'Except I never put my head under the water, so while they cleansed my body of the effects of the battle with Rabten, they didn't cleanse my mind.'

'If the tree spirit pursues you, then you must be extra careful.'

'That's just it. My mind feels lighter. Free again.'

'Then maybe the shock of the cold water released whatever was holding you.'

'I don't know. I'm sure Jadeja knows more than he's saying. I'm convinced he's hiding something.'

'Jadeja is working for the Shaman-Master. He has no reason to lie to us.'

'Doesn't he? I mean we still know so little about him.'

'Eilidon, he has proved himself time and again. Just look around you. He did all this. He looked after us.'

'And I am grateful. It's... I don't know. There's something, that's all.'

She went and found the rest of her clothes, most of which were quite dry and got dressed.

Jadeja returned.

'The coracles are gone. I swear they were laughing as they went.'

'Thank you,' said Caderyn. 'I have kept my promise. Now if you would be kind enough to pass me my clothes, I think we should be moving.'

'After you have eaten,' said Jadeja, passing him the last of the fish.

While Caderyn ate, Jadeja and Eilidon repacked their belongings and put out the fire. Once everyone was ready Jadeja led them on, a little unsteadily at first. They stopped several times to allow Caderyn to rest and for he and Jadeja to confer on the best path to take.

The land was dry and the temperature rose as the day went on. By mid-afternoon they were sweltering. Up ahead they could make out two lines of cypress trees with an opening between them.

'Be watchful and let me do the talking,' said Jadeja.

At the base of the trees that stood either side of the opening were two colossal cat heads. No bodies were visible. They looked as if the earth had swallowed them whole, leaving only their heads above ground. They were rust and grey in colour, having large mosaic eyes with irises of the brightest blue. Each cat stared straight ahead and their expression was unwelcoming.

'Why have you come here Jadeja, Shaman-Master Apprentice and who are these strangers with you?'

The voice was deep and unsettling.

'I seek the firestone for my Master. My companions are the Paladin, Eilidon of the Web and Caderyn of the Bow.'

'Step forward Paladin Eilidon. Stand between us.'

She moved to stand between the two heads. Rotating slowly, they appraised her carefully.

'You may pass.'

Jadeja nodded to her and she walked beyond the guards to the entrance, to await the others.

'Caderyn of the Bow step forward.'

His examination was brief and he was allowed to pass.

'Step forward Jadeja, apprentice to the Shaman-Master.'

The heads stared at him.

'It is forbidden. You must remain with us.'

'But why?' asked Caderyn. 'He is our leader. He must be allowed to accompany us.'

'It is forbidden,' growled the cats. 'You may enter. He may not.'

'Caderyn go. I am fine. I will wait here.'

Reluctantly, Caderyn turned and passed through the entrance, leaving Jadeja sitting miserably with the guards. The cat heads now turned towards him, fixing him with their gaze. He was unable to move.

Eilidon looked at Caderyn who gestured to move forward. They crossed a pristine lawn and ascended a marble staircase to the Temple. The building was square with a domed roof made of shimmering red tiles. The walls were carved from white marble inlaid with rubies. All around the outside were giant statues of golden cats sitting up on their haunches. Eilidon tensed when the heads turned to watch their approach. To the right of the door was a fountain of crystal-clear water sunk into the marble.

'We must leave our weapons and wash our hands and feet before we can go in,' said Caderyn.

'Is that wise?'

'Wise or not it is the only way we will be allowed to enter here.'

Reluctantly, Eilidon removed her blades. Then taking off her shoes, she washed her hands and feet in the fountain. Caderyn did likewise, laying down his bow and arrows and his blades and cloak. He removed his shoes and completed the ritual. Once they had finished, they approached the Temple doors.

'Exalted and glorious Maur. We come with great need. Will you grant us entry?'

Caderyn then bowed, indicating to Eilidon to do the same. For some moments nothing happened, then slowly and silently the Temple doors opened and a disembodied voice spoke to them.

'Welcome Caderyn of the Bow and Eilidon of the Web. We are honoured that the Shaman-Master sends us two of his Paladin. But where is the third?'

'She has returned to our Master. That is all we know,' replied Caderyn.

'Come forward. Stand on the fire square.'

Caderyn started to move.

'No. Eilidon first.'

Caderyn pointed to a white tile in the floor edged with red diamonds. Immediately Eilidon stepped into it, a golden flame surrounded her, engulfing her body. Although she could see the flame, she felt no heat. It was not burning her, it was cleansing her aura. The flames flickered and danced until they were satisfied and then they stopped as abruptly as they started.

'You may sit.'

Eilidon saw a group of red and amber cushions. She sat and waited. It was Caderyn's turn to stand among the flames while they performed their dance to cleanse him. Once satisfied, he too was allowed to sit. They were joined by a large ginger cat with burning red eyes.

'I am Birali, servant and guardian of Maur's Temple. You have been cleansed. You may state your business'

'We seek the firestone. Our Master has great need of it,' said Caderyn.

'The firestone is sacred to Maur. You cannot just remove it,' said Birali.

'I know, but the Jhankhira sends his messenger to retrieve it. He will try to steal it.'

'I know of whom you speak. He has tried many times, in many disguises, to enter here. Each time his way is barred.'

Eilidon listened to this and thought of Jadeja. *Why had he been stopped at the entrance?*

'The Jhankhira grows stronger. He has the bottle of Isfahan. This is why he seeks the power stones. He wants to open the bottle. My Master wants to perform a ceremony of banishment to prevent the demoness from ever harming the world. He has sent his apprentice, Eilidon and I to bring the stone to him.'

'Where is this apprentice?'

'Your guards would not let him pass.'

'Only those whose aura is pure may enter here.'

Eilidon glanced towards the gates, wondering what impurity surrounded Jadeja.

'If the Temple of Maur is truly required to relinquish the firestone then it will do so. If you can reach the stone the Temple will give it up to you.'

'What must we do?' asked Caderyn.

Birali rose to her feet.

'You must pass through the corridor of lights. If you make it to the end without any light touching you, the firestone will reveal itself to you. Come I will show you the way.'

Eilidon stood as well.

'Only one may take the test.'

Birali looked deeply into her eyes, the myriad lenses of the spider gazed back at her.

'If he fails you may try.'

Eilidon sat back down, watching Birali lead Caderyn to a plain marble door off to the side of the chamber. Birali opened the door.

'You must pass through the lights.'

'If I touch them what happens?'

'Then the Temple will remove you.'

Birali bowed letting him pass through the doorway, closing the entrance behind him. Caderyn had noticed a stairway and began descending. He had to feel his way as he was now in total darkness. He counted fifteen steps and then the floor levelled out. In the far distance, he could make out a faint orange glow and he knew that was the direction he needed to move towards. He was about to step forward when a line of lights appeared. They remained stationary until he moved, then they began oscillating from side to side. At first they moved in unison, but with each step he took, their movement changed. They began moving in a curved motion like the writhing of a snake. This was easy for him to dodge, but then each light separated itself from the line, swinging from side to side at different speeds. Just when he thought that he had worked out the pattern and taken a step they changed again, beginning to move in three lines, in, out, in, out, faster and faster. Then reforming into one long snake, before separating again. He had to dodge and weave, duck and bend. It took all of his agility and skill to avoid them. Another change confronted him. It looked as if the lights were spinning round and round each other. He was momentarily confused. *This is impossible*, he thought. Trying to pick the right way to move he leant too far forward and touched a light. The passage was immediately ablaze with dazzling white light which totally blinded him. When his vision cleared, he was in a heap on the lawn outside the Temple. Knowing that he had failed, he gathered up his shoes and weapons and headed back to Jadeja waiting at the gate.

'Eilidon of the Web, your fellow Paladin was unsuccessful. Are you prepared to try?'

'Yes Birali. I am ready. Show me the way.'

She stood up and followed the cat to the marble door.

'To retrieve the firestone, you must pass through the lights without touching them. If you fail, the Temple will remove you and the firestone will remain here.'

Eilidon nodded. Birali let her pass and closed the door behind her.

Finding herself in darkness Eilidon remained motionless until her spider eyes had adjusted. Seeing the steps, she began her descent. Once again, the line of lights appeared and began moving the moment that she did. First the snake, then the separation. In and out, faster, slower. She recognised the rhythm.

Of course, the dance of the fireflies.

She remembered sitting in the trees at home watching the ritual dance of the tiny creatures. At first their movements had looked random, but the longer she watched the more she could see the pattern and the rhythm. She recognised that same pattern here among the lights. Now that she knew the dance, she could negotiate her way through the line without touching any of them. Reaching the end, she turned and bowed, at which point the lights reformed their line and disappeared. Instead of darkness Eilidon was rewarded by a blaze of orange light, as the firestone lit up in welcome.

Birali appeared at her side.

'My compliments Eilidon of the web. The firestone awaits you.'

Birali indicated to her to lift the stone off its plinth.

Bowing to Birali, Eilidon took the jewel. It was the size of her palm, a beautiful red gem with a dancing orange flame at its centre.

'Guard it well Paladin. I hope one day you will return it.'

Eilidon wrapped the stone in a silken pouch decorated in runes and placed it inside her jerkin.

'With my life,' she replied.

Birali then led her back up the stairs and out through the marble door.

'The blessings of Maur be upon you. May your path be swift and true.'

'Thank you. I look forward to the day when I can return this to you.'

160

'The Temple of Maur will welcome you. Now you must hurry, there is darkness in the air.'

Eilidon bowed once more and exited the Temple, retrieving her boots and blades as she left.

21

Outside Caderyn was pacing up and down. Jadeja was still held motionless by the guards, unable to move.

'Something's coming,' said Caderyn.

Jadeja was released, jumping quickly to his feet. A large black mass was moving towards the Temple.

'A wolf pack,' said Caderyn.

The cats turned to Jadeja.

'You may join your companions. Leave now. We will hold them.'

The two boys ran across the lawn, meeting Eilidon halfway.

'I have the stone…' she stopped and pointed.

The boys saw the cat heads rise from the ground on human bodies. One wielding a sword, the other an axe. The golden cats from outside the Temple, backs arched and tails high, joined them. Each one in battle mode.

The leading wolf launched itself at the guards who ran it through with a sword. A second was cut in half by an axe. The following pack broke and a full-scale assault began. What the wolves lacked in size they made up for in numbers. The ankles of the giant guards were vulnerable

162

and several pairs of wolf fangs sank deep into the flesh, weakening their opponents. Unswayed, the temple guards continued to hack through their enemy. The golden cats were also unyielding in their defence of the temple; razor sharp teeth and claws tearing wolves asunder. The battle was harsh and bloody.

'We have to leave,' said Caderyn.

'Shouldn't we stay and fight?' said Eilidon.

'No. The stone is more important,' said Jadeja.

'We can't outrun wolves,' said Caderyn

'No, but I know who can.'

Jadeja reached into his mind and called to Chito.

Chito of the Plains, our hunters are here at Maur. We ask you to carry us to safety.

An answering whinny came back to him.

'The back gate,' said Jadeja. 'Follow me.'

He led them behind the Temple to a single statue of a woman with a cat's head, sitting cross-legged on the grass. In her hand she held a white marble egg. Jadeja placed his hand over the egg and pressed down. There was a sharp click and a trapdoor opened in the ground behind the statue, revealing a stairway.

'In!' he ordered, pushing first Caderyn then Eilidon down the stairs before following quickly behind them and closing the entrance.

'How far down does this go?' called Caderyn.

'Only under the cypress trees. It is not far but it will allow us to get away unseen.'

They descended about twenty feet and found themselves in an earthy passageway interspersed with tree roots. The dim light was difficult to see by, but once Caderyn's eyes had adjusted, he found his way easily. It was the stale air that he struggled with, forcing him to take short shallow breaths. He wondered where the light was coming from then realised that it was tiny glow worms.

After fifty feet or so the ground began to rise again and the roof of the tunnel became lower, making them crawl the last ten feet or so. They reached a dead end.

'There is a lever,' said Jadeja.

Caderyn felt the ground in front of him but touched only earth.

'I can't find anything.' As he spoke his foot caught on a tree root. He kicked at it trying to free himself and was rewarded by another sharp click. The ground in front of him swung open. Wriggling through, he inhaled deeply, glad to breathe the fresh air again.

He pulled Eilidon through, then Jadeja. The sound of screeching cats and howling wolves reached their ears.

Wolf after wolf attacked the gate. The axe and sword of the giant guards cut them down, one after the other. Any that they missed were set upon by the enormous, hissing and spitting golden cats, jaws drawn back, incisors tearing at their flesh. Certainly, no wolf was going to enter the Temple on this particular day.

'I hope the guards hold them off long enough for us to get away,' said Eilidon.

'So do I,' said Jadeja. 'I have no wish to encounter Rabten again just yet. Come on'

They ran towards a small grove of trees. There Chito was waiting for them with three sturdy palominos.

'These are my fastest ponies and they will permit you to ride.'

'Thank you, Chito. Your help will not be forgotten.'

Caderyn helped Eilidon and Jadeja onto their steeds, then mounted his and away they rode. The ponies were swift and the battle cries from the Temple grew fainter.

They galloped through the night. The ponies carrying them to the edge of the plains. At dawn, tired, exhausted and dripping with sweat the ponies stopped, their weary riders slipping from their backs.

'Thank you. Thank you. We are indebted to you,' said Jadeja.

The ponies whinnied their reply, turned back to the plains and home.

'What now?' asked Eilidon.

'Shang To,' replied Jadeja. 'Although I hadn't intended on coming this way. The ponies have brought us safely away from Maur but we will have to take a route that I had hoped to avoid. We should keep moving. The cats may have held the wolves at bay, but they won't be the only thing that hunts us.'

'I'm sorry Jadeja but I need a short rest. Can we at least take ten minutes?'

'Five, Caderyn. No more.'

During the brief stop they assessed the food and water situation. The water bottles were full from the river but food was not so plentiful. There were some apples and pears and nuts taken from the garden, but that was all.

'I'll eat as a spider so those rations last longer.'

'That will make a difference,' smiled Caderyn. 'Thanks.'

Jadeja headed east, leaving the burnt amber of the plains grasslands behind them. Without trees, the land was hostile to birds and they saw and heard none. For the most part, the only sound they were aware of was the trudging of their feet or the occasional cricket. They didn't stop until the last light of the day was gone.

'We can't make a fire. The smoke would give us away, so it's going to be a cold night,' said Jadeja.

'Lie down gentlemen, close together. I'll cocoon you. It won't be comfortable, but it'll be warm.'

The two boys lay down and Eilidon began encasing them in silk.

'Now I know what a dargon feels like when she catches one,' said Caderyn

When she had finished with the boys, she spun her own web to catch her breakfast in. Positioning herself in the corner of it, she slept.

At dawn, Eilidon was awoken by a strong vibration in her web. Looking down she saw a large locust caught in the threads. She shot forward and injected it with venom, then wrapped it while the venom did its work and turned the unfortunate creature into locust smoothie. Leaving her breakfast to marinate she returned to human form and extricated the boys from their sticky bed. While they ate a meagre breakfast of an apple and a handful of nuts, a large spider feasted on locust.

'We may have to join you in eating insects if we don't find more food soon,' said Caderyn.

'There are worse things to eat. Although right now I'm struggling to think of any,' said Jadeja.

'Instead of thinking about your stomachs, gentlemen, I suggest we get moving.'

'Yes majesty,' said Caderyn, who was rewarded with a kick on the shin.

The terrain they now had to cross was a series of gullies. The land had been worn away by some ancient force. Jadeja bent down to touch the red-brown sandstone, letting the particles slip through his fingers. It felt totally dry. The only greenery was the occasional gorse bush. It was hard going. They climbed the ridges then went down into the next gully. Up and down, up and down. It was exhausting.

'How much further?' panted Caderyn.

'I am unfamiliar with this landscape but we are heading for that mountain range,' said Jadeja, pointing to a line of peaks in the far distance. 'I reckon another day or two if we keep up this pace.'

'Not without some proper food. And our water is getting low.'

'When we get to the other side of this gully we'll scan for water. There may be a stream. If we see any vegetation we'll know that water must be near,' said Jadeja.

They pressed on, Jadeja bringing up the rear, wondering if his legs could manage to climb another ridge. When they reached the top, they found themselves on a small plateau with a few scrubby bushes.

'This doesn't look too promising,' said Caderyn.

'Stand still,' said Eilidon and proceeded to climb up his back and onto his shoulders. From this height, using her multi-faceted eyes she could see much further.

'Anything?'

'Three more gullies and then there is a greener area. I can't make out exactly what it is, but it's definitely green.' She climbed down.

'Three more,' moaned Jadeja.

'We should make it by early evening. Come on my friend.' Caderyn patted him on the back.

They walked across the plateau then scrabbled down the sandstone into the next gully. They startled a large lizard. Eilidon threw a blade, killing it before it had time to disappear into one of the many cracks in the rocks.

'Supper,' she said triumphantly.

'Thanks. I think,' laughed Caderyn.

Picking up the unfortunate creature, they crossed the gully and began the ascent of the other side. Jadeja started gathering up small pieces of shrub.

'What are you doing?' asked Eilidon.

'Kindling,' he replied. 'I'm not eating that thing raw.'

'Don't overburden yourself.'

'This is light my lady and will start a fire quickly.'

She left him to it and concentrated on finding good footholds. By the time they had crossed the third gully, Jadeja had filled the fishing net with suitable materials for a small fire.

'Good job you kept that,' said Caderyn.

'I had hoped that we would be able to do more fishing. Still it has proved very useful.'

The sight that greeted them was not what they had hoped for. Instead of lush green foliage and fresh water, it was dome shaped rock. The surface appeared to be divided up into a mass of smooth, flat faces like the facets of a diamond. Each one reflected the sunlight, giving off a green luminescence.

'No wonder you thought there might be water here,' said Caderyn. 'I've never seen anything like it.'

Eilidon looked around her with a growing unease. The rock formation reminded her of something. Jadeja was about to move forward when she stuck out an arm and held him back.

'Don't move.'

'But my lady, there may be water nearby. These rocks might....'

'They're not rocks Jadeja. They're eyes. Now the landscape makes sense. We need to move... quickly.'

'They began backing down the ridge they had just climbed. At the bottom of the gully Eilidon turned and ran,

168

followed by a pair of very puzzled boys. The ground began to shake and they were hit by loose pieces of rock falling from above them.

'Is it an earthquake?' shouted Caderyn.

'Worse. It's an azdhar.'

'A what?'

Caderyn's question was answered by the shadow that fell over the sun.

'That,' screamed Eilidon.

The creature that now hovered in the sky was a colossal lizard with bat-like wings. The body was the same grey-brown colour as the landscape. Its green eyes shining out from a flat face. Two nostrils opened and closed as it tried to identify this new scent it had picked up. There were two sets of lids over the eyes. One closed over the front as the other opened over the side of the eye, giving it panoramic vision. When it caught sight of its prey the mouth opened to reveal layer upon layer of vicious teeth.

Caderyn loaded his bow, turned and fired his first arrow which landed in the creature's underbelly as it swooped down towards them. Diving under an outcrop of rock they were just in time to avoid being impaled on its teeth. With a cry of frustration, the azdhar flew up and circled round, ready for another attack.

Jadeja was ready with his sling shot.

'I'll aim for the left side, you take the right,' he shouted to Caderyn whose bow was already reloaded. The barrage of shot and arrows only served to enrage the beast as it flew down towards them again. This time the creature used its enormous claws to loosen rocks and stones above them starting a small landslide, forcing them to break cover. They ran back along the valley.

'There,' shouted Jadeja, pointing to a large boulder they could hide behind. They watched the azdhar fly up and circle around ready for another onslaught. The terrifying beast hurled itself at them scooping the boulder up in its enormous jaws and spitting it back at them.

'Look out!'

Jadeja almost got crushed as the rock smashed into the hillside just above him, raining huge fragments onto them.

'We need to get it on the ground. While it's up there it has too great an advantage,' said Eilidon.

'And how do you propose to do that?' asked Caderyn.

'Aim for the wings. If we can damage them it will have to land.'

'I have an idea,' said Jadeja.

Using some of the kindling he had gathered earlier he quickly started a small fire and attached dry kindling to several of Caderyn's arrows. Picking up on his plan, Caderyn dipped three arrows in the flame. As soon as they were alight, he spun and fired them at the azdhar flying down for yet another assault on them. The arrows hit and the flames ate into the dry and ancient skin that made up the creature's wings. Driven berserk by the pain that it was in and struggling to fly with damaged wings the giant creature crashed to the ground. The boys felt its hot breath. The eyes glared out from their sockets casting venomous glances towards them. Nothing had ever inflicted this much pain onto it before.

'Okay, now what?' asked Jadeja as the monster advanced rapidly towards them.

'Aim for the eyes,' shouted Eilidon.

Jadeja fired his sling shot.

'Caderyn, keep it focused on you two. I'll kill it.'

Jadeja loaded his sling again and again, timing his shot to land after Caderyn's arrows. Every shot further enraging the azdhar which he knew was intent on eating them. Caderyn was across the gully and firing at the right eye so Jadeja aimed several stones at the left. Howling in pain the azdhar turned from left to right trying to seize its attackers, teeth gnashing and biting while the enormous tail thrashed the ground, making the earth shake violently.

Eilidon, now a spider, climbed unnoticed onto its back. She moved cautiously, aware that if she was thrown off by its threshing movements she would be squashed in an instant. Creeping forward she reached the head where she found what she was looking for, a small smooth patch of pulsating skin. This was the creature's heart. Throwing out a sticky thread to secure herself she became human again and took out her sharpest blade. Sensing the weight on its back the azdhar reared up throwing Eilidon off balance. Luckily her thread held but she had to climb back along its body as it continued to jerk about, each movement threatening to throw her to the ground and almost certain death. With supreme effort, she managed to climb up once more. This time she plunged her blade deep into the heart, twisting the knife for maximum effect. The azdhar raised its head, shuddered violently, then fell heavily back to the ground and lay still. The movement threw Eilidon backwards, she tried to grab hold of something to save herself. Instead her head hit the azdar's hard outer skin, knocking her unconscious. When the creature halted, she was left dangling over the side of its body.

The two boys rushed forward. Caderyn climbed swiftly up the side of the lizard, cutting Eilidon free and lowering her down to Jadeja who carried her further down the gully away from the dead azdhar.

'Is she ok?'

Jadeja felt her neck for a pulse.

'She's alive. There is a large swelling on the back of her head.'

Caderyn rested her head in his lap, calling on healing spirits to revive her, then they waited anxiously until she came around.

'Is it dead?'

'Most definitely my lady. Thanks to you.'

'How did you know what to do?' asked Caderyn. 'That was brilliant by the way.'

'There is a famous story told by my people of a fight between an azdhar and Lya, a mighty warrior of the Arachne. The azdhar attacked our people, killing and eating them. None could stop it. Legend tells of how Lya spun a giant web to catch the creature but it proved immune to his venom. While it sat imprisoned in his web, Lya climbed over its body and located the pulse point. Recognising this as the way to kill it, he jumped down to fetch his sword. Back in human form he mounted the creature and drove his blade through this weak spot, killing the azdhar and cementing his place as a hero of our people.

I remembered the tale from my childhood and gambled on it being true. The azdhar I recognised from the many pictures we have, particularly the eyes. Although until today I wasn't one hundred percent convinced that such a creature existed. Everything about this landscape matched the stories. In the tales, the azdhar created furrows in the ground with its enormous body. There it sat and waited for prey, catching it unawares as it did with us.'

'Well almost,' said Caderyn. 'Thanks to your quick thinking we were able to get away.'

Eilidon shivered.

'I'll make a fire. We should set up camp. The day is drawing to a close,' said Jadeja.

While he made a fire pit and started a fresh blaze, Caderyn walked the length of the azdhar's body retrieving as many of his arrows that he could find. Already the blood that oozed from the top of the creature's head had attracted a swarm of flies. Inspecting the teeth, Caderyn began prising one free from the mouth and took it back to the camp.

'Arrow heads,' he explained.

'By the way Eilidon, if you'd prefer not to eat lizard there is a swarm of bluebottles over at our dead friend.'

She got up slowly, disappearing for an hour or so, only returning when she had eaten her fill of fat and juicy flies.

The boys roasted their lizard in the fire then tucked into its tough and leathery meat. It wasn't particularly pleasant but it filled their bellies.

'Shall we camp in this gully tonight?' asked Eilidon.

'We may as well,' said Caderyn.

'Definitely my lady. I do not relish the thought of more climbing today.'

'That's settled then. You two sleep, I'll take first watch,' offered Caderyn. 'Probably best to extinguish the fire though.'

Caderyn perched on a rocky ledge just above them, bow in hand. He sat watching the stars begin to appear in the sky and wondered at the vastness of it all. Around two o'clock he woke Jadeja and then lay down staring at the heavens until sleep took him.

Jadeja too, was aware of the stars that night. His eye was drawn to a small cluster over to the north. They appeared to form a figure of eight. While he watched they split into two separate circles like distant eyes staring down at him.

He was held, ensnared, unable to look away. Slowly the eyes became an entire face. One that he recollected but did not want to see. A voice filled his head.

'Jadeja. Jadeja.'

There it was, calling and calling to him.

'Jadejaaaaa. Come to me little one.'

The voice pulled at him, drawing him closer and closer.

'There you are. I have missed you.'

The eyes were penetrating his very being, pinning him to the rock, sucking at his soul. He was powerless to resist, losing himself into darkness.

'That's the way. Follow me. This is where you belong.'

He felt the darkness enveloping him. *I am lost* he thought, as he slipped deeper under the spell. He held out his hand to embrace the dark then a tiny light broke into his mind's eye. Then another came and another, until the connection was broken by a thousand tiny lights dancing around his head.

The voice from the stars sighed heavily.

'Next time boy. Next time.'

And then silence. Jadeja came out of his trance and watched the fireflies as they danced around him. He realised that they were eating away at a black shroud that surrounded him. Once it was gone, he could move freely.

'Thank you, my tiny friends, again you have saved me from myself.'

The fireflies dance continued briefly before they disappeared.

Shaking off his drowsiness, Jadeja pulled out his flute and began to play, calling the spirits to protect them. This time he noted, they did not dance gaily, instead they formed a circle around the three of them, hands entwined to create a barrier. When that was done, Jadeja put away his flute and allowed himself to sleep and dream of Suremaana.

22

Somewhere, high up in the Temple at Shang To, Suremaana also dreamt. Her dream was troubled. The Artisan stood before her asking his question over and over.

Will you betray the one you love?

Again, she felt the silver snakes writhing up her arms, holding her to his table. Then she switched to the inner Sanctum of the Temple, a place filled with sacred lights. There a figure in black struck the mighty gong, filling the building with its sound. Only it wasn't the calming and healing sound that usually emanated from this beautiful instrument, it was a harsh and bitter note that penetrated her soul. She found herself running toward the figure as it raised the beater to strike again. This time the sound made the very fabric of the building start to shatter. Cracks began to appear in the walls. The roof split and darkness seeped into the sanctuary. Knowing that a third strike would mark the end, she grabbed the arm that held the beater. The hooded figure turned to face her.

'Jadeja!' she screamed.

Her shout brought the elder Gardeer into her chamber.

'Wake up child. You are dreaming again.'

Slowly Suremaana awoke, her pillow soaked with tears.

'What was it that has so upset you?'

Opening her eyes Suremaana recounted her dream.

'I can't believe that he is evil. He was always so gentle and kind.'

'Our dreams are not always true child. Sometimes they show us our worst imaginings and our deepest fears. Perhaps you fear the connection you have with this boy.'

'Eilidon does not trust him. There is something hidden from her that she cannot fathom. I should have listened to her.'

'Perhaps, but if your heart tells you otherwise don't ignore it.'

'Do you think that they are safe? It has been so long since I heard from them.'

'The Master says that they are on their way here. I'm sure you will see them again soon. For now, I will give you a valerian tea. That will clear the clouds from your mind and allow you to sleep peacefully.'

Gardeer left the room, returning shortly afterwards with the tea. They sat quietly while the liquid cooled sufficiently for Suremaana to drink. Once she had finished, she lay back down and closed her eyes, drifting quickly off to sleep again. Gardeer waited quietly with her for a few minutes before returning to her own chamber. For the rest of the night Suremaana's sleep was deep and peaceful.

Since their arrival at Shang To, Gardeer had been her only company. After a brief meeting with the Shaman-Master to fill him in on the events of their journey, he and the rest of the Elders had been in a tight enclave deep in meditation. Only Gardeer had been allowed to leave the meditative circle to accompany Suremaana.

Anxious about the fate of her friends, but powerless to help them, Suremaana worked her frustrations off by undertaking a rigorous training regime. Each day she practised kicks, tumbles and spins. She ran and ran through the Temple gardens or swam in the moat, ending each day so exhausted that sleep was easier to come by.

Gardeer cooked and prepared hot scented baths for her to sink into at the end of a day's training. Sometimes they would sit together and talk, Gardeer telling her about the lake people and Suremaana talking about the Serpentae, particularly her mother.

'She was a gifted Paladin.'

'My mother? Father never told me much about her.'

'It was long before he met her. She was much older than him, although you would not have known to look at her. She remained youthful right up until her death.'

'I wish I had known her. She died when I was two.'

'That was the agreement she made with Orochi, the Serpentae Goddess. When she married your father, she was too old for child bearing, although she had not revealed this to him, hoping that her love would be enough to sustain them, which it was for many years. However, your father longed for a child and your mother, Vasuna, became consumed with guilt for not being honest with him about her age. In desperation, she went to Orochi's Temple. There she begged and pleaded with the goddess to grant her a child. She made many offerings and sacrifices until eventually the goddess yielded to her pleas. She told Vasuna that she would grant her wish but the price would be her life. It was to be at the time of your birth, but at the last minute the goddess relented and said that she could have two years with you. Vasuna agreed and I would say that the next three years were the happiest your parents had ever known. From the moment she conceived, until your second birthday your father was blissfully happy. Your mother too, but she knew this joy would soon be over. A week after your birthday she returned to the Temple where she gave thanks for your being and then died at the goddess's feet.

When they found her, she was carried to your father who was distracted with grief. For two years he remained locked in his chambers, seeing no one, not even you. On your fourth birthday, you were playing hide and seek with your nurse and you wandered into his rooms. Your intrusion was greeted with a yell to his servants to take you away. You were frightened but you didn't show it. When the nurse appeared to get you, you asked her,

Who was that angry man?

Hearing your innocent question and realising that his own, so longed for child did not know him, brought the king back from the edge of darkness. He called his servants again and bid them run him a hot bath and shave him. Then cleansed and renewed he came to find you.'

'I remember. I made him dance with me. He lifted me high in the air and spun me round.'

'Your innocence and free heart gave him new hope and new life.'

Suremaana smiled at the memories.

'And now he is alone again.'

'Yes, but he knows that your time as a Paladin will end when you are twenty-one and you will return to your people. That sustains him.'

'How do you know all this Gardeer?'

'Because I was your nurse. The Elders sent me when they heard of Vasuna's death, they knew she had been my friend.'

179

'Then why don't I remember you?'

'You were so young and your father filled your life from that day. I returned to my people and did not see you again until I arrived with Hamroon to escort you here.'

Suremaana remained quiet.

'Thank you,' she said and squeezed Gardeer's hand.

'You remind me so much of her, apart from your extraordinary red hair.'

Suremaana stroked her tresses and smiled, 'This is the result of Jadeja saving my life.'

Her mind drifted, picturing his face full of concern. Gardeer's voice pulled her back.

'You have her gift for tunnelling. That is rare. You move like her too.'

'Were you a Paladin?'

'No. I was chosen to train, which is where I met your mother. Unfortunately, I didn't pass the final test. There are not many who do.'

They were interrupted by the sound of a gong.

'The Shaman-Master summons me. I'm sure your friends are safe. Stay strong in your belief.'

Gardeer left to join the other Elders in the inner Sanctum.

Suremaana wandered off and climbed the watch tower at the entrance to the Temple. At the topmost window she sat herself on the ledge and stared out over the winding path that led to the Temple gates. She thought over the story of her mother and wondered what it would be like to love someone so much that you would make such a sacrifice for them. To her surprise and annoyance, images of Jadeja filled her mind, the warmth of his touch and the vulnerability behind his eyes. *Stop this* she told herself. *You are a Paladin and personal relationships are forbidden. You took an oath of loyalty to the Shaman-Master.* Then she coiled a length of her new red hair around her fingers and Jadeja occupied her mind again.

23

The morning after the battle with the azdhar, Eilidon woke with a renewed vigour. Killing the beast had fired her up and restored her inner defiance that had been dented by her encounters with the three sisters.

I am Paladin and I am strong, she repeated to herself.

Returning to the azdhar's body she made a web to capture the flies busily laying their eggs on the decaying corpse. She walked the length of its body and cut a small piece of skin from its tail. This was her token and proof that she had defeated the enormous creature.

By the time she returned to the camp, the boys were awake and breakfasted on what rations they had, although an apple and a few nuts were not going to fill them up. Eilidon felt guilty, having just gorged herself on bluebottles.

'Ah Eilidon, we need to get moving. We still have a long way to go and I feel vulnerable here.'

'You're right Caderyn. If we climb up and cross the gullies we will be away from this place quicker.'

Jadeja moaned. 'Not more climbing. I think my legs have only just recovered from yesterday.'

The other two laughed.

'Listen to the old man. Perhaps sir would like a piggyback,' offered Caderyn, bending down.

Jadeja looked at him, then realised that he was joking.

'No. I'm fine.'

They gathered their belongings and began climbing the side of the gully. At the top, they surveyed the terrain.

'Only three more,' said Eilidon. 'We can clear this by noon.'

Striding out purposefully, she led the boys onwards, scrambling down into the next gully. Although the going was difficult there were plenty of footholds and handholds and they made good progress, crowning the last ridge as the sun reached its highest point. What lay before them was a circle of enormous dome shaped mountains. Their surfaces looked so smooth and uniform it seemed like a giant potter's hand had shaped them all out of a single mould. The sides of each dome rose sheer and impenetrable. Jadeja shivered, remembering the last time he had stood here.

'We can take the path round the mountains. It is easy to navigate and will only take a day or so,' he said.

Eilidon looked at the ring of mountains.

'Surely it will be quicker to go through the middle? It looks like a straight path.'

'NO! You do not pass the guardians,' said Jadeja.

'Why not?'

'This is the Valley of the Winds. See the guardians at the entrance.'

She looked where he pointed and saw two enormous v-shaped, thin faces, carved into the rock. Each face had high cheekbones and a long nose under which full lips were pursed as if whistling. Slender ears ran down the side of each face. One ear was adorned with a mossy stud on its upper lobe.

'When you pass, the guardians call up the winds and the voices.' said Jadeja.

'What voices?'

'The Drogas, as these mountains are called, are the resting place of the Drogmas, an ancient people. It is said that their souls inhabit the domes. Anyone trespassing here will be tested. If you are strong you will pass safely through the valley.'

'And if you fail?'

'If you fail my lady, the Drogmas will claim you as theirs. Which is why we should go around them.'

'What do the voices do?'

'When the whistling starts you are assailed by a rising wind. Then the voices start questioning you or trying to deceive you. They tap into your consciousness and feed on your fears. They want you to stop or turn around. Once you falter, they have you. To pass through you must keep moving forward. It is all illusion, but when you are in there it feels real.'

'Sounds like you have been here before Jadeja.'

'Once my lady. I vowed that I would not come back.'

An image of the three sisters flashed into Eilidon's mind. 'Probably best if we go around,' she said.

Caderyn was unconvinced. 'I think we should risk it. If the voices do as you say then Rabten and his followers will not go in there. That must give us an advantage.'

'Advantage or not, I will avoid going through there,' said Jadeja.

'I have an idea,' said Caderyn. 'Show me your runes.'

Eilidon and Jadeja pulled back their sleeves to reveal the runes that the red bird had placed there before they left the Shaman-Master's house in Simniel.

'These were given to us for a purpose. I believe if I invoke the spirits and we combine our runes we can call up enough protection to get us through there.'

'It is too much of a risk,' said Jadeja.

'Not with the bird to protect us.'

Jadeja was not convinced. 'We go round,' he said and strode off. The other two followed. I'm doing the right thing said Jadeja to himself, even so, something pulled at his mind. *Coward, coward. You are risking the mission because you are afraid. If you fail at this what else will you fail at.* Dark laughter filled his head. *Worthless maggot.* He saw the Shaman-Master's face filled with disappointment. *I trusted you Jadeja.* Then the laughter again. *Not long now boy. Soon you will be mine. Take the long way round. I'm waiting for you.* 'Out. Out,' he yelled, pushing the voice back into the recesses of his subconscious.

Caderyn swallowed his objections and followed Jadeja. Eilidon for her part was relieved to avoid the mountains.

He was right about the terrain. It was easy going. Too easy. *The Drogas are treacherous,* he thought. *Something is not right.* A movement to his left made him stop. Eilidon was already aware of it, Caderyn too. Something was manoeuvring in the ground. He felt its presence like a dark fog in his mind. The earth shifted, forming concentric circles, surrounding them. Fear rose like bile in his throat as he felt this new threat fix its attention on him. A page from the book of Thaddeus opened up in his head and he realised with horror what approached. Eilidon and Caderyn were motionless, fearing where to step, looking to him for guidance. He tried to recall the words on the page, the correct incantation to banish it, but his mind had emptied of knowledge and was filled only with panic. The circles at their feet tightened. *Think, think Jadeja.* The earth shifted again and he saw rising from the mountainside a black nicovar serpent. A giant beast from the darkest realms of the spirit world. It raised its head like a king cobra ready to strike and held his gaze. Suddenly the words came unbidden to his mouth and he shouted out.

'Corth fawl, Corth fawl. Belorrial rioch.'

The serpent was momentarily confused as the ancient words blocked its way.

'RUN! Back to the guardians,' screamed Jadeja to the other two, then repeating the words again, he sprinted after them.

The incantation was incomplete and he knew it would only keep the snake at bay for a brief time. *Long enough for us to enter the path I hope.* He yelled 'The entrance.'

Before he had time to see if they had heard him, he felt the incantation break and knew that the giant serpent was bearing down on him. Glancing behind he saw the mighty jaws open and blackness spew forth threatening to engulf him. He joined the Paladin as they passed the guardians, the serpent's black shadow unable to cross the entrance.

'Right, let's get this over with,' said Caderyn. 'It can't be worse than what we just faced.'

Jadeja hesitated, looking at his companions. He knew what awaited them, but now there was no choice about it. He saw the determination on Caderyn's face and realised that he would be all right, Eilidon however, he was not so sure about. Summoning up all of his courage he led them on. As soon as they moved the whistling began. At first there was a soft note that rose and rose to a high-pitched warning. Then silence, the kind of quiet and stillness that occurs just before a storm. There was no movement. No sound. Just a sense of oppression in the air. They walked on with an ever-increasing sense of dread.

Suddenly the earth began to shake and the sand was whipped up around them by a whirling gust of wind.

'It begins,' said Jadeja. 'Remember, it is all illusion. Keep moving forwards.'

The first gust dissipated only to be followed by swirls of air, trying to slow them down. Bending their heads, they pushed on.

Next the voices started.

'Caderyn of the Bow, we see you. We see you. The Master wants you. Caderyn. Follow us. The Shaman-Master is in dire need of your help. Listen. Can you hear him call? You must go to him.'

The Shaman-Master's voice filled his head.

'Caderyn, the Jhankhira is here. You must come. I cannot defeat him alone. He overwhelms me. Caderyn… Caderyn.'

The voices continued, alternating between the Shaman-Master and the call to follow him. He felt himself falter, desperately wanting to turn and follow the voices. Raising his arm in front of his face he allowed the runes to form an invisible barrier between him and the wind, blocking out the voices, allowing him to keep going.

'Jadeja. Jadeja. We know your name. We know who you are. We remember you. Come with us. We will show you. You will finally know the truth.'

The voices filled Jadeja's head with all the questions he wanted answers to. They promised to show him. He shook his head.

'You're not real. I won't listen to you.'

'Listen to me then, little one.' It was Rabten's voice.

'Listen to me. Come with me. The path is open. All you have to do is follow it. Follow me. Follow your heart.'

He could feel himself being overwhelmed.

'No, no, no,' he yelled. 'Leave me alone.'

'Why should we leave you? We know you want to follow us. We know you want answers.'

Try as he might he couldn't block out the voices on the winds.

Rabten's voice echoed in his head once more, laughing at him, he felt like a small vulnerable child again. In despair, he raised his hands over his ears, allowing the runes to glow and wrap around him, lessening the sound, so that he could keep going.

For Eilidon the voices on the wind were less of a problem. Their frequency was similar to the vibrations on a web and so she found herself able to absorb the sound. The voices continued to swirl around her, sensing a resistance. Smiling defiantly, she strode forward. However, the winds were not so easily beaten. Just when she thought she would make it through the valley unscathed, she felt it. The familiar blast of icy coldness she had last experienced on the river. A deep sensation of horror engulfed her. She knew what was coming. There they were, the three sisters.

'We have come back for you, Eilidon of the Web. You will not evade us this time.'

She felt their icy breath on her neck. Saw their bony fingers reaching through the winds. She tried to tell herself that they were not real, that it was all an illusion, but the cold enveloped her. Her steps faltered as the three sisters barred her way.

'Not so brave now, are we?'

'No friends to protect you.'

'No river to carry you away from us.'

188

'Why don't you turn and run? We like a chase.'

Biting cold pressed into her face as the rimy fingers touched her.

'Run Eilidon. Turn and run. They will take you. It's the only way.'

The voice was Jadeja's. She hesitated. The sisters eyed her greedily.

'Come, the forest awaits,'

'No, turn and run. Run!' Jadeja's voice was there again.

Fear encompassed her. The desire to flee became stronger. She knew what would happen if the sisters took her. They smiled menacingly. Pressing ever closer to her face.

Somewhere in the recesses of her mind Eilidon knew they were an illusion - still the urge to flee was overwhelming. The winds twirled and twisted, their icy blast was paralysing. The sisters embraced her. Again, she heard Jadeja, 'Turn and run, it's the only escape.'

The strength of the winds increased wrapping her in a vortex from which she could not escape. Utterly defeated, she started to turn away from the sisters. A hand grabbed her arm. Fearing the worst, she closed her eyes and screamed in abject terror. The grip tightened. Slowly the runes on her wrist began to flare and she realised that it was not an icy hand, but a warm one. She opened her eyes. It was Caderyn, the runes on his arm ablaze. The sisters melted into the ether and the winds dissipated. The spell was broken. Allowing herself to be led by him, the voices gradually faded from her mind. Together they moved forward until they reached the end of the valley. When they passed between the last two Drogas the wind stopped, releasing them to the land beyond.

24

Exhaustion took each of them and they collapsed to the ground.

'Thank you,' mouthed Eilidon.

Too drained to speak, Caderyn simply raised an arm in acknowledgement.

Jadeja sat with his head in his hands. He could feel his heart thundering uncontrollably. *Breathe,* he thought. *We are through and the Nicovar is behind us,* but he couldn't stop himself shaking. He clutched his amulet. The eagle comforted him, until gradually his fear subsided. Looking across at the others he noted how white Eilidon's face was and even the usually fearless Caderyn was hunched up in a ball to hide his horror at what they had just survived. *I must change the mood* he thought and scrambled to his feet and began climbing up the side of the Droga. Thinking he'd gone mad the other two called after him, then they saw where he was headed. About a third of the way up, perched on a ledge was a solitary tree, laden with fruit. Jadeja picked as many as he could carry and climbed back down.

'Figs,' he said, passing them around.

They were delicious, soft and ripe and very nourishing. Jadeja was pleased to feel the tension lifting slightly. Once they were full, they packed the remainder for later and continued on their journey. Jadeja thanked the tree for her bounty.

'It feels like the figs are a reward for making it through the valley,' he said, trying to lighten the mood. The strain on Eilidon's face clearly visible.

'Perhaps,' replied Caderyn. 'I'm just glad that we did make it, although it was a close call for you Eilidon. If I hadn't grabbed your arm, I think you would have turned.'

'I know. I'm sorry. I was weak. I won't be again.'

There was a steely determination in her voice. She hated the fact that fear had got the better of her.

'You were not weak, my lady. The Drogmas are very strong and we were ill prepared to pass through there. Unfortunately, the nicovar left us no choice.'

Jadeja's words only served to deepen her resolve never to give in to fear again.

Beyond the Drogas the land sloped downwards and was firm underfoot. Here and there scrubby bits of grass began to appear. Slowly they encountered signs of life. Bushes with dark green leaves sprouted up from the earth. Off to the left a family of rodents appeared.

'We must be getting close to water. There is more vegetation here,' said Caderyn, calmness returning to his demeanour.

'Let's hope so. My water bottle is empty,' said Jadeja.

Cresting a low ridge, a carpet of purple flowers spread out before them. He pointed to a small group of moose, grazing to their right.

'There will definitely be water nearby if the animals are gathering,' he said.

A scruffy little brown bird hopped about in the flowers, pecking at tiny insects. Allowing themselves to relax just a little, they strolled through the flowers, heading towards the moose, which scattered at their approach. Before them lay a lake of vivid aquamarine, with streaks of rust where particles of iron dust had been washed into the water. Jadeja took a tentative sip.

'It's fresh.'

He quenched his thirst, then filled his bottle, taking care to avoid the copper coloured streaks. The other two did likewise.

'If we skirt the edge of the lake we should come to the Valley of a Thousand Smokes. From there we can find the mountain path to Shang To,' said Jadeja.

'The Valley of a Thousand Smokes?' said Caderyn.

'An old volcano. You'll see what I mean when we get there.'

'Should we camp or move on while there's still light?' asked Eilidon.

'Keep moving. There is still an hour of daylight left. The more distance we put between ourselves and the Drogas the better,' said Jadeja.

They walked around the lake, heading for its eastern tip. The vegetation thickened, the water encouraging plants and trees to grow. Because of the volcanic nature of the area there were none of the usual lakeside plants, like bulrushes and willows on the eastern side. Instead the shore was rock and shingle which made it easier to negotiate.

They continued until the sun had long set, before settling down a few metres from the lake under an acacia tree. Eilidon was too exhausted to make a cocoon for the boys, so they wrapped their cloaks tightly around themselves and huddled together for warmth.

'We should move at dawn,' she said. 'My senses are on edge. The sooner we reach Shang To the better.'

'I agree,' said Jadeja. 'If we cross the valley and reach the mountain path, we should be there the day after tomorrow. The Master needs us and the firestone. I will take first watch. I'll call up some spirits to guard us.'

He pulled out his flute and began to play.

Whether it was the music or simply tiredness, Caderyn and Eilidon were both asleep within minutes. Once they were under, Jadeja moved along the lake shore until he was hidden from view. He took out a small ornate bell that he had secreted inside his tunic. The bell was barely the size of a thimble and was made from animal horn, intricately carved with eyes and flames.

Jadeja removed his shoes and cloak and washed his feet and hands in the lake. Using a stick, he drew a circle on the ground and placed the bell and his flute in the centre. Very carefully he lit some dried sage leaves that he carried with him in a pouch within his tunic. Once they were smoking, he passed them up and down his body to absorb and remove any dark energy. He sat in the centre of the circle facing north. Picking up the miniature bell, he rang it gently.

'I call upon the powers of the north and the element of air. Enter my circle. I have need of you.'

Putting down the bell, he sat perfectly still. A gentle movement of air filled the circle as he felt the presence of the spirits.

'What awaits me at Shang To and will I be equal to it?'

In answer, he felt the north wind rush round his head clouding his vision. When the mists cleared, he saw Rabten

193

striding towards him, then being pulled back by an invisible hand. Next, he saw the Jhankhira, locked in battle with the Shaman-Master. He heard his master's voice urging him to complete the ceremony.

Only you can do this Jadeja. We are relying on you.

Then he saw her. He heard her calling his name, like she had always done. He wanted to run to her. To embrace her. To fall into her darkness. Into oblivion.

The winds subsided and he awoke from his trance. Hands shaking, he picked up the bell and rang it one more time, stood and bowed and stepped out of the circle, ending the connection. The bell and flute he put away then resumed his watch, mulling over what he had just seen. Fear and dread consumed him. The strength of his enemy was terrifying. *I cannot do this. I will fail Master. Why do you demand this of me?*

Unable to settle, the next two hours were spent pacing anxiously before waking Caderyn to take over from him. Sleep evaded him for much of the night, his mind flitting from one catastrophe to another. Eventually, exhausted, he slept.

The next morning, after a breakfast of figs, they continued, reaching the eastern tip of the lake around noon. There they climbed up and over a rocky outcrop and stared down into a deep valley. The rock formation on the right-hand side looked like a series of flying buttresses, the kind you might find on a gothic cathedral. All along the floor of the valley, steam was rising, sometimes in gentle wisps, at other times high pressure jets rose up like the smoke from a fast-moving train. The heat from the jets was in stark contrast to the coolness of the lake shore.

'The Valley of a Thousand Smokes,' said Jadeja.

'We have to cross that?'

'Yes, my lady Eilidon. I'm afraid we do.'

'Let's go then.'

She began heading down into the valley, quickly followed by the boys. Clouds of vapour soon engulfed them and they had to peel off layers of clothing because of the heat. Sweat poured from Jadeja, sapping his energy. Caderyn stripped down to his undergarments and was still overheating. The terrain was not easy. Eilidon had a near miss when a jet of steam rose up suddenly in front of her. She uttered several words in a language Jadeja did not understand.

'I think that's Arachne swearing,' laughed Caderyn, picking his way carefully to avoid getting scalded by another jet.

Even the ground was treacherous, turning to pools of volcanic mud in places, bubbling up and threatening to suck them under if they stepped in one.

A yelp from Caderyn stopped them.

'Are you okay?' asked Jadeja.

'Yes. It was hot, that's all.'

He turned towards them, face spattered in mud where a pool had bubbled up and sprayed him. Eilidon burst out laughing.

'I believe volcanic mud is very good for the skin. Purifying.'

'Oh really. Then perhaps madam would like to try.'

He bent down and scooped up a handful of the stuff and smeared it on Eilidon's face. She immediately hit back with a flick of her wrist, catching Caderyn full in the face. Jadeja tried to step in between to stop them and was unceremoniously knocked backwards into the mud. The indignant look on his face produced gales of laughter from the other two.

Caderyn stuck out a hand and hoisted Jadeja to his feet, black mud dripped of his trousers and vest.

'Sorry my friend. Are you hurt?'

'Only my pride,' replied Jadeja. 'Come on. Let's keep moving. I can clean this stuff off when its dry.'

He marched on, testing the firmness of the ground at every step, not wanting to lead them into a patch of sinking sludge. When they reached the end of the valley they were rewarded with a geyser of warm water. Jadeja slipped off his muddy clothes and stepped in.

'This is heavenly,' he said, lying back and enjoying the warmth and the cleansing. Caderyn followed him in but Eilidon declined, stopping only to wash her face and hands. Jadeja rinsed his clothes and lay them on the warm ground to dry while they ate a small meal of figs and nuts.

The sun was beginning to sink and the fading light threw some strange shadows in the steam. Ahead of them loomed the Katai Mountain, at the top of which was the Temple of Shang To.

'We will be there tomorrow,' said Jadeja. 'I am not as familiar with the path on this side of the mountain. It is less used than the other one, although I believe the two intersect about halfway up.'

'In that case, we should rope together, so no one slips off a ledge.'

'A wise precaution my lady.'

Sensing the tension in his voice, Eilidon said, 'The path will be safe enough, if we're careful.'

'I'm sure you are right my lady.'

But it wasn't the path that Jadeja was nervous of. It was what awaited him at the Temple.

25

At daybreak, they took the mountain path. Eilidon had made a strong silken rope which they tied around each other like an extra-long umbilical cord.

Caderyn went in front, Jadeja second and Eilidon bringing up the rear. Once they had left the steam jets behind, the air became noticeably cooler and thinner. The path, such as it was, took them in a zig-zag pattern up the mountain. Although unfamiliar to him, Caderyn was a skilful tracker and could make out the route. Thankfully it wasn't the snow season, so whilst there was the occasional ice patch, for the most part they were walking over rocks.

Jadeja sensed that the mountain welcomed them. Caderyn was always able to find footholds and an easy way around any boulders that blocked their path. Progress was fast and by midday when they stopped for a short rest, they were surprised by how far they had come. Gazing back down the mountain the steam jets now looked like harmless wisps of smoke rather than the boiling hot plumes that had threatened to scald them. In the far distance, they could just make out the circle of Drogas. Eilidon shivered at the memory.

'This path is easier than I expected. We should be at the intersection soon. It will not be long from there,' said Caderyn.

'Good, apart from seeing my Master again, I am looking forward to a decent meal,' said Jadeja, trying to conceal the tension in his voice.

'Boys and their stomachs!'

'It's all right for you. You've been feasting on flies and locusts. Jadeja and I are on figs and too many of them can have the wrong effect,' said Caderyn.

Eilidon smiled, feeling slightly guilty that she had managed to eat reasonably well, while the boys were making do on very slim pickings.

Suddenly Caderyn sprinted ahead taking Jadeja so much by surprise he almost fell over as the rope between them became taut.

'Hey, slow down,' he called. 'You might have warned me.'

Caderyn was forced to stop by the rope that bound them.

'Sorry. This is the intersection. I recognised the carving.'

He stood in front of a rectangular stone sculpture appreciating the face deep in contemplation. The eyes were closed and the mouth was set in a welcoming smile. A band with three lines of round coils covered the forehead like an elaborate headdress. The whole thing stood on a rectangular plinth filled with water from a trickling stream, filtering through the rocks behind it.

'The welcome stone,' said Jadeja. 'We must drink.'

One by one they knelt at the stone scooping up handfuls of the cold, refreshing water. Thanking the mountain for the gift, Caderyn allowed himself to relax, finally feeling that they were safe. This was his undoing. Although they had reached the welcome stone, they had not yet passed it. Turning back to the others he felt a violent push from behind and found himself plummeting over the mountainside.

'Caderyn!' yelled Jadeja, watching despairingly as the young man toppled over the edge. The fall came to an abrupt stop as the rope tightened. The sudden jolt caused Caderyn to slam into the rock. Screaming with pain he felt the bones in his leg shatter. Jadeja staggered to the cliff edge, dragged forward by the boy on the end of the rope. Eilidon braced herself against the weight and prevented Jadeja tumbling after him. Peering over he could just about make out the shape of Caderyn dangling precariously on the end of Eilidon's silken rope. Behind him he could hear the roar of the creature that had attacked him. A huge rock dweller, a being so old it appeared to be made from the rocks it lived in. Vaguely human in shape, it had fists of stone that could smash a man's skull with a single blow. The same fists that had pushed Caderyn over the edge were now bearing down on Jadeja as he tried to hold his friend and haul him back up.

Eilidon screamed to Jadeja.

'Secure the rope. Secure the rope.'

'I can't.'

She tried to stall the rock dweller by throwing stones at him and swinging up above it, throwing a web over its face. While these distractions slowed it momentarily, they were not going to hold it back.

'Jadeja, we must run.'

'Nearly done. Okay it's secure.'

Jadeja cut his line, side- stepping a hammer blow that smashed into the ground where he had been standing.

Grabbing his hand, Eilidon pulled him passed the welcome stone and onto the Temple path.

'What about Caderyn?'

'We must wait until that thing retreats. Did you secure the rope?'

'Yes, but Caderyn?'

'My rope will hold. We can't help him until that creature's gone.'

Caderyn felt the line slacken a little. *Jadeja's cut it*, he thought. *I'm still hanging so he must have secured it, but if it gives way, only death awaits me.* With the rock dweller still smashing the path he knew no one was coming. Desperately trying to ignore the pain and nausea that threatened to overwhelm him, he focused on the mountain. Rocking his body backwards and forwards he got the rope to swing but misjudged the distance and crashed his already injured leg into the rock face.

'Aaaaaaargh. Aaaaaaaaaaaaaaaaaargh'

A few minutes later Caderyn tried again. His second attempt was more successful.

His fingers grappled with the rock, but his grip loosened and he swung back again. *I can do this,* he thought. He rested a while, hanging dangerously on the end of the rope. The noise above quietened. The beast had moved on. Mustering up all his remaining strength he made a third attempt. This time he managed to keep hold of the rock and haul himself onto a ledge. He tried to stand but the pain shot through his leg like a firebrand. Sinking back down, he felt the rain begin to fall.

High above him Eilidon and Jadeja were waiting anxiously for the rock dweller to finish its rampage and go on its way. Once the impediment in its path was gone it had lumbered on down the mountain soon blending in with the landscape.

Cautiously Jadeja and Eilidon made their way back to the welcome stone. Seeing that the way was clear Jadeja went to the place that he had secured the rope.

'No, no, no,' he cried, holding up the limp thread to Eilidon.

'If he has cut it, then he must have managed to get back on the mountain. I think it will be quicker and safer if I go down. You stay here and keep a look out for that thing.'

She transformed and disappeared over the mountainside. Jadeja marvelled at the speed with which the giant spider let out a thread to descend, stopping now and then to crawl behind a rock. She found a semi-conscious Caderyn on a narrow ledge and nearly went tumbling over the edge herself, as in his rather groggy state he tried to waft away the spider that hung above his head.

Dropping down at his side, she became human.

'Hey you.'

Recognising her voice, he smiled.

'It was all going so well.'

'That's what happens when you get cocky.'

She examined his leg. His thigh bone was shattered into many pieces and each time he moved a shard would penetrate the flesh around it.

'I am going to bind your leg as tightly as I can to prevent the pieces of bone from moving. It's going to be painful. Here chew on this.'

She took a piece of dried bracken root from inside her tunic.

'It will numb the pain a little.'

He took the root gladly. The taste was aniseed and bitter, but as he chewed he felt himself drifting off, shutting out the agony, at least temporarily.

Eilidon wove a tight net around his leg that prevented the shards from moving. Her biggest problem now was how to get him back up the mountain. They couldn't leave him here exposed to the vagaries of a rock dweller or other hostile creatures. They had to get him past the welcome stone. There it would be safe enough to leave him while they went to get help.

She knew she wouldn't be able to carry him on her own and the path wasn't wide enough for two. So, wrapping him in a cocoon with threads at each end, she took them up to Jadeja and between them they were able to slowly, slowly haul him back up to safety. Once they were clear of the welcome stone an exhausted Eilidon sat down.

'I'll stay with him. You go and get help.'

'My lady, I think it would be safer to stay together. If we can fashion a stretcher using your cocoon and some branches, I think that we can get him there. I know that rock dwellers do not usually cross the entrance, but I don't think we can take that chance.'

'You're probably right. I'm just tired.'

'I will make the stretcher while you rest my lady. I'm sure I can find what we need.'

Leaving her to recover he went off to find some wood. There wasn't much. This high up there was mostly gorse and heather. He found a wide shelf that because of its sheltered position had managed to sustain a few sturdier plants including a bracken tree with many thick branches. Apologising to the tree, Jadeja told it of his need and asked for permission to take some of its wood.

'Although I don't know how I am to get branches with only a knife.'

A sudden movement off to his left startled him. He spun round, knife in hand. A mountain goat appeared from a cave entrance concealed at the back of the ledge. Tentatively he approached. There was little of interest, except right at the back, a pile of firewood some previous traveller had thoughtfully collected. He also found a stash of dried fruits and nuts. Grabbing what he needed he returned to Eilidon.

'I found a cave. Someone had left firewood and a small store of food,' he said, showing her the fruits he had brought back for them.

'That will be the Elders. They'll have left it for travellers too weary to begin the final climb.'

'Do you want to rest there or press on my lady?'

'Move on. His leg is badly broken and needs attending to. It's going to take all the skill of the healers to mend it,' she replied.

Jadeja and Eilidon began attaching the branches to the cocoon, fashioning four handles, two at each end. They picked up their load and began carrying Caderyn on his makeshift stretcher. It was slow going. Caderyn was heavy and the air was thin, making their breathing laboured. Arms and legs were aching from the strain. The lack of oxygen was burning their lungs. They worked out a system of five minutes walking, five minutes resting. This allowed them to make maximum progress. Caderyn tried not to complain even though he was in agony. Every time they put down the stretcher, however gently, pain would shoot through his leg. He tried to call on the spirits to ease the journey, but he could not focus. Jadeja saw his face but stopped himself from thinking about it, knowing that the best way to help him was to keep going.

They came to the archway before the temple gates. This had been hewn out of the mountain. Above them was a vaulted ceiling, lovingly crafted by an ancient people, in such a way that it showed off the majesty of the rock. Jadeja marvelled at this gateway and the people who had made it. He wondered about the history this archway could tell. Just inside was a recess that housed an old hand bell. Calling to Eilidon to put Caderyn down, Jadeja rang the bell three times to indicate that they needed help. An Elder and a group of soldiers quickly arrived.

Bowing low, Jadeja told them of Caderyn's injury. Seconds later he was hoisted up by the soldiers and carried swiftly back to the Temple. Eilidon and Jadeja progressed more slowly to the Temple gates.

From her ledge high up in the tower, Suremaana had heard the bell and rushed down to see who approached. Caderyn was whisked passed her and taken straight to the healers. He just managed to acknowledge her as he went by. Seeing her friends approaching she ran to them, hugging Eilidon so hard that she could hardly breathe. Turning to Jadeja she was torn between hugging him and a more formal greeting. In the end, a little awkwardly, she hugged him too.

'I'm so relieved you're here. I saw Caderyn. What happened?'

'A rock dweller. His leg is badly broken. I am hoping that the Elders will be able to fix it,' said Jadeja.

'I'm sure they will, they are very gifted. You need a good rest. The peace of the Temple will help. First I will take you to Hamroon for a proper meal and you can tell me all about your journey.'

They followed her through the gate into the tranquil gardens of Shang To. Jadeja though, felt only trepidation for what lay ahead.

26

Caderyn was rushed into the healing chambers where the elder, Rowen, was waiting. He was very gently laid on a bed for her to examine. First, she took off his clothes then, using a tuning fork she tapped it on his leg, the note telling her exactly where the breaks and fractures were.

'This is going to be difficult to mend young Paladin, but not impossible. As long as you are patient.'

He managed a weak smile in answer.

'I am going to give you a strong sleeping draught because I have to cut into your leg to pull the bones back together. Do you understand?'

He nodded.

Rowen went to prepare the herbs. Caderyn banged his fist into the bed in frustration at his carelessness. To get so close to home and then have this happen was too much, especially when he knew the Shaman-Master wanted his Paladin by his side.

Rowen returned and administered the sleeping draught, chanting over him as he drifted off into the deepest sleep. Once he was under, she opened up his leg and began the intricate job of knitting together his shattered bones. The operation was long and complicated and she had to call on many healing spirits to help her. When she had finished and sewn up the wound she sat and chanted over him again, praying for his recovery.

Suremaana took the other two down to the kitchens, where Hamroon was waiting with bowls of steaming hot stew.

'My dear Eilidon, how wonderful to see you. Come my dear, sit down and eat. You seem to have wasted away.'

Eilidon tucked in heartily. Although she had fared better than the boys, she was still extremely hungry.

'Jadeja, come young man. Eat. Eat.'

Despite his worries, Jadeja too gobbled down a bowl of the delicious stew. Suremaana studied him carefully.

Could he really be a traitor? she thought. *I can't believe that he is.*

He caught her eye and she flushed slightly, as he smiled awkwardly at her.

'How have you been my lady? I…We have often wondered if you were safe.'

'I am well, Jadeja. My journey here was very uneventful and I had the privilege of visiting my father. How about you? I think perhaps you had a harder time of it.'

'We certainly did,' said Eilidon. 'As well as nearly drowning we had to fight off an azdhar and…'

She was interrupted by a messenger asking for her to take the firestone to the Master.

'I'll let Jadeja fill you in on the rest,' she said, standing up to go.

Jadeja took up the story of their journey from Porphyra's garden to Shang To. She exclaimed at the giant cats at the Temple of Maur and was horrified by the azdhar. He did not say much about the Valley of the Winds, not wishing to recount the terror of the voices. When he had finished, he yawned loudly.

'Suremaana, why don't you show Jadeja to his chambers. A hot bath has been prepared for him,' said Hamroon.

'Won't the Master want to see me?' asked Jadeja.

'Not tonight. He will speak with you tomorrow. For now, you should rest.'

Feeling somewhat dejected, Jadeja followed Suremaana out of the kitchen and across a small courtyard, into a set of rooms carved into the mountain. Climbing a stone stairway that led to the sleeping quarters, he felt his mood lifting slightly at the familiar sight of the deep cavern beautifully lit with golden braziers. Doors on each side of the cavern opened on to individual chambers, simply furnished with a wooden bed, a chair, table and a trunk for clothing and other personal belongings. At the farthest end of the cavern were the bathrooms. An underground water source flowed into a pool. This water was then filtered through a series of wide pipes suspended just above hot coals which heated it, providing hot water for the baths. The used water was then fed into a further system of pipes suppling the irrigation for the Temple gardens. It was a very efficient system.

Suremaana showed Jadeja to his room.

'My chamber is just across the way. The baths are at the end, but you must know that.'

'Yes. Thank you, my lady.'

She hesitated a moment in his doorway.

'I...I missed you,' she said shyly.

He looked at her longingly.

'I missed you too.'

If only you knew how much, he wanted to add but somehow couldn't voice. So many thoughts filled his head. How beautiful she looked. He wanted to take her hand but was uncertain if she would welcome that. They remained still, looking at each other, not sure what to do next. Each one afraid to say or do the wrong thing.

'I better go and take my bath.'

'Yes, yes. I'm sorry. I shouldn't detain you. I will go and check on Caderyn shortly. He must be in a lot of distress.'

She crossed to her chamber, which she entered after a last look back in his direction.

In another part of the Temple, Eilidon was sat with the Shaman-Master who took the firestone from her.

'You did well Eilidon, to take this from Maur. I don't know anyone who has passed the test before.'

'I recognised the dance of the fireflies from all my nights sat in the trees back home.'

'I always knew you were highly intuitive. That is why I chose you to be a Paladin. You can sense things where others cannot.'

'Yes Master, I have always been able to read people. Except...' she hesitated

'Go on child.'

'Except Jadeja. Master I know that he is your apprentice and he has proved himself many times on our journey, but there is something about him. Something hidden that I cannot see and it troubles me.'

The Shaman-Master looked at her for a long moment.

'Eilidon, I value your counsel and I understand your concern. Let me just say that in the days ahead when our enemy appears, Jadeja will reveal his true self. Until then we must watch over him. He has had a difficult life and does not give his trust easily. I believe he has forged a friendship with Caderyn which the young bowman may need if he is to walk again.'

Eilidon exclaimed.

'I knew his leg was bad but I thought the healers would repair it!'

'Rowen has done her best, but the damage was extensive. I fear his leg may never be truly mended. We can only hope that it will be strong enough to support him.'

To her surprise Eilidon found herself crying. The exertions of their long journey and the terrors they had faced suddenly overwhelmed her.

'I'm sorry Master. I do not wish to appear weak.'

'Eilidon my child, you are not weak. This is simply your aura shedding the weight of your encounters. Go now and rest. We have prepared your old chamber.'

She bowed to him and retired to her room, where she slept deeply.

The Shaman-Master held up the firestone. In his hand, the flame inside danced and burned brightly, recognising the essence of the man and his innate goodness. He communed with the stone for a while and then took it and placed it in the inner Sanctum with the air stone from Simniel and the earth stone that belonged to Porphyra and Yangchen. The water stone was kept in the Temple. The Jhankhira would come for them, bringing with him the Bottle of Isfahan that he intended to open.

The Shaman-Master prayed in the Temple that they would all have the strength to overcome what lay ahead.

27

When morning came, Suremaana looked for Jadeja, but he was not in his chamber or in the kitchen.

'He is with the Master,' said Hamroon. 'Did you need him?'

'Oh no. I just wanted to check if he slept well. Eilidon too,' she added quickly.

'The lady Eilidon was up an hour ago. I believe she is in the healing rooms.'

'Thank you Hamroon. I will go and check on Caderyn also.'

Bowing, she left the kitchen, grabbing a hunk of bread on her way out.

Rowen greeted her warmly when she entered Caderyn's room.

'How is he?'

'In a great deal of pain I'm afraid, but that is to be expected. His leg was broken in several places. I think it will cheer him up to see you.' She stood to one side to let Suremaana pass.

He smiled weakly. 'Still got the red hair then?'

'Yes. They didn't recognise me when I got home. A very diligent soldier tried to arrest me for swimming in the royal pool.'

'I'm sure you soon put him right.'

'I certainly did, but that is only minor compared to what you have been through.'

Caderyn and Eilidon exchanged looks.

'It wasn't that bad. I got over-confident and didn't see that rock dweller. Rowen says I'm going to be in bed for weeks. I think I'll die of boredom.'

'Probably,' said Eilidon.

Rowen came back in.

'Ladies I must ask you to leave. I have to dress his wound and then I will be giving him a sleeping draught.'

There was a moan from Caderyn.

'You can be quiet young man. It is important that you do not move that leg for a few days and sleep also helps with the healing process. Ladies you may visit him again in the morning.'

Seeing it was pointless to argue, the girls left.

'What shall we do now?' asked Eilidon.

'Combat training. The guards will be practising. We can join them.'

They headed to the courtyard where the Temple soldiers were exercising.

'I think this is just what I need,' said Eilidon.

Jadeja was sat with the Shaman-Master in his chamber.

'I have read the runes and journeyed to the lower world. The Jhankhira will come here to stop the ceremony and take the stones himself to open the bottle. He knows that we have them.'

'He will send Rabten first, Master. He has been following us for many days.'

'Yes Jadeja, I have seen it. They are gathering their forces. Rabten was taken aback by your use of his raven. He did not expect that. He will be keen for revenge.'

'I will be ready Master. I have been practising my chants as you instructed.'

'Oh Jadeja, my boy. If only Rabten were the worst of what awaits us. What awaits you. For now, we must build our defences and plan our strategy. The banishment must take place at Spring Equinox on your…On the exact day. We must also wait for the fifth element to arrive.'

'The fifth element, Master?'

'Something we need for the ceremony. I am not sure when it will manifest, but now that you are here, I believe the time will be soon.'

Jadeja, still puzzled by this reply, looked quizzically at his master. *What does he mean, now that I am here?* The Shaman-Master's expression gave nothing away.

'The Jhankhira is a few weeks away yet. Take this time to rest and revise the lore. I think also that Caderyn is going to need your friendship too.'

'Yes Master. Thank you.'

Jadeja returned to his chamber to contemplate what lay ahead. His visions haunted him. The voice that kept calling to him in his sleep was getting louder. He had hoped that the Temple would have blocked it out, but it had not. Taking out his red stones, he placed them in a circle around him, then he stood and called in the powers of the North, South, East and West and the elements of air, fire, earth and water. When he felt their presence, he asked them for guidance, for protection from the voice and for strength to face his enemies. He sat in a trance for half an hour, allowing the elements to fill his mind. Coming around, he found a dull white stone pendant in his lap. Holding it by the leather strap he inspected it carefully. There was nothing remarkable about it. However, as soon as he held the stone in his hand it emitted a powerful and blinding white light. He let go quickly, dropping the pendant on the floor. The light vanished the moment he stopped touching it. Wrapping it in a cloth, he took it straight to the Shaman-Master.

'Master please forgive my intrusion but I must show you this.'

He placed the pendant on the table. The Shaman-Master observed it for a long time, picking it up and turning it over. A faint glow emanated from the stone when he first touched it. He smiled.

'How did you come by this?'

Jadeja explained about the powers leaving it for him. The Shaman-Master nodded.

'So quickly,' he muttered. 'Will you touch it?'

Jadeja was hesitant. Reaching out nervously he took the stone. This time there was no blinding light. In fact, there was nothing at all. Jadeja was puzzled. The Master watched him.

'You were expecting something else?'

'When I first held it, it gave off a bright white light, but this time nothing.'

'The first time, the stone was reacting to you. Now that it knows your touch it does not need to reveal itself. It has been sent for you and you must wear it at all times, although to do so puts you in greater danger. The Jhankhira wants this, the fifth power stone. It has come to you now. I was afraid that it would.'

'But why me Master? Surely it should be yours.'

'You saw the way it reacted to my touch. Compare that to its reaction to you. No Jadeja. It is you that it belongs to. The light stone is yours. You will know why when the time comes. I only hope that I have prepared you sufficiently. I would have preferred to have had more time to train you, there is still so much that you need to know. So much that I have yet to tell you.'

A very confused Jadeja put the pendant around his neck and tucked it under his tunic, where it lay next to his skin. He felt a warmth flow through his body and settle in his heart.

'Go and find your friends, but I would advise keeping the stone secret. It is not time for it to be revealed.'

Bowing low, Jadeja left, pondering all that had happened that morning. He was so lost in thought that he bumped straight into Suremaana, knocking her over.

'My lady, I am so sorry. I seem to have a habit of doing this to you. Here let me help you.'

He took her hand and pulled her to her feet. The touch of his fingers sent a shiver through her.

'It's fine Jadeja. I wasn't watching where I was going either.'

They stood looking at each other.

'I...I was going to walk in the gardens,' he stammered. 'Would you like to join me?'

'Thank you. That would be, that would be nice.'

She realised that she still had hold of his hand. Blushing, she apologised and let go.

He smiled awkwardly at her and they walked off to the gardens side by side. Occasionally their shoulders would touch or their arms brush against each other as they walked the grounds. A large spider sat in one of the trees watching uneasily. Their closeness worried her.

In the days that followed Suremaana and Jadeja spent more and more time together. Each morning he was up early so that he could watch her training with the Guards, admiring the fluidity of her movements and the speed and agility she possessed. Some days she taught him some fighting moves and in return he showed her how to fire a sling-shot. He listened attentively while she told him of her people and her father, the sound of her voice driving out the dark thoughts crowding in his brain. He never reciprocated. Somehow, he couldn't open up about his past. It wasn't from any caprice on his part or any macho display to try and draw her in, it was simply he was unable. Although being with Suremaana eased his inner turmoil, there was always an air of melancholy about him, which only served to intrigue her more.

She discussed his reticence with Eilidon also, which only increased her suspicions. She warned her friend against investing too much time in him.

'I can't help it,' Suremaana told her. 'I have a connection with him and even though he won't open up I know that he feels it too.'

Eilidon, not relishing closeness of any kind, remained sceptical.

'I'm not the best person to ask for advice on these matters. All I can tell you is something about him is hidden from me and I think you should be very careful.'

Hearing this, Suremaana remembered her dream. Part of her knew that she needed to be cautious but she also knew that Jadeja had captured her imagination. Her head was filled with thoughts of him and she couldn't stop them.

'I'll try.'

Eilidon sighed sensing that Suremaana was already too heavily invested in the relationship.

'Your oath of loyalty to the Shaman-Master does not allow for personal relationships.'

'It's not,' said Suremaana, but she knew she was lying.

I'll just have to watch him more carefully, thought Eilidon.

While the girls were having their conversation, Jadeja was sat with Caderyn who really was restless and impatient, incarcerated as he was, in the healing rooms. Rowen had kept him sedated for the first week to ensure as little movement as possible. Now he was more awake and in dire need of distraction. Jadeja had taken to playing Umar with him, an ancient game of strategy similar to chess. They were sat engrossed in a match.

'So, how are the girls? I haven't seen either of them for a couple of days.'

'I believe they are well. The lady Eilidon often disappears on her own.'

'And Suremaana?

'She is very well. We trained together again this morning.'

'I get the sense that you two are spending quite a bit of time together.'

Jadeja fidgeted awkwardly in his chair and looked down intently at the board. Caderyn watched him and grinned mischievously.

'Is there anything that you would like to confide in me?'

Jadeja hesitated, then spoke.

'I er, yes. The lady Suremaana seems to enjoy my company.'

'And you hers, I'm guessing.'

Jadeja blushed.

'I'm happy for you my friend. Just tread carefully. We Paladin are not supposed to form attachments. Even if we can't help it.'

Jadeja nodded.

'She has my utmost respect. I would not presume to have anything other than friendship with her. I am just grateful that she is willing to spend time in my company. As to an attachment, I cannot say how she feels, but I know that I am drawn to her.'

'Well that's the most open I have ever heard you be, you don't usually give anything away.'

Jadeja sat uncomfortably as if the revelation weighed heavily on him.

'I…I feel that I can trust you. That is a rare thing for me.'

'Then I am honoured,' smiled Caderyn.

He looked at his friend and wondered again what kind of life this strange young man had experienced.

The game continued in silence for a while, each contemplating the conversation they had just shared.

'How is your leg? Is it mending?'

'Not as quickly as I would like, but then I did smash it up pretty badly. I'm not allowed to get up for another week at least. I am not sure that I can last that long. I'm sick of looking at these walls.'

'The week will pass and then I will take you out of here myself. It is best not to risk the healing process. Or Rowen.'

'I know. I know. It's just that I'm used to being active, being permanently indoors does not sit easily with me.'

'I have been studying. I have to help the Master with the banishment. Would you like me to bring you some books? At least if your mind is occupied the time will pass quicker.'

'Thank you Jadeja. I would appreciate that. Perhaps you could ask the Master for advice on what aspect of lore I should study.'

'I will do that when I next see him.'

He wasn't sure when that would be as the Shaman-Master had rarely spoken to him since their meeting about the stone, but he didn't disclose this to Caderyn. In truth he was disappointed that the Master hadn't been more pleased that he had completed his mission. He had barely said thank you to him for bringing the stones and the Paladin safely to Shang To. He wasn't one to expect praise but so much of him longed for approval and acceptance. *What have I done wrong?* he asked himself. *Is it because of Caderyn's injury? Surely the Master does not blame me for that?*

His mood darkened and he was unable to concentrate on their game, so he was relieved when shortly after that Rowen ushered him out of the room leaving her free to tend to her patient. He wandered into the gardens and sat under a willow tree to meditate. Instead of finding calm in the stillness his thoughts were invaded by Rabten's face, looking at him with a sneering grin. *Not long now little one. Not long now.*

The words echoed round and round in his head and he felt himself shiver violently which woke him from his trance. Suremaana was sat beside him.

'I didn't want to break your concentration. You looked so peaceful.'

Jadeja winced at the irony of her remark.

'Not really. I couldn't settle.'

'Do you want to come and train with Eilidon and I?'

'Not today, if that's okay?'

'Of course. I'll see you later.'

He heard the disappointment in her voice and felt bad rejecting her, but the need to be alone was greater. Once she had gone and he felt sure that no one else was near, he took out the light stone. Today it glowed gently. He regarded it carefully. It felt light in his hand, yet he sensed a great depth to it.

'Why have you come to me? I am not a Paladin or a great Shaman. I am merely an apprentice.'

He felt his gaze being drawn into the stone. There he saw a child emerging from darkness. It was only the briefest image, but it remained long enough for him to recognise the face.

28

In the last days leading up to Spring Equinox the Shaman-Master kept Jadeja in the library studying the history of the light stone. The more he read, the heavier the responsibility of guardianship sat on him. He barely saw Suremaana or Caderyn, having so little spare time.

His dreams worsened. Instead of protecting him from the approaching demoness, the stone drew her in. He asked the Shaman-Master about this. He remained silent for some time, searching for the right words, weighing up how much to disclose to his young apprentice.

'My boy, it calls to her because for many years it was the source of her power. It is the reason she became the Lamenter.'

'But according to the lore, the stone only truly responds to the chosen bearers. Surely she is not one?'

'No, she isn't. Her connection to the stone was through her child. It went to her without resistance because she carried the next true bearer. It would have become fully bound to her if we had not stopped her from performing a sacrificial ceremony.'

Jadeja felt his body go cold as the realisation of what his master was telling him hit home. Flashes of memory, a stone, the eagle, the three sisters, caused his knees to buckle and he sat down.

'I'm sorry. I should have told you the truth when I found you, but you were so weak and frightened. When you grew strong and settled, I wanted to protect you. I didn't want to burden you with this knowledge.'

The Shaman-Master looked anxiously at his young apprentice who sat motionless, trying to process what he had just heard.

Jadeja stood up slowly, then turned and threw the books on the floor.

'That is why you made me your apprentice. You used me to get to it. You wanted control of the light stone. I always wondered why me, with all my failings. You knew why she called. All those nights when the darkness came and you abandoned me to it.'

'No Jadeja, I always tried to protect you.'

'That's why you sent me to collect the power stones, so you could come here and plot how to take the light stone from me.'

His mind whirred, going over and over scenarios in his head.

'Suremaana, is she part of your scheme? Did you order her to pretend to like me so that I would do anything she asked?'

The Shaman-Master shook his head.

'And Caderyn? Is his friendship false too? At least I know Eilidon doesn't like me.'

'No Jadeja, I did not order either of them to like you, their friendship is genuine and I am not plotting to take the stone off you. But part of the reason I wanted you to be my apprentice was because I knew you to be the next bearer.'

'So that you can control it…me,' screamed Jadeja.

'No. No, my boy, so that you can control it. It is a great responsibility and I wanted you to be prepared.'

'I don't believe you.'

The stone flared at his neck, filling the room with light.

'Please Jadeja. Please calm down. The stone is powerful and responds to your anger.'

'Are you afraid Master? Are you? Well I have been afraid my whole life. You were the one person I thought I could trust and now I find that our relationship was built on lies and half-truths. I am merely a tool in your plan. You need the stone and me to banish my… the demoness. When I have done what you want, do you intend to banish me too?'

The Shaman-Master knew that his next words were pivotal.

'No Jadeja. I want only to help you. And yes, I do need the stone to banish the Lamenter. We couldn't do it when we captured her because the light stone went back to the elements and without it, her imprisonment was incomplete. I had hoped that the stone might come to me so that I could perform the banishment. It knew of our need and has helped us before. I thought if you completed the mission to bring the other power stones here, the elements might allow the light stone to be used without burdening you with it just yet. I see now, that it was never their intention. The stone is yours and only you can banish Lamenter.'

'Why now? Why Spring Equinox?'

'Because that will be your sixteenth birthday.'

Jadeja remained motionless.

'There is something else you should know. I …'

'Enough. I don't want to hear it. I hate you. I hate the temple. I hate all of this.'

Pulling the stone from around his neck he threw it at the Master and ran out of the library. Lost in a whirlwind of emotions, he had no idea where to go or what to do. He ran and ran, through the temple, the grounds, out of the gate and down the mountain, only stopping at the welcome stone. Here he screamed like a wounded animal.

'WHY? WHY?'

His shouts echoed back at him, mocking his pain. Then laughter, that familiar voice jeering at his torment. He sat, letting the angry tears flow.

The eagle amulet he wore fell forward and he grasped it like an anchor. The vastness of the landscape reflected back the enormity of what he now knew. The blue and pink of the sky and then deepening red held no beauty for him any longer. Everything was black and cold. The evening air made him shiver. The diabolical nature of his discovery pressed down on his shoulders like giant's hands, gradually crushing the life from him. All that he had come to know, to love, now felt false and tainted. *Suremaana? Caderyn? Was none of it genuine?* He was utterly lost.

A single firefly danced merrily round the welcome stone. Bitterness choked him.

'Are you mocking me too?'

Little by little it came closer to him and settled on his hand. In response to this signal the air around him filled with fireflies until his entire body was encased in their protective light.

The Shaman-Master, looking out from the watchtower, saw what was happening. He went back to the sleeping quarters and left the light stone on Jadeja's bed, where, several hours later, soothed by the fireflies, the boy returned and put it back on.

Although the fireflies had placated him, for the next few days he isolated himself, seeing no one, trying to come to terms with who he was and what he had to do. Suremaana missed him greatly and wondered at the gulf that now existed between them. She confided in Gardeer.

'The Shaman-Master prepares him for the banishment and his mind is full.'

'Too full even for me?'

'Yes, my dear, even for you. Be patient with him. He will need you after Equinox.'

'If we survive the onslaught we all know is coming.'

Gardeer placed a reassuring hand on her arm.

'We are well prepared my girl. Well prepared.'

Suremaana managed a half-hearted smile and went to combat practice. Gardeer found the Shaman-Master.

'Has he spoken to you?' she asked.

The Master shook his head.

'He keeps his own counsel, but I know the eagle accompanies him and that is a comfort.'

'Do you think that he will complete the banishment?'

'I hope so Gardeer. I hope that we can prevent her release and he can perform the ritual from the rune chamber without having to face her.'

'And if we can't?'

'If we can't keep her contained, we must pray that he will find the strength to overcome her.'

29

The first indication that something was wrong was the lack of birdsong in the morning. The dawn chorus was always rousing and joyful, the birds welcoming in the new day. As Equinox dawned, there was nothing, only the empty silence that occurs immediately before a storm, when the birds take shelter and ready themselves for the deluge.

Eilidon picked up on it first. Her senses prickled and she knew that the threat was imminent. She roused Suremaana and then went straight to the Shaman-Master. He was already up when she entered his chambers.

'He is here, Master.'

'I felt it too, Eilidon. You must ready the guard. There will be a fierce battle, of which sort I don't yet know. No doubt an aerial bombardment. Prepare our defences. Send Suremaana to lead the guard. You lead the archers, I will gather the Elders. We must protect the inner Sanctum.'

'Yes Master, and what of Jadeja?'

'Send him to me. I have need of him.'

Eilidon left to carry out her orders, first stopping at the healing rooms to check on Caderyn. He too was aware of the threat.

'I can't sit here and do nothing.'

'Well you can hardly get up and fight now, can you?'

'I can still fire my bow. Get me to the tower. I can shoot from there.'

'Certainly not, young man. You are not to put any strain on that leg of yours. It is at a crucial stage of its recovery.'

'Rowen, I can't sit here while the Temple is under attack. I am Paladin. It is my duty to protect it.'

'Right now, it is your duty to mend. The Temple is well defended.'

Rowen would not be swayed.

'I have to go,' said Eilidon.

'Good luck,' he called.

He waited until Rowen had left and then inched slowly to the edge of the bed. He swung his good leg over the side, then very carefully lifted the other broken limb. The pain from the movement made him wince. He sat with his good leg on the floor, the bad one hanging loosely next to it. Gingerly, he pushed himself up, trying to keep all the weight on his good leg. The change in position sent such an excruciating pain through his body that he fell backwards onto the bed. He tried again. This time he managed to stand, but as soon as he tried to put any pressure on the broken leg the pain overwhelmed him. He let out a scream of frustration just as Jadeja entered the room.

'Don't you start telling me I shouldn't be moving. I am Paladin. I took an oath. I cannot be in my sick bed at this time of crisis. And where have you been? I haven't seen you in days.'

Jadeja looked at him.

'I had things on my mind. Caderyn, I...I... I came to bring you this.'

227

He produced Caderyn's bow from under his cloak. The quiver of arrows he took off his back.

'Now where do you want me to take you?'

Caderyn took his bow with hungry hands. Touching the wood filled him with renewed vigour as the boy and the bow became one.

'To the top of the tower, but I am afraid you will have to carry me. My leg is too weak.'

Jadeja bent down so that Caderyn could climb on his back. Again, the change in position was agonising for him. Once Caderyn was steadied on his back, Jadeja set off to the watchtower. This tall edifice looked out over the mountain and the lands below and was the perfect vantage point to spot an enemy. Caderyn knew the tower well. It was from here that he had honed his natural affinity with the bow.

Climbing the stairs was long and difficult. Jadeja had to stop many times, but eventually they reached the lookout room at the top, an unremarkable square brick room with windows on all four sides, each furnished with a wooden seat.

'Which one will you take?'

Caderyn surveyed the room, then stilled his mind and waited.

'That one,' he said, pointing to the east window. 'They will come from that direction.'

Jadeja lowered him carefully onto the window seat.

'Open the benches.'

Jadeja did so and found them full of arrows. These he placed around Caderyn until he was encased within a wooden fortress of deadly spears.

Caderyn grabbed his hand.

'Thank you, my friend. I could not countenance my fellow Paladin putting themselves in mortal combat while I lay in bed doing nothing.'

Jadeja nodded, trying to keep his own fear for all of them and particularly himself, under control. When he left the room, he took out one of his red stones and placed it at the entrance, calling on its protective power to block the doorway from enemies. Turning on his heels he sprinted down the stairs and headed for the Temple.

The Master and the Elders were in the Sanctum. The four power stones were sitting inside a protective circle of energy. Jadeja felt the light stone against his chest. He looked to the Shaman-Master who smiled warmly at him.

'Dear boy, thank you for coming, our need is great. The Jhankhira will attempt to retrieve the stones and open the bottle. We have to complete the banishment before he can release her.'

'What must I do, Master?'

'Jadeja, go to the rune chamber and begin the ritual. Stay out of sight. The Jhankhira must not find you.'

Jadeja stared at his master.

'I will do as you ask, for the sake of the temple.'

The Shaman-Master went to speak but Jadeja silenced him.

Hamroon took a solemn Jadeja down a dark passageway that led to a small chamber whose walls were covered in runes, many of which glowed. He noticed different runes light up as he entered.

'You will be safe here. The runes will call up protective spirits if anyone tries to enter. The lore books that you need are over there.'

Jadeja saw the collection of books in a corner of the room already open at the relevant pages.

'I am sorry the elders cannot be here to assist you but we must work with the Master and focus on defeating the Jhankhira. Trust him boy. He knows what he is doing. He truly loves you.'

'Does he Hamroon, or is it all an act so that I will do what you all want me to?'

Hamroon stayed quiet, weighing up whether to divulge what he knew. Sensing the boy's pain and doubt he decided to tell him.

'You are his brother's son, so yes, he truly loves you.'

'Then why did he abandon me? Why was I left alone for so long?'

'He has looked for you since the day you were born. We couldn't find you. He searched and searched. Even when he was called upon to be the Shaman-Master he would not complete the ceremony until he had found you and knew you were safe.'

'He could have told me that he was my uncle.'

'I think he was ashamed that he had not protected you. In his mind he failed you, and did not deserve your affection. I must return. There is food and drink and you can study the runes, they will speak with you. Now I must go. Bless you child. Be strong.'

Hamroon closed the door. The entrance melted into the wall and was no longer visible. Runes appeared on the door, blending it seamlessly with the walls, so that it was impossible to tell where the entrance had been.

Weighing up this new information, Jadeja sat on the cushions in the centre of the room. *Master, Uncle. Can I do this?* His mind switched to Caderyn high in the tower, ready to fight. And Suremaana, she would be risking her life leading an army and here he was locked in a room, alone. All of them at risk and all of them relying on him. *What if*

*they don't survive? Caderyn is already injured and can't leave the
tower and Suremaana.... Suremaana.* He banged the floor,
causing many of the runes to flare.

'I have to get out of here,' he yelled.

The runes danced around as if teasing their captive. He
tried to find the door but couldn't. With his anger
mounting he felt the stone heating up against his chest.
Crossing to the books he sat back down and began the
ritual.

Back in the Sanctum the Shaman-Master was deploying
the Elders. Hamroon and Gardeer he sent to work with the
archers. Rowen and Elise to the guard. The others he kept
with him.

'We must form a circle around the stones. Call up your
spirits. Prepare them to attack. The Jhankhira must not be
allowed in the centre. I do not know in what form he will
come. We must be watchful. He is very cunning and he
wants the stones above all else. We have prepared for this
my brothers and sisters. We will hold strong. We must give
Jadeja the time he needs.'

The Elders bowed and formed their circle, chanting
together,

'Shre Ma
Jay Ma
Shre Shre
Jay Jay
Ma Ohm'

Calling upon the powers to guard the Sanctum. The
Shaman-Master rang Ima, the bell of protection and closed
the circle.

30

Suremaana led her troops to the main Temple gates. All were wearing their full armour, thick leather body plates overlaid with bamboo and stitched together with protective spells. On their heads they wore helmets of the finest steel covered in burgundy leather. Full visors covered their faces. They stood in silence, rank after rank, waiting.

High up on the Temple walls, Eilidon was positioning her archers. She knew the first attack would be aerial and it was her job to repel it. Her armour was a silver, silken body suit, intricately woven and infused with venom on minute barbs, barely visible to the naked eye. The lightness and suppleness of the suit belied its strength and concealed its menace. Senses on high alert, she knew it was time.

Caderyn saw it first, perched as he was high up in the watch tower. The large black shape began to appear on the horizon. He sounded a small horn that hung on a hook just above his head. The note rang out, a clarion call to the troops assembled below, that the assault was about to begin.

The black shape resembled an enormous raven. Caderyn's hawk-like vision soon saw that it was made up of hundreds of smaller birds flying in formation. His first arrow brought one down.

Eilidon was ready, ordering her archers to fire their first volley, hitting multiple birds. *Too many are coming,* she thought, but she kept her doubts to herself, instead ordering her men to fire again and again. The bird numbers were so great that their formation held. She tried to fight off the feeling of being overwhelmed, keeping the archers firing into the bottom layer of birds, helpless to stop a fresh wave flying down from the top. They landed in the courtyard, turning into soldiers the moment their feet touched the ground.

Suremaana, alert to the invasion, turned her army ready to face them. At a sign from her, they sprang into action. The elite troop of martial arts fighters struck first, kicking and spinning with such speed, the enemy barely knew what hit them. The swordsmen followed up.

Despite the archers' best efforts, a second wave of birds made it to the ground, where Suremaana and her troops were engaged in fierce hand-to-hand combat.

High above in the watchtower, Caderyn fired at the heart of the giant raven-shaped cloud of birds, knowing that Rabten was up there somewhere. When he spotted him, he set his arrow. Sensing the danger, Rabten turned his gaze towards Caderyn, who hesitated for the briefest moment. That was enough for Rabten to evade the arrow and fly down to land.

The Elders, Rowen and Elise had called on many spirits to aid them. Soldiers who had fought valiantly in life now rushed to the assistance of the elders in death. The sounds of their battle cries filled the air. Each of the soldiers was faced by a spirit of the Jhankhira's. They were closely matched, tearing at each other with blade and axe. Eilidon ordered half her archers to fire at the sky and the other half to fire down at the soldiers on the ground in a desperate bid to protect Rowen and Elise and prevent them being overrun.

The Temple guards fought well but they were heavily outnumbered. Blood ran freely in the courtyard as more and more guards lost ground. Seeing the danger of total annihilation, Suremaana and Eilidon gave the signal to pull back to the inner courtyard. The soldiers retreated rapidly, carrying their wounded the best they could. Once they were safely within, the four Elders created a protective spirit barrier to hold off the Jhankhira's forces.

'It will not keep them out for long but it will give us chance to regroup and plan our next attack,' said Hamroon.

Reaching his men, Rabten realised what the Elders had done and began an incantation using his inverted dreamcatcher to draw the power from the barrier. Eilidon was alert to it straight away.

'Hamroon, Rabten is weakening the barrier. Can you counteract him?'

'We will do our best, but I fear his power is greater than ours.'

Caderyn stared down at the courtyard. He knew that Rabten was down there, but his men had formed a shield barrier over him to protect him from any stray arrows while he chanted. Caderyn loaded his bow and fired anyway, his arrows bouncing harmlessly off the shields.

He watched and waited hoping for an opening to appear, knowing there was little else he could do. He was so busy studying Rabten's men he was unaware that he was being watched. Then he felt it, cold and black. He turned his head. The Jhankhira stood before him, a stray feather on the floor giving away how he had entered the room. He noted the full Shamanic clothing, except his tunic and his bells were black. The belt was inlaid with cauris shells and the tusks of wild hogs. Some sort of charms were hanging off it. These were metal cases housing disembodied malevolent spirits harnessed to his will, although Caderyn did not know this. Two strings of miniature heads criss-crossed his body, a gruesome reminder of his evil intent. On his head, he wore a band of tall black feathers.

'So, bowman, here you sit in your eerie, firing your arrows at my disciples. I'm surprised you do not fight with your fellow Paladin. Soon my men will overrun the Temple and your Master too. He is powerless to stop me.'

'We shall see,' replied Caderyn.

He moved to fire his bow but the Jhankhira raised his hand, muttering some ancient words and set the bow alight. Caderyn threw an arrow at him which he merely parried away, then lunged forward, grabbing Caderyn by the throat and lifting him effortlessly off the seat.

'You see boy, I will not be stopped.'

He dropped Caderyn. The searing pain from landing on his broken leg was so great, he blacked out. The last thing he saw was the Jhankhira heading for the doorway where Jadeja's red stone flared up and barred his way. Momentarily puzzled by this, the Jhankhira resumed his bird form, flying from the window and across to the Temple, landing just as Rabten broke down Hamroon's barrier and the combat began again.

31

Leaving his soldiers to do battle, Rabten joined his Master at the Temple. Together they tore down the spirit blockades that the Elders had placed across the doors and entered. The Temple was eerily silent, holding its breath, waiting for the attack.

'They will be in the inner Sanctum, guarding the stones. Foolish man. He has no idea how powerful I have become. He still believes that he can defeat me. You must enter at the rear of the Sanctum and strike when I give my signal.'

'Yes Master. I will be ready.'

Wrapping his cloak tightly around himself, Rabten disappeared down a side passageway.

The Jhankhira took a small bottle from inside his tunic. The seal was held in place with a fine gold thread. Gazing through the dark green glass, he spoke quietly to the swirling, inky black cloud within.

'Soon, my love. It is almost time.'

Very gently he replaced the bottle and took a small vial containing a white powder from his belt. Using a dagger, he made an incision across the palm of his hand and let the blood fill the vial, mixing it with the powder. This cocktail he then smeared down the strings of heads that criss-crossed his torso. Next, he took the smallest of his bells and rang it in a circular motion up and down his chest. He then replaced the small bell and rang its neighbour. Just one note. When the sound had dissipated, the heads began to rouse. One by one they stirred, until all of them were awakened.

Smiling with satisfaction, the Jhankhira strode on towards the inner Sanctum and the waiting Shaman-Master. A few drops of blood fell from his hand leaving a trail of black burns on the Temple floor.

Eilidon sensed the unease emanating from the Temple.

'He's in there,' she shouted across to Suremaana. 'We have to go to the Master.'

Leaving Hamroon and Rowen in charge of the army, the two Paladin sprinted for the Temple. A couple of Rabten's men tried to bar their way. The first was brought down by a blade to the neck, the second, by a scissor kick so fast, he didn't see where it came from.

The two girls entered the temple.

'Blood,' said Suremaana, pointing to the black stains on the floor. She bent down to touch it.

'Don't!' ordered Eilidon. 'If that is the Jhankhira's blood it will be very potent and deadly.'

Suremaana withdrew her hand just as a wisp of smoke rose up from the mark, feeling for her flesh, then vaporising to nothing.

'Thanks.'

Each drop of blood they encountered gave off black vapour as they approached it. Both girls, aware to the danger, proceeded cautiously, senses heightened as they tracked their quarry.

In the Sanctum, the Shaman-Master and the Elders waited, focusing their energies on holding the protective circle around the stones. The firestone flared.

'He is here,' said the Shaman-Master. 'It begins.' As he spoke the doors to the Sanctum were thrown open.

'I have come for the stones Vikander. And this time you will not stop me.'

He took the largest of his bells and rang it so loudly, the vibrations made the walls shake. As one, the heads around his body began to chant ancient words of evil, over and over, in constant rhythm, calling up spirits long departed.

The Shaman-Master was ready for this. Reaching for the bell he wore on his right shoulder, he rang it three times. Immediately three giant phoenixes appeared, wings spread, forming a spirit barrier in front of him.

The Jhankhira smiled. 'So predictable. Did you think I would not be prepared for this?'

The heads stopped their chant and the metal discs on his belt began to open. From within them there emerged hideously deformed black demons, each one larger and uglier than the one before. With a howl, the Jhankhira sent them forward to attack.

The Elders drew on their own protective spirits to fight the demons. They had to guard the stones. The Jhankhira directed his demons from one elder to another like a conductor guiding his orchestra. They slashed and tore at their victims. All the time the Elders sang a song of power to keep the circle intact, the Shaman-Master's voice singing the loudest. The Jhankhira laughed mockingly.

'Do you really think that this will stop me?'

Drawing his sword, he advanced on the Shaman-Master who called the three phoenixes to form a shield around him.

'You will not release her,' said the Shaman-Master.

There was a cry from behind him and he felt the circle break. He glanced back and saw the elder Nireen being consumed by three of the demons. He sent one of his bird spirits to close the circle again.

'You will have to do better than that.'

With a wave of his hand, the Jhankhira sent out another demon.

'I am powerful Vikander. You have not been paying attention. Too busy hiding in your Temple. You think your birds will stop me. You think your elemental powers can prevent what I am about to do. My demons are strong. Listen to the screams of your Elders.'

The Shaman-Master did listen as another of his circle fell and he had to send another phoenix to close the gap. The Jhankhira grinned.

'Come Vikander, let us fight like we used to in the training grounds. I always had the measure of you then. Let's see if you have improved.'

Before he could bring his sword down, a blade penetrated his hand causing him to drop his weapon. With a roar of anger, he spun around to see Eilidon launching another attack. He sent a demon to encircle her and pin her to the wall, from where she could only watch helplessly as the fight continued.

Suremaana was the next to try, somersaulting towards him at speed. Even though she was quick, he detected the movement and knocked her backwards with a wave of his hand, a surge of black energy forcing her away.

The Jhankhira and Shaman-Master engaged in battle. Drawing his sword, the Shaman-Master thrust his blade at the Jhankhira who rebuffed it with ease.

'Still useless with a sword. You never were one to do the fighting.' The Jhankhira caught the Shaman-Master on the arm as he failed to sidestep in time. He thrust again but this time the Shaman-Master was equal to it. The demons continued to press the Elders, trying to break the circle. Suremaana staggered to her feet and was about to try again when her eye detected a movement at the back of the Sanctum. There in front of the sacred gong was the robed figure from her dream, poised to strike.

'Nooooo!' she screamed. 'Jadeja. No!'

She sprinted towards him. The Jhankhira bellowed, 'Now,' and the figure struck the gong.

The sound that echoed through the chamber was harsh and cruel. The vibrations stopped the Elders, drowning out their singing and filling their hearts with blackness. Outside the fighters came to a standstill, unable to continue with the sound ringing through their heads.

In his chamber Jadeja felt the tremors but the runes protected him from the worst of the effect. Only the Shaman-Master remained standing, using all of his strength and power to resist the gong.

'That instrument is sacred. How dare you infuse it with your blackness.'

His anger was so great that he came at the Jhankhira like a dervish, his blade moving so fast it was almost invisible. The Jhankhira was equal to his attack. Indeed, he seemed to relish it, aware that all the time he was draining the Shaman-Master of his ability to protect the stones.

The figure at the gong raised the beater to strike again. Knowing that a second strike would finish them, Suremaana somehow got to her feet and launched herself at the man. In her weakened state, she only managed to knock him off balance. He turned to face her.

'Rabten,' she uttered. The relief that flooded her that it wasn't her beloved Jadeja, gave her new strength. This time her kick did not miss. She caught him full in the throat knocking him to the floor. Seizing the beater, she brought it down over her knee and broke it in two. The effect of this sent a huge shock wave through her body rendering her unconscious.

Rabten took up the broken beater and struck the gong once more. Although the sound was less powerful now, it was still strong enough to finally break the circle. The Shaman-Master stood and looked at his enemy.

'You will not win.'

Before the Jhankhira could seize him, the Shaman-Master rang the smallest of his bells. In contrast to the gong, this note was pure and sweet and soothing. The Jhankhira grabbed it, silencing it. Then with a wave of his hand, a demon lifted the Shaman-Master and bound him to the wall.

'I want you to witness this, Vikander, as I undo all you have worked to keep safe. Including your heart.'

He stepped into the circle of stones, then took out the bottle.

'Don't do this. She is the Deceiver. The Lamenter of Souls. She will betray you too.'

'Vikander, you always were bitter that she chose me over you. After all I have done for her, she will be mine again.'

The Shaman-Master watched despairingly, as one by one the Jhankhira touched the power stones with the bottle, calling on their powers to undo the binding. He placed the bottle in the centre of the circle, took a black feather from his headdress then reopened the wound in his hand and wrote a series of runes in blood on the floor to finish the undoing process. Slowly, very slowly, the gold threads that held the stopper in place, began to unwind.

The Jhankhira paced anxiously, eagerly awaiting the opening. High on the wall the Shaman-Master watched helplessly. When the final thread was undone the heavy gold stopper began to push upwards, the inky black cloud forcing its way out. The stopper fell to the floor and the demoness, howling in triumph, was released into the Sanctum. Circling high in the air like an ominous storm cloud, she writhed and whirled, before descending to the ground, where she reformed into a grotesque and abominable figure. The face was monstrous, looking as if all the evil in the world dwelt there.

'Free at last!' rasped the demoness.

Looking up, she stared straight at the Shaman-Master. Her gaze pierced his soul.

'Foolish man, to think that your bottle would contain me forever. My disciple was always going to defeat you. I have trained him too well.'

The Shaman-Master looked down at her.

'It will not last,' he said.

The demoness merely laughed, then reformed into a staggeringly beautiful woman, with long lustrous black hair, deep, black eyes and full red lips. Despite himself, the Shaman-Master was intoxicated by her beauty, recalling once more the effect she had had on him as a young man.

Striding towards the Jhankhira she kissed him deeply, passionately. He melted into her arms, returning the kisses with all the ardour of lovers finally reunited after a long separation.

'My love. I have waited so long for this moment.'

'You have done well, my Jhankhira. Where is your agent Rabten?'

'I am here oh Great One.'

She beckoned Rabten to her and looked him over carefully.

'You are a fine specimen.'

She gazed at the young man, admiring his lean, muscular body and the handsome face beneath the tattoo. She passed a hand over his head.

'You have the making of a powerful Jhankhira.'

'My Master has taught me well.'

'Indeed he has. I can sense that you are very skilful, and strong.'

Returning to the Jhankhira she stood before him, noticing the crows' feet around his eyes, the furrowed brow and the lines around his mouth. Although he was strong, there wasn't the tautness of a younger body.

'Take off your bells and belt. Remove your headdress.'

He looked at her somewhat puzzled.

'You dare to disobey me,' she yelled.

'No my love, but I may need them. In case of further attack.'

She ran her fingers seductively down his face.

'You will not need them for what I have in mind,' she answered coyly. 'Here let me help you.'

She gently lifted the headdress from him and then the string of heads, before kissing him again as she undid his belt and let it fall to the floor.

'I am yours my lady, as I always have been, throughout the long years of waiting.'

'And that has always been your weakness. You have served your purpose today just as you did years ago. Now it is time for a change.'

Reaching to his heart, she pulled the soul from his body and consumed it, leaving the flesh to fall to the floor where it burst into flames, until only a pile of ash remained. The belt, headdress and heads, she picked up and gave to Rabten.

'You are my Jhankhira now.'

Rabten threw off his cloak and put the ritual garments on, gloating in triumph.

The demoness then marched over to the Shaman-Master.

'Now Vikander. Where is my son?'

32

The Shaman-Master stared back at her unflinchingly.

'No matter. I will find him. I know you have him here, Rabten has been following him. He will soon reveal himself and then Vikander, you will regret crossing me.'

A moan from Eilidon drew her attention.

'Ah, the spider, caught in your own web now. Do you like my demon? Can you feel his breath? Bring her down to me.'

The demon obeyed and stood Eilidon in front of his mistress. She studied Eilidon carefully, noting her lean muscles and sensing her physical strength. Eilidon stood her ground as the Lamenter penetrated her mind, forcing her back, protecting her innermost thoughts from invasion. When it was over the Lamenter stood back.

'Your senses are heightened and you have great skill with a blade. I had not thought about a spider, but I see now that there is much you could bring to me.'

'I will bring you nothing,' spat Eilidon.

'Perhaps not, but your child will bring me much. Rabten, take her. You must breed with her before she reaches eighteen. The combination of your gifts and hers will give me a potent disciple.'

Rabten smirked at Eilidon.

'It will be my pleasure,' he said, running his hands through her hair.

'Shall I take her now mistress, here in the Sanctum?'

The Lamenter smiled.

'Later, we have other work to do first. Demon, take her to a chamber and see that she does not escape.'

Eilidon was dragged away to a chamber where her fighting clothes were ripped from her, leaving her bruised and angry at the humiliation. She tried to transform, but the demon prevented her. All she could do was sit and wait.

The Lamenter raised herself up to face the Shaman-Master. A trail of black vapour twisted around his head and then penetrated his ear, swirling around his mind, grasping at his thoughts. He fought back with a protective bird spirit, the dance playing out in his head. The ebb and flow of the tug-of-war between the two spirits causing his body to thrash about uncontrollably.

The Shaman-Master was strong and well-versed in repelling evil, but this being was particularly virile. He looked into the depths of his mind and called forth a dragon, a most powerful protector. The Lamenter was equal to it, calling up a griffin so large, the dragon was soon engulfed.

The Shaman-Master summoned a bear, hoping that its immense strength would block the way to his deepest thoughts. She read him again and matched his bear with one of her own. The battle in his head was ferocious as the two bear spirits tore into one another. He knew that he had to block her, to give Jadeja more time. There was still a chance he could complete the ritual without facing her.

The pressure in his mind was intolerable as he fought to stop her gaining access to his secrets. He sensed his bear was weakening. The black demon had superior strength.

'You are faltering Vikander. Why not save yourself the torment and reveal to me where he is?'

Her words rallied him and his bear fought back savagely, tearing the black bear asunder. The Shaman-Master looked at her.

'Never.'

Incensed, she drew herself up and transformed into the hideous figure that had first emerged from the bottle, then with the speed of a falcon she entered his mind.

He felt the blackness descend on him and infiltrate every pore of his body, paralysing him physically and mentally as she probed him for answers. This time he could not stop her and she found what she needed. She saw too how he had once loved her, when she had been just a young woman, when they had been Paladin together. She remembered his touch; how gentle he had been. How he had tried to stop her from opening the gateway; stop her becoming the great one she was meant to be. How he had fought her then and continued to fight her now, betraying her instead of coming with her. Anger returned and she wrapped herself around his soul and extracted the information that she needed.

Returning to her womanly form, she kissed him fully on the lips.

'Thank you, Vikander.'

She left him, a broken man, hanging on the wall.

'Come Rabten, our boy is this way.'

33

High up in the watchtower, Caderyn stirred, slowly remembering what had happened. Feeling his leg, he realised that all the healing work Rowen had done was wasted. He knew the bones had broken again. He removed his waistcoat and tore it into strips, then taking four arrows he cut off the tips and tails and using the shafts, put together a makeshift splint, tying them in place with the strips of fabric. He couldn't stand, but he hoped that by holding the bones still he could prevent further damage, all the time fighting the searing pain coursing through his body.

He somehow hauled himself back up on to his window seat and surveyed the scene below. He had been unconscious when the gong had sounded and so had not felt the worst of its effects. Looking down on the courtyard he could see a mass of bodies. Nothing appeared to be moving. He stilled his mind and tried to reach the Shaman-Master. All he encountered was blackness. He couldn't make the connection. He tried again, this time using the bird runes on his wrist to try to connect with the Master's phoenix. Nothing. The red bird was gone. Everything was black.

Fearing the worst, Caderyn came out of his trance and pondered what to do next. Over in the doorway the red stone began to glow. Moaning with pain, he somehow shuffled over there and picked it up.

'Jadeja. A stone of protection.'

Caderyn placed Jadeja's stone onto the runes on his wrist and began chanting:

Awen. Awen Awen
Mogh Way Wa

This time the runes did respond, but only weakly. He reached out once more to the Shaman-Master. The blackness had dissipated and he could sense his Master, but only just. He knew that something terrible had happened to him.

Caderyn my boy, she is here. Eilidon… was all he got before the connection was lost. The Shaman-Master's specific reference to Eilidon worried him. Once again using the red stone and the runes on his wrist he forced his overwrought mind to still itself. When he was calm he chanted, calling on the runes to connect him with Eilidon. In her prison on the other side of the Temple, Eilidon felt her runes flare; she stopped her incessant pacing of the room and sat down on the bed. Allowing the anger inside her to subside she felt the call from Caderyn. It was the first time they had communed in this way so the connection was weak, more of a sensation than a conversation. Nevertheless, it gave her strength. Reassured by the link, Caderyn used it to send further protection to her runes enabling her to resist her demon guard and transform. She built a web and waited for Rabten's next move. Drained of all energy Caderyn relinquished the connection. Cursing his damaged leg, he returned to the window, lifted the seat, found a spare bow, and waited.

Locked within the chamber of runes, Jadeja held the light stone high and began the incantation of banishment. The stone flared, filling the room with its light. The longer he chanted the stronger his voice became and he began to feel more confident in his ability to get to the end. He felt a change in the atmosphere and he knew his friends and Master were in grave danger. He tried concentrating again but he had lost the rhythm. The runes on the walls were frantically flashing, responding to a signal. Faster and faster, forming and reforming until they revealed a doorway. Leaving the books, he concealed the light stone within his tunic and exited the room. Having no clear idea of where he was, he stood, bewildered for a moment. Calming his mind, he allowed the spirits to guide him. Turning left, he found himself at the top of a stairway. He ran down it and came to a small door that opened on to the courtyard. He was unprepared for the carnage that met his eyes. Bodies strewn everywhere. His first instinct was to run. So much blood. *Courage Jadeja, courage.* Clenching his fists, he began checking the bodies for signs of life. He found Hamroon, semi-conscious and dragged him clear. His eyes scanned frantically for Suremaana, hardly daring to believe that she could have survived. He saw no sign of her or Eilidon.

Caderyn, he thought.

Running as fast as he could, he crossed to the watchtower and began to climb the stairs. Inside the room Caderyn heard the approaching feet and steadied his bow.

'Caderyn. Caderyn. Are you safe? It's me, Jadeja.'

Caderyn lowered his bow as his friend entered the room.

'It's a good thing you called out, or I would have shot you.'

'What happened?'

'I don't know. The Jhankhira came here. He attacked me and damaged my leg again. I passed out. When I came to, the fighting had finished. Where have you been?'

'The Master had me locked in a chamber of runes performing the banishment. I would have stayed there but I was let out. I haven't been to the Sanctum yet, but I think I need to go there.'

'Take me with you. I can't stay in the tower and I can't leave without help.'

'You are probably safer here.'

'Perhaps, but the spirits sent you to me for a reason. I may still be of some use.'

Reluctantly, Jadeja agreed. Caderyn grabbed two full quivers, crossing them onto his back. He slung his bow on top of them. Once more the two friends counted the steps.

The descent was slow, with many stops, but eventually Jadeja staggered out into the courtyard. Allowing him to recover a little Caderyn directed him to a secret entrance.

'Back door,' he said.

Moving cautiously along, they both fell silent, sensing the catastrophe that awaited them. The passageway ended at a small door. Jadeja had to stoop to enter, a tricky operation with Caderyn on his back. It opened onto a small antechamber. Ritual items were kept here: headdresses, goblets, dried sage and beaters for the sacred gong. Jadeja reached for a beater before laying Caderyn down on a pile of cushions. A heavy velvet curtain screened the room from the Sanctum. Jadeja nervously drew back a corner. He was ill-prepared for what was there. The sight of the

Shaman-Master suspended on the wall, looking old and wizened hit him like a hammer blow.

'Master.'

The Elders were either dead or dying on the floor and there in the centre of the circle the bottle of Isfahan, open and empty. He felt utterly helpless. *I failed again*, he thought and fought back tears. To his left, he saw Suremaana, lying motionless. He rushed to her side, picked her up and carried her through to Caderyn.

'Can you help?'

Caderyn passed a hand over the unconscious girl.

'Yes. I will revive her. The Master?'

'Defeated. The bottle is open. She is here.'

'I know,' answered Caderyn. 'I know.'

'I failed them, Caderyn. I was supposed to complete the banishment before the Jhankhira could release her.'

'You haven't failed Jadeja. The enemy was stronger than we had anticipated. We are still here. It is up to us now, although how useful I can be, I don't really know.'

Caderyn's words rallied Jadeja and the light stone flared at his chest giving him succour.

Leaving him to help Suremaana, Jadeja searched the antechamber until he found a small vial of silver liquid. Taking two of Caderyn's arrows he touched the tip of each one with the light stone and then poured a few drops of the silver liquid over them. Carefully replacing the vial, he spoke to Caderyn.

'I am going to need you to help me defeat Rabten and the Jhankhira. I will move you behind the gong. You should be unseen there. Do you have the strength to fire your bow?'

'If the Temple needs me, I will find it.'

'I have tipped these two arrows with mercury and light. If you can pierce the Jhankhira's heart with one of them, you will kill him. The same for Rabten. I am going to summon them. You will know when it is time.'

Jadeja carried him behind the gong and shielded him with a protective aura. Although his leg was throbbing, Caderyn's years of training allowed him to switch his focus away from the pain and onto the Sanctum. All he had to do now was wait.

Crossing to the Master, the emptiness in the older man's eyes made him weep, despite their recent hostilities.

'She has done her worst to you. I will stop her Master.'

He returned to the gong, taking out the beater he had collected earlier. He struck it three times, loud and clear. The first two notes were pure and sweet, sending out a calming vibration. The third, was a warning. He went and touched each of the power stones, making an invisible link between them. Once the circle was complete, he stood in the centre and laid out his red stones, only remembering at the end that he had left one in the tower. He trusted that they would still protect him. He watched to see who would answer his summons.

Rabten was the first to come.

'So little one, you finally show yourself, instead of hiding away like a coward while your friends do battle. You never did have the guts for a fight.'

Jadeja ignored the taunt.

'I see you are the Jhankhira now. Who did you betray this time?'

Rabten laughed.

'My mistress realised who was the more powerful man.'

'Is that why she wants me Rabten. Because I am more powerful?'

Incensed by this jibe, Rabten called up a reptar, a giant lizard spirit, to attack. Jadeja was ready and repelled it with a red flame from his stones that consumed the beast with ease.

'I see you have acquired some skill little one, but you are still just a boy.'

Anticipating another assault, Jadeja steeled himself. Rabten sent out a black cloud that became a colossal raven. The bird flew to the ceiling, focusing on its target, ready to attack. Jadeja called on his red stones. One by one they sent out a beam of light to form a protective canopy over him. When the bird dived it hit the beams and dissipated into the ether.

A furious Rabten then reawoke the strings of heads, whose chanting called forth the demons from his belt. This time Jadeja touched each of the power stones, which sent out guardians to fight off the demons. Satisfied with his defences, he drew his sword and advanced on Rabten who laughed and took out his blade.

Rabten was taller and had a greater reach, but Jadeja lunged and dodged with fierce intent.

'You have some skill with a blade little one, but you will not kill me.'

'I don't intend to,' replied Jadeja. Then with one swift movement he cut an opening in Rabten's tunic, withdrawing his sword, just as a silver arrow pierced the new Jhankhira's heart. Jadeja reached in and pulled Rabten's soul from within and placed it in a small jar he had taken from inside his tunic. Once contained, he placed it inside the sacred circle for safekeeping. He then removed the Jhankhira's headdress from Rabten's body and placed it on his own head, before returning to the centre of the circle.

Caderyn fell back down, the effort of standing to fire the arrow taking the last ounce of his strength. He hoped that Jadeja would be able to finish the battle without him.

34

Standing in the centre of his protective circle, Jadeja waited for the onslaught that he knew would come. He was expecting a whole host of demons to be sent for him, so he was unprepared for the sweet voice that now filled his head.

'There you are my boy. I have been searching for you all these long years. Helpless to protect you because I was locked away. You have heard me calling. The Shaman-Master never told you. I wonder why? He wanted you for himself, to keep you away from me. Yes Jadeja, I am your mother. But you knew that, didn't you? He kept you away. He had no right to do that. It was not his choice to make.'

He remembered the anger he had felt at the Shaman-Master's confession. He had stopped him from knowing who he really was. *She wants me,* he thought.

'Yes, you have felt my presence. I know you tried to resist me. I had to come for you. A mother's love for her child overrides all else. Darling Jadeja, I am here now. Come to me. Let me make up for all the lost years.'

The voice was soothing and tender, reaching in to the part of his soul that remembered what it was to be a wandering child, isolated and abandoned, feeling again the emptiness and isolation.

'Yes, you know what it is like to be alone, my poor boy. I am here now. Your mother is here. Kept away from you by the Shaman-Master and his Elders. Yes, they didn't tell you, did they? Kept your true identity from you. Kept me from you. You owe them nothing Jadeja. They have given you nothing, they have only taken away. I would not have abandoned you if I had been free. But they did. They left you alone. Once they had captured me, no one bothered to take care of you. You were left to fend for yourself. Those days are passed. I am here now. Open your heart and come to me.'

He opened his eyes and saw the Lamenter in all her beauty, standing in front of him, arms open, ready to embrace him.

'Mother.'

The word sounded strange on his lips, having never had cause to utter it before.

'Yes my boy. Here I am, kept from you by the Shaman-Master. You think he took you in out of kindness. No. He took you in because he knew who you were. He wanted to hide your identity from you. To prevent you from seeking me out. To prevent you from being reunited with your family.'

Again, he felt her words pressing home, promising him the one thing that he was denied as a child. Sensing the upper hand, she pressed her advantage.

'Come to my embrace dear boy and I will show you your father. We can be the family that you always wanted. You can have the family that the Shaman-Master always denied you. You can have the love that he kept from you. You can belong.'

The words filled his head. Memories of a lost childhood, of a lonely aching emptiness. The pain of always being the outsider, being mistrusted and shunned.

All the time these images were playing out in his head, the Sanctum was filling with darkness, until the only thing visible was his mother's smiling face and her arms reaching out to him. How he longed to feel a mother's warm embrace. To know that he was loved and wanted. She knew that he desired this above all else and she would provide it, if only he would let her. He took one step forward, then another.

The Lamenter smiled.

'That's it my boy. Almost there. Your mother wants you.'

He faltered. *Why didn't she say loves instead of wants?* The stone around his neck flared gently and memories of the Master's kindness came back to him, then Suremaana's face. Suremaana, her smile, her touch. He put his hand to the stone and in that moment, he saw through the Lamenter's flattery and knew why she was also named the Deceiver of Souls.

'I may be your son, but you will never be a mother to me. Now get out of my head.'

Realising that she had lost the connection, the Lamenter's rage took hold and she sent her darkness to envelope him so tightly he could barely breathe. He pushed against it with all of his will, but still the darkness gathered, squeezing tighter and tighter, a vice compressing his being. The malevolence in the air was palpable. The Lamenter kept him rigid, unable to move.

'Is this what you prefer? Your weakness is pathetic. No child of mine could be so easily overcome. I will destroy you Jadeja.'

The stone on his chest flared momentarily, sending a burst of energy through him, allowing him to use his arms. Sensing victory, the Lamenter towered over her victim, poised to consume his mind. In the moment of her final attack, Jadeja's hand pulled out the stone concealed under his tunic. Immediately the blackness was driven back by a glorious luminescence. Bright, dazzling white light exploded into the room, shielding Jadeja from the evil will of the Lamenter. Screaming in anger, she pulled herself up to her full height and unleashed a torrent of black spirits against him.

'So, you already have the light stone. It belongs to me. I want it back.'

'You are not worthy of wearing it.'

She laughed pityingly as he fought off the demons.

'You understand nothing boy. It is my stone, my birth right, and I will call it back to me.'

She then began singing a lament; a powerful outpouring of grief over the loss of the stone.

The storm immobilised me.
The bright time covered in shadow.
On the day of separation
Heaven and earth trembled.
The darkness grew,
The sun was eclipsed.
We were torn asunder.
Jewel of my heart
Alas, that we were parted.
How long shall I wait until the light returns?
How long must I languish in darkness?

The singing went on and on, plaintively calling to the stone. Her voice permeated through the walls, filling those that heard it with the deepest sorrow. Caderyn put down his bow and wept copious tears. The Shaman-Master sobbed. Jadeja faltered, her words in his head. The stone appeared to be fighting its own battle, torn between its new master and its old one. Slowly the demons vanished, until once more it was just Jadeja and the Lamenter face to face. Stepping closer to him, she continued calling to the stone,

You are my lifeline.
My being is utterly broken.
How long must I mourn?
When will my desolation end?
I weep. I beg for life.
You will make a choice.
Help me to live
Or die, once again.

Now she was inside the circle, drawing the light from the stone towards herself where it was absorbed by darkness. Jadeja stood under the canopy created by his red stones, but it was incomplete. With the power of the stone waning he struggled to hold her at bay.

Somewhere in the antechamber Suremaana stirred. The Lamenter's voice began to invade her consciousness. To try and protect herself she transformed, her serpent form less susceptible to the words. She slid from behind the curtain to see a beautiful woman singing to Jadeja, reaching out to him. He appeared to be enjoying the song. He was staring, bewitched.

She is beautiful. The most beautiful creature I have ever seen. He is sure to want her, thought Suremaana.

She felt an overwhelming sadness start to take hold.

Somewhere in her memory she heard a voice. Remembered the question. *Will you betray the one you love?*

She looked again. This time her vision was clear. Jadeja wasn't reaching for the woman, he was being consumed by her.

Carefully, silently, enraged by what she was witnessing, Suremaana slithered unseen across the Sanctum. The Lamenter was unaware of her approach, all her attention focused on retrieving the light stone. Jadeja felt his strength of will fading. He sensed that he was losing the battle. He felt his life's essence being pulled from him as the Lamenter drew the stone towards her. Just when he thought that he would succumb, something entwined itself around his body and two fangs pierced his neck. Immediately, a large red bird spread its wings in front of him, forming a barrier between him and the Lamenter, who momentarily ceased singing. In that instant Jadeja seized the stone in both hands and shouted out,

'I am the chosen wearer.

I call upon the lights of the world

To surround me, to protect me.

And to banish you into darkness once more.'

In one final attempt to reach the stone the Lamenter tore through the phoenix making Suremaana bellow with pain. Before the Lamenter could touch the stone, the room began to glow as millions and millions of tiny lights filled the Sanctum, until Jadeja was entirely bathed in totally impenetrable white light. More and more lights appeared, surrounding the Lamenter, pressing on her, squeezing her, shrinking her, draining her power. Gradually forcing her down, eating up the blackness, until Jadeja was able to pick up the bottle of Isfahan. Uttering these words,

'Che meanth doreth va
Che beroth heaant sa
Che govorg rianth na
Deamon berorg ga.'

He pushed her back into her prison, resealed the bottle, passing the lightstone over it three times to add an extra layer of protection. To complete the banishment, he held the bottle over each power stone in turn, invoking their powers and the light stones to send her into the depths of the spirit world from where she could not return.

'Begone, Lamenter. The light stone is mine.'

Once the demoness was secured within her prison, he sat and wept bitter tears, for the mother he had never known and would never have.

35

With the Lamenter back inside the bottle the lights began to settle on the floor around Jadeja, waiting until his sorrow lessened. When his tears stopped the lights moved on to the Shaman-Master now laying on the floor, having been released from the demon that had pinned him to the wall. Jadeja crossed to him.

'Master, I am sorry. Hamroon told me who you are. I... I was too quick to judge.'

The Shaman-Master looked up at him, squeezing his hand tightly and smiled.

'You are the Master now, Jadeja. Your apprenticeship with me has finished. Can you lay me in the circle please? I fear that I am too weak to walk.'

Jadeja picked him up and carried him to the centre of the circle. He then called on the elements to heal him. Fire for vigour, air for breath, earth for succour and water for cleansing. Finally, Jadeja placed the light stone on the Master's forehead to draw out any remnants of the Lamenter's darkness. When he had finished the Shaman-Master was much restored.

'I am sorry my dear boy, that you had to face her alone. I had hoped to prevent her release, but I underestimated how powerful the Jhankhira and Rabten had become. You must have many questions which I will try to answer when you feel ready to ask them.'

'Thank you Master, but I did not face her alone. Suremaana…'

He stopped, realising to his horror, that he had forgotten her. He began frantically searching for her, finding her across the other side of the Sanctum, the force of the Lamenter's attack having thrown her backwards. She was barely breathing. Scooping her up in his arms he rushed back to the circle with her. Once more he called on the elements to heal her. Again, he used the light stone to draw out the darkness, like sucking venom out of a snakebite. Several times the stone flared, fighting with something. When it eventually stopped Suremaana opened her eyes. Without a moment's hesitation he bent down and kissed her gently on the lips. She responded, putting her arms around him and holding him tightly.

'I love you,' she whispered.

'I love you too, my lady. I have done from the moment I saw you. Thank you for saving me. Saving us.'

'It was the Artisan's question that made me realise what I had to do. I had to give you your protective spirit back.'

'She could have killed you,' he muttered.

'Perhaps, but she would definitely have taken you if I had done nothing. I am Paladin. It is my duty to protect the Shaman-Master and the Temple. The fact that I love you just made it easier for me to step in.'

'My lady, she was my mother. I…'

To stop him speaking, she kissed him again.

'Jadeja,' said the Shaman-Master, 'There is much to do. Suremaana, see to Caderyn and then find Eilidon. She was taken by one of the Lamenter's demons. To a bed chamber I think.'

The pair stopped their embrace and slightly red-faced, they separated, Jadeja to see to the Elders and Suremaana to find the other Paladin. Caderyn was slumped by the antechamber. His face was dirtied from the tears the Lamenter's voice had drawn out of him. His body was exhausted, drained of all energy by her black lament. She retrieved some cushions from the antechamber and placed them under him to make him more comfortable. Then she took a ceremonial robe and draped it over him to keep him warm. She could do nothing to lift his despair.

'I'm going to find Eilidon. The Master and Jadeja will get to you when they can.'

He sank down onto the cushions and began to cry all over again. Leaving him to his sorrow, Suremaana set off to find Eilidon. After trying several doors, she came across one that was locked. With no sign of a key her only option was to force the door open. Crossing to the other side of the corridor, she ran at the door launching a powerful kick. The door flew open. At first glance she thought the room was empty, then turning, she saw a web above the entrance.

'Eilidon, come down.'

Confident that Suremaana was alone, Eilidon dropped to the floor.

'Get me some proper clothes.'

Suremaana took off her outer tunic and gave it to Eilidon, who put it on gratefully.

'What happened? Why are you locked in this room?'

'I was a trophy for Rabten.'

She shivered at the memory.

265

'What happened to him? How did you defeat the Lamenter?'

'It was Jadeja. He did it.'

Eilidon stopped. 'Jadeja!'

Suremaana nodded.

'He has the light stone. It was him she wanted. Or rather, his stone. She was his mother.'

With this information Eilidon now made sense of the guards at Maur refusing his entry. They knew he was connected with the demoness. She also realised why she had been unable to read him.

'Where is he now?'

'He is with the Master in the Sanctum trying to revive the Elders. Get dressed and meet me back there.'

'Caderyn?' asked Eilidon.

'Injured, but alive.'

Suremaana returned to the Sanctum where she found Jadeja and the Shaman-Master trying to save the Elders. Two were past help and had been laid out in ritual pose for the passing over ceremony. The others were starting to revive. Jadeja looked exhausted. Each time the light stone was used on an elder, it took strength from him. Suremaana took his hand.

'You can't do this for everyone,' she said. 'There must be another way.'

'My lady. My…The Lamenter, has caused extensive damage. I must do what I can to repair it. It is my responsibility.' He squeezed her hand. 'Thank you for your concern.'

'Did you find Eilidon? Was she safe?'

'Yes Master. She will be here shortly.'

'When she gets here, I want you both to go and find Hamroon, Gardeer, Elise and Rowen and bring them here. How is Caderyn?'

'He is suffering from a deep sadness and his leg is severely damaged. I left him near the ante-room.'

'Thank you Suremaana. You have proved yourself a worthy Paladin.'

Before she had time to reply, Eilidon arrived. The first thing she did was approach Jadeja.

'Suremaana told me that it was you who defeated the Lamenter. I am sorry that I doubted you. Can you forgive me?'

Jadeja looked at her.

'My Lady, many times I doubted myself. You were right to be cautious. The enemy tried to control me. You did what any Paladin would do. You protected. There is nothing to forgive.'

'Thank you Jadeja.'

She bowed low, then left with Suremaana to find the four Elders.

Outside, the courtyard was strewn with bodies. The Jhankhira's forces had melted away when the Lamenter was reincarcerated, but many of the Temple guard lay dead. Without the adrenalin of battle Suremaana faltered at the sight of so much death. She scanned the ground for Gardeer and Hamroon. *Could they have survived this?* she thought. The scent of blood fixed itself to her snake tongue. There was no escaping it. Steeling herself, she began searching. Spotting a familiar colour, she knelt down to move a dead soldier, revealing Gardeer underneath. After feeling for a pulse her long exhale made her realise that she had been holding her breath. She lifted Gardeer easily and carried her inside, stroking her hair gently as she lay her down in the sanctum.

When Eilidon found Hamroon he was more of a problem. His size made him too heavy for the two of them to carry. In the end, they constructed a makeshift pallet and dragged him between them. Once he was safely inside, they went back out for Rowen and Elise.

Rowen, they found by the Temple gate, her face contorted in pain. She had an open wound to her left shoulder. Eilidon spun a web to seal it, then very carefully carried her back to the Sanctum. Suremaana continued to search for Elise, eventually finding her. She had suffered multiple sword wounds. *Dear Elise, so gentle, so kind, you did not deserve such a death.* Knowing that she was beyond help, Suremaana lifted her body and took her back to the Sanctum, to be laid to rest with the two Elders who had not survived. Jadeja was still trying to revive the others, but his strength was waning.

'Master, I will not be able to save them all. I am draining the energy from the light stone. Soon it will be finished.'

'Her wounds have cut deeper than even I expected,' replied the Shaman-Master. 'Come sit in the circle. We will find another way.'

Jadeja sat in deep meditation and called on the spirits for guidance once more. Suremaana watched as tiny lights began to dance around him, drawn to the stone and drawn to him. One by one they infused his body with light until he appeared to be wearing a cloak made up entirely of these tiny creatures. He stood up and crossed the Sanctum. Reaching for the beater he had used earlier, he raised it and then struck the sacred gong. A long pure note rang out through the Temple and Suremaana realised that this was the true meaning of her dream.

Jadeja struck again and again. Each note sent out a wave of healing. He carried on, bathing everyone in beautiful restorative sound, washing away the Lamenter's darkness, cleansing the Temple and its inhabitants. Tears ran down Suremaana's face as she watched the young man that she loved revive the soul of the Temple.

After he finished, he bowed to the lights giving them instructions. Each one left him and went to heal guards, Elders and the other members of the Temple community. Several of them landed on Caderyn, sensing that his need was great. First they drew out the sorrow, then they worked on his leg, repairing it as much as they could. He was still unable to walk, but the pain subsided. Eilidon bound it firmly, then she and Jadeja carried him down to the Shaman-Master.

'My Paladin, I thank you. We have come through the darkest of days. Thanks to your bravery we were able to defeat our enemy. I am sorry that I could not reveal Jadeja's true identity to you. Even he did not know. I thought the burden would be too much for him. I had hoped that he would not need to know just yet, but the Lamenter had other plans.

Jadeja, you are the light bearer and you have proved yourself more than worthy. You will make a great Shaman-Master when the time comes. For now, there is much work to do here and then you will be required to spend time in seclusion with the monks of Sanghar to learn the lore of the stone. You carry a great responsibility and you must be schooled in its secrets. For now, I offer mine and the Temple's unending gratitude.'

Jadeja bowed, accepting the tribute with his usual humility.

Epilogue

The restoration of the Temple and its people took many weeks. Rabten's soul was dispatched to the deepest prison and his body was taken away to be burnt, along with his Shamanic garments. The bells were removed from the belt then taken to the rune chamber by the Shaman-Master. He carried out a ritual cleansing of each bell, returning them to the ways of the light and placing them on a new strap ready for their next Master.

Caderyn was once again confined to bed until his leg mended. This time no one dared to move him. Rowen placed a spirit guard in his room that threatened to attack anyone that so much as touched him. It did allow Jadeja to play umar with him, which was a welcome distraction, although his visits were far too infrequent for Caderyn's liking. Jadeja had little spare time. He and the Master had many rituals to perform for the deceased and for the renewal of the Temple.

Eilidon, as promised, took the firestone back to the Temple of Maur. On her arrival the guardians at the gate rose up to their full height and bowed to her. The golden cats formed a guard of honour up the steps to the entrance of the Temple, where Birali greeted her warmly.

'The Temple of Maur is truly grateful for the return of its sacred firestone. Its blessings will rain upon you.'

Eilidon accepted the tribute humbly and entered the Temple.

Suremaana was reminded by the Shaman-Master that as a Paladin she was forbidden from having a relationship with anyone, but for a few weeks, both Master and Elders discreetly ignored seeing her and Jadeja together, knowing that their lives would soon be separated. When Jadeja's departure did come, it was a time of mixed emotions for all of them.

Caderyn limped down to the gates to see him off.

'Until our paths meet again may the spirits guide and guard you, my dear, dear friend.'

'Thank you Caderyn. It is hard to leave my friends behind. May the light always be upon you.'

The parting with Suremaana was the hardest of all. They were glad for the days they had shared, but the pain of goodbye was unbearable.

'We will meet again my lady. Hold fast until then. You must fulfil your oath as Paladin and I must follow my path. Remember you will always have my heart.'

She held him close to her one last time. 'And you mine,' she whispered.

'I am to visit my father again before returning Porphyra's stone. I will take comfort in that.'

'That will be good for you, my dearest lady. Think of me often.'

'Come Jadeja, it is time.'

'Yes Master. Will you walk with me a while, Master and apprentice together for the last time?'

'It would be my honour.'

With a final bow to the Paladin, Jadeja left the Temple.

Acknowledgements

Firstly, I must thank the wonderful members of StoryVine Writers Group, Sue Newgas, Jenny Heap and Rowen Wilde, for their support, encouragement and critiquing. I couldn't have written this book without you. Rowen your insightful edits really helped to improve the quality of Paladin.

Thank you to my young readers, Noah Johnson, Edward Smith and Ketan Reddy, for your enthusiasm, feedback and positivity. You really motivated me to get this book out.

Thank you to The Hilary Johnson Authors Advisory Service. The editorial report helped to turn this into a much better book by making me shift the focus and improve the story.

Thank you to the agents who were encouraging in their feedback, even if they didn't sign me and to Pirates Publishing house in India for believing in the book and shortlisting Paladin for publication.

A special thank you to Alan Sharpe for designing a brilliant cover, check him out at sharpesketch.com. And to my son Phillip, for being a critic and helping me with my technology issues. I promise I will improve.

And finally, a big thank you to you, for buying my book and posting a review (if you have) on Amazon and Goodreads and spreading the word. Your support means so much.

36667413R00164

Printed in Poland
by Amazon Fulfillment
Poland Sp. z o.o., Wrocław